Into the Brown Mountain Lights

Brown Mountain Lights Book 3

CC Tillery

Spring Creek Press

First Edition

ISBN 13 **978-0-9894641-7-8**

Published by **Spring Creek Press**

Cover Photography and Design 2019 by Kimberly Maxwell

DEDICATION

In loving memory of our mom, Margie Clark, for the numerous gifts she gave us during her life. We love her more than we can say and miss her more with each passing day.

Chapter One

Late Spring 1861

Dazed and Confused

I watched in horror as the light sucked Jackson's right hand and arm into the dark brown center, my mind screaming, "It's the wrong light, get away!" Fear surged through me like a jolt of electricity as I yanked my body to the side in a frantic attempt to break his hold on me. God only knew where I would end up if he managed to drag me in with him. His fingers loosened, slipped a few inches down my arm then banded around my wrist again. Screaming with frustration, I planted my feet firmly in the ground and pulled against him, to no avail.

Thunder rumbled and the wind picked up, blowing my hair across my face, partially blinding me. The air smelled of ozone as twin ribbons of panic and terror tangled together, forming a roiling ball of fire in my stomach. But fury, sparking an equally fierce blaze in my heart and mind, drove me to fight back. I would not, could not go with him.

I shook my head to clear the strands of hair from my eyes and saw the light expand, elongating to form a door-like opening into the dull brown of the center. It looked inviting

1

somehow, almost friendly, but I knew if I allowed Jackson to drag me in behind him, I would be lost.

It had Jackson firmly in its grip now, slowly drawing him in. I could see nothing but the left half of his hateful face, his left arm and hand with his fingers tightly clamped around my right wrist in an unbreakable hold, and his left leg and foot. He looked like he'd been sliced neatly in half with one vicious slash of a razor-sharp cleaver.

The one eye still visible to me narrowed then glinted with determination as his teeth clenched with fierce fervor and I knew he would take me with him if I didn't get away. I couldn't let that happen, even if it meant I would leave this insufferable time. Frantic to break free, I screamed, "No," a long keening wail that mixed eerily with the wind howling through the trees, and was rewarded with the distant sound of someone shouting back. Unable to make out the words, I thought it might be Josh—please let it be Josh—but wasn't sure. Even so, he sounded too far away to be of any help.

Still, I called out, screaming his name as I thought, you're on your own, Lizzie, he'll never get here in time, it's going to be up to you to save yourself. The fact that I didn't know whether I could or not terrified me and with that terror came a strengthening sense of my own determination, an unholy desire to cause this man unbearable pain.

My mind focused on my rage, I dug the heel of my left boot into the soft, spongy ground, lifted my right leg and kicked at him as hard as I could, praying it would cause him enough pain to loosen his grip. But the skirt of my long dress tangled around my leg, throwing off my aim and limiting my motion. He grunted when my boot collided with his calf but his fingers remained tight and firm around my wrist as his body was slowly drawn into the light.

Gathering my skirt in my left hand, I braced myself and started to kick at his groin but jerked my leg to a stop before my foot made contact. The light was too close to chance. It would probably grab on, suck me in with Jackson. Changing direction, I aimed for the side of his knee, putting all my strength behind it, and heard the satisfying crack as his kneecap shattered and his leg snapped backwards in a direction it shouldn't have been able to bend. His mouth opened in a silent scream, reminding me of how I'd tried to scream when my light had me. I wondered if his body had gone numb as mine did, hoped it hadn't and that he could feel the pain I inflicted on him. But if it had, would that numbness be enough to cause him to loosen his grip? I could only pray so.

He would have fallen if the light hadn't held the right side of his body upright. Still, without support, the left portion of his body remaining outside the light jerked downward, enough to pull me off-balance and send me tumbling to the ground. I landed on my knees and finally, finally, his grip loosened enough to allow me to pull myself free. I let out a triumphant whoop as I scrambled away, crawling like a baby, desperate to reach safety, trying to put as much space between myself and Jackson in case he still had enough in him to grab me again.

When I reached what I judged to be a safe distance, I sat back on my heels, covered my mouth with my hands and tried to hold in the hysterical laughter bubbling up in my throat, watching as the light drew Jackson in so that only his left forearm and hand were visible, the last clenched in a tight fist. Wondering vaguely if he thought he still had my wrist in his grasp, I stared in awe as his hand disappeared into the center and the light seemed to tighten in on itself then vanish as suddenly as it had appeared.

I did it, I thought, as wild joy burst through me. Giving in to the feeling, I curled my body into a ball, hugging myself, as the urge to laugh deliriously warred with that of shedding tears of relief. God, I wouldn't have believed it if I hadn't lived it. I had defeated Constable Jackson. I lifted my head just as Josh burst through the trees.

"Lizzie!" He fell to his knees and drew me into his arms, cradling me against him. "Lizzie, Lizzie, my love, my darlin, are you all right?" He pulled away to look at me. "What happened? Where are you hurt?"

The hysteria finally spewed out like an erupting volcano and all I could do was laugh uncontrollably for several minutes as tears rained down my face. Josh ran his hands over my body, searching for injuries, while I tried to calm the frenzied feelings churning inside me.

I heard someone crashing through the trees from the other direction, Abbie yelling. "Lizzie? Lizzie, I'm comin."

I needed to control myself but I couldn't do it yet, though the pressure in my chest eased some when Josh's hands slowed and he pulled me back into his arms. With that, the hysteria and its accompanying irrepressible urge to laugh settled a bit.

Abbie sank to her knees in front of us, carefully setting down the lantern she'd brought. "Lizzie, what happened?" When I didn't answer, she shoved furiously at Josh. "What did you do to her? Let her go." Her hand clutched at my shoulder. "Lizzie. Talk to me, ya hear me? Tell me what he did." Grabbing my other arm, she shook me hard.

Taking a hitching breath, I only got out a few words before I dissolved into laughter again. "Not Josh. Constable Jackson, he, he—"

"He what?" Abbie demanded, glancing around. "Where is he?"

Drawing in another gasping breath, I looked at her. "He's gone. Oh, God, Abbie, he's gone. Jackson is gone." I laughed again as I whispered the last, though I wanted to shout it to the world.

"Gone? Gone where?" She looked around then stood up and put her hands on her hips in a surprisingly good imitation of her sister Sarie, which amused me to no great end, although I managed to contain myself. "Gone where, Lizzie? Pull yourself together and tell me."

I pointed toward where the light had been. "There was a light. It was pulling him in and I kicked him and it … it took him." Another giggle broke through then I just sat there and tried to breathe deeply, struggling to compose myself. I sensed Abbie's and Josh's curiosity, their need to know what happened, but both remained quiet, giving me time to calm down.

Vaguely wondering if my encounter with Jackson hadn't heightened my senses, I stared at the dark sky overhead, thousands—no billions, zillions, an infinite number in the universe, my mind whispered—of stars glittering like ice crystals on a bed of black velvet. The night seemed to pulsate around me with the songs of insects and tree frogs backed up by a slight rumble of thunder in the distance. I could smell the pine needles on the ground beneath me, sweetened by the smell of wild roses and violets drifting on the pureness of the spring air, carried by a capricious breeze that in turn caressed and slapped my heated cheeks. I smiled to myself, thinking I was alive and Constable Jackson was gone. I wanted to shout it to the heavens. I had defeated my nemesis and sent him on his merry way to hell—at least I hoped with all my heart that was where the bastard ended up.

Josh still held me in his arms, and when he shifted slightly, I looked up at his handsome face. "Thank you," was all I managed to get out before my eyes filled with tears and I buried my head in his shoulder, breathing in his comforting smell of horses, hay and man. My man, I thought, smiling.

The smile dropped away when he said, "Why did you kick Constable Jackson into the light, Lizzie?"

Okay, way to burst my balloon, Joshua, I thought irritably as I shook my head and drew away from him. "Why shouldn't I have? Because I'm a girl? Let me tell you something, Josh. Never underestimate the power of a desperate woman who doesn't want to go where a man's dragging her. I'll bet there were plenty of cave women who would have attested to that."

When he gave me a puzzled look, I inwardly sighed, wishing I didn't have to explain everything all the time. "Supposedly cave men used to hit women over the head with their clubs before they dragged them by the hair to their caves." I said, shaking my head, unsure if it were true or not. "Well, that's what the cartoons showed, at least."

Abbie gave me a confused look. "What in tarnation's a cave man, Lizzie, or a cartoon?"

"I'll tell you later. My point is, I would think more than a few would have objected to being treated like that and fought back. Which is why the men had to hit them on the head in the first place, to knock them out so they would go peacefully. Well, screw that. Screw that, Josh!" I shouted the last.

Josh winced but I didn't let that put an end to my tirade. My emotions were so churned up, I didn't think anything could stop me right at that moment.

"It's not like I held out my hand and said, 'Here, take me with you, Constable Jackson, please take me with you.' He grabbed my hand and wouldn't let go, the son of a bitch. When I realized it was the wrong light, I fought back. I wasn't going to let him take me through that damned light so I did what I had to do to—" I broke off when I saw the hurt in Josh's eyes, realizing he and Abbie didn't know what happened between me and Jackson and I must sound like a raving lunatic. "Oh, God, I'm sorry, Josh. Just ignore me. I don't know why I said that." I waved my hands around my head then used them to cover my face again. "I'm a little bit crazed right now."

Abbie dropped down beside me. "Was it your light, Lizzie?"

I took a deep breath as I shook my head. "No, the center was dark brown instead of black. When I saw the light, I ran toward it, hoping it was mine and I could go through it to escape him—Jackson, I mean."

"Why was you wantin to get away from Constable Jackson?"

"He was trying to make me tell him where Viola was. I got away from him but he chased me. When he caught me, as I was struggling with him, he stumbled into the light. He had hold of my right wrist and I couldn't break his grip so I kicked him as hard as I could. But my skirt tangled around my leg and threw off my aim and it didn't stop him. So I drove my foot into his knee as hard as I could." I shuddered, Josh's arms tightening around me. "I actually heard his kneecap shatter. Oh, God, it was a horrible sound. I hope I never hear it again but I can't tell you how glad I am I heard it tonight." I knew I was babbling but couldn't seem to stop. It seemed the hysteria wasn't finished with me yet. "Lord help me," I groaned, "somebody slap some sense into me."

Abbie, impatience practically radiating from every pore of

her body, said. "I'm goin to if you don't start makin some sense." Instead, she grabbed my shoulders, giving me a hard shake, which helped. "What happened to that jackass? How did you get away from him?"

"When I kicked his knee and he didn't let go, I thought I was a goner. But he went down, or the left side of his body which wasn't supported by the light dipped down because of his knee, you know? It wouldn't hold him up and he took me down to the ground with him." I held my wrist up, grimacing as I noted the purpling bruises encircling it. "That's going to hurt tomorrow. Anyway, when he hit the ground, his grip loosened a bit so I jerked as hard as I could and was finally able to pull my hand free. I got away as fast as I could and the light ..." I shrugged. "It took him in, it just absorbed him, and then it disappeared and him with it. He's gone, thank the good Lord and all the angels too. Jackson's gone." I reached out for her hand. "He won't be bothering us anymore, Abbie."

Abbie looked around as if searching for the man. "Where do you think he went?"

I shrugged again. "I don't know, some other time and place, just like I did. I really don't care just as long as he's not here to bother us anymore." I put my arms around her and hugged as tight as I could, lowering my voice to a whisper. "I'm so glad you're here, Abbie. I think ... " A shudder went through me, remembering the violence in his eyes, his superior strength as he manhandled me.

She drew back, giving me a concerned look. "What did that low-lyin polecat do to you, Lizzie?"

I shook my head. "It doesn't really matter now. The only thing that does is he's gone and hopefully won't be coming back anytime soon." I turned to Josh, suddenly remembering where he had been headed when Jackson caught me. "Where's Viola, Josh? Is she all right?"

Abbie's lantern provided enough light that I could see confusion warring with concern in his expression as he studied me for a long moment before saying, "I hadn't made it to Pokni's place when I heard you scream. After that, I didn't think of anything else except getting back here to you." He cupped my cheek in the palm of his hand. "Lizzie, are you sure you're not hurt?"

Smiling at him, I rubbed the back of my head where Jackson had ripped the hair loose. "Other than a few bruises and a partial scalping, I made it through unharmed. I'll probably feel like I've been run over by a mack truck ... um, I mean kicked by a mule tomorrow, but right now, I'm okay. I mean, fine, I feel fine."

He gave me a questioning look. "How did you meet up with him, Lizzie? You never said."

"I think he was watching us, Josh. He suspected we were helping Viola escape up north and tried to force me to tell him where she was."

He nodded, lightly tracing the bruises on my wrist. "And he hurt you." His fists clenched. "I'd give my soul to see that man again. I'll kill him if I do."

"Oh, Josh, what happened to him is even worse. He's gone to a different time he won't be familiar with, and he's injured at that, with no one to help him. I only wish I could know where he ends up. I hope the light took him to some prehistoric land where there are mean, nasty cave men and huge dinosaurs and other big animals that will have Jackson for a tasty little snack. Or maybe to the future where aliens have taken over the earth and they'll run all kinds of ghastly and painful experiments on him to try to figure out where he came from." I grinned at that image. "Yeah, I like that even better than the idea of him becoming a meal for a surly Tyrannosaurus Rex."

Abbie picked up the lantern then stood, brushing off her skirts. "Don't rightly know what aliens or dinosaurs or that other thing you said are, but as long as he's gone, I ain't gonna cry about it. I just hope those poor things don't get a bellyache from eating his sorry soul." She looked up as lightning flashed overhead. "Rain's gettin close. We better get on home."

I smiled at her as I raised my hand. "Here, help me up. I'm not going to complain, either. In fact, I have a feeling I'm going to spend quite a bit of time cooking up a lot of grizzly fantasies about where he ended up and what happened to him when he got there."

Abbie took one hand, Josh the other, and they pulled me to my feet.

I grasped their hands hard. "I'm so glad he didn't drag me into that light with him." My voice trembled and I stopped myself, afraid I'd begin to cry from the immense feeling of relief sweeping through me.

Abbie gave me a reassuring smile. "Me too, Lizzie."

Josh kissed my cheek. "Me as well."

As I stood there smiling at them, the first raindrop fell. Josh gave my hand a bolstering squeeze. "Let's get you home, Lizzie. You should rest. I think I'll wait until the storm passes then go get Viola. She'll travel better if it's not raining."

"Oh, I forgot. I had her shawl and clothes with me. Jackson grabbed them away from me but he dropped them while we were fighting. We need to find them, Josh. Viola has little enough as it is and she'll need her shawl for the trip. It gets cold up north even at this time of year."

"We'll look for it on the way back to your cabin. Shouldn't be too hard to find if we follow the path you and Jackson took."

"We didn't follow the path. When I was trying to get away from him, I ran into the woods."

Josh nodded. "All right, so we'll start from here since this is where you ended up. I'm a pretty good tracker, and I'll bet y'all left an easy trail to follow. If we don't find them right away, I'll look for them when I go get Viola. Once the clouds clear, it'll be easier to see in the moonlight."

Abbie fell into step with us as we headed back. Like me, she seemed fascinated with the fate of my nemesis, as she said in a musing tone, "I can't help but wonder where Constable Jackson went."

"Wherever he ends up, he's not going to have an easy time of it with that shattered kneecap and the added hindrance of not knowing where or even when he is." I smiled at her. "Unless he finds an angel like I did."

She grinned at me. "I ain't no angel but it's sweet of you to say. Mayhap he'll end up wherever Pa is if'n that's what happened to him. They never cottoned to one another. More like hated each other's guts. Knowin Pa, he's likely to put a bullet through him soon's he sees him than say anything, even hello."

Josh gave a derisive snort. "That's too good for him."

I laughed. "You're right. Dying's too easy. Constable Jackson needs to suffer for a good long time if for no other reason than the way he treated us. And that's how I'm going to think of him." I stopped as a gust of wind blew the spitting rain horizontal, carrying Viola's raggedy shawl with it.

Josh snagged it out of the air and handed it to me. "Let's take a minute here, look around and see if we can find her other things. What else did she have, Lizzie?"

"Not much, just an old, worn dress and a snaggle-toothed comb."

Josh, who apparently had superior night vision, stepped off the path and pulled Viola's spare dress from where it was caught in a blackberry bramble then brought it back, studying the ground as he walked. "I'll look for the comb later, and if I can't find it, maybe Pokni has one she can have."

"We can give her one of ours, Lizzie," Abbie said, as she handed Josh the lantern then took the dress from him, "and get another one next time we's in town."

With another flash of lightning and an angry grumble of thunder, the rain picked up. I shivered as I nodded. "That'll work. Right now, we'd better get a move on before the heavens open up."

We ran, jogged really, as I didn't have the energy for anything more, and when I saw the welcome light shining from the windows of our cabin from the lantern Abbie must have left burning inside, I slowed, sighing in relief. Like being in Josh's arms, just seeing the cabin brought a warm wave of comfort. I all but jumped up on the small porch, opened the door and could have wept when I saw the fire burning in the fireplace.

Home. I was home. Or at least it felt like it. Even though I detested this time and all it stood for, I had Abbie and Josh and for the moment was happy to be here.

I followed behind Abbie as she went directly to the

hearth, stirred the flames until they flared up, then hung the teapot on the hook.

She handed Viola's dress to me. "I'll make some tea and then we're gonna sit down and talk about what happened tonight."

"I don't know what else I can say, Abbie. I've already told you what happened. The only important thing is that Jackson's gone and I'm safe. We're all safe."

"Mayhaps." She lowered her voice to a whisper. "But I want to know what he did to you, what he said to you." She pointed a finger at me before I could deny anything. "Jackson may be gone but I reckon there's more to the tellin than what you told us."

I glanced over my shoulder at Josh, who had placed the lantern on the table and was now watching us, his forehead furrowed.

Abbie followed my gaze. "You don't want to say nothin in front of Mr. Josh? Ain't that right?"

"No, no, it's not that exactly. I just ... I was so scared, Abbie. I've never been that frightened in my life and I don't want to think about it anymore tonight." I looked once more at Josh, whose expression hadn't changed. "Not tonight, okay?"

Abbie nodded, giving me a look that said she wasn't finished with me yet.

I slipped my arm around her waist, kissed her cheek. "Thanks."

Josh cleared his throat, his eyes on the window. "Storm's moving to the west and the rain's slowing down. I reckon I better be on my way and not keep Viola waiting any longer than I have to."

I smiled at him as I put Viola's shawl and dress on one of the rockers in front of the fire. "Won't you stay for a cup of tea first?"

"No, I should get on my way while I have the moonlight. I'm hoping we won't have any more storms tonight, but if we do, I'd like to get Viola as far on her way as I can, at least to the first stop."

Abbie said, "Hold on, Josh. I'll go get a comb for Viola."

"I'll wait right here, Abbie."

When he held out his hand to me, I crossed the room to clasp it in mine. "Promise me you and Viola will be careful."

"Lizzie, are you sure you're feeling all right? I can stay and get Viola started on her way tomorrow."

I shook my head. "You'd best go on tonight. I'm sure Viola's anxious to get started. The sooner you go, the sooner you'll get back." I hesitated. "Josh, Abbie had one of her … feelings the other day. She thinks Viola won't make it, that she'll die on the way. I don't suppose there's any way we can check on her progress, is there?"

He thought about that for a moment then squeezed my hand. "I know the first few stops she'll make. I can ask the conductors to send word back if anything happens to her."

"If that places you in more danger, I'd rather you didn't."

"It won't be any more dangerous than what I'm doing already but it will take time. We may not know for weeks."

"All right." I sighed. "I'm going to miss you and I'll worry about you both. How long will you be gone?"

"I'll miss you too, Lizzie, but it shouldn't be more than a night, maybe two, depending on how quickly Viola can travel and if it's safe. I'll do my best to get back here tomorrow." He stared at me for a long moment. "I know you don't feel up to talking about what happened with Jackson tonight, but I hope you will tell me at some point."

I nodded. "There's not much more to tell, Josh, but we'll talk."

He took my chin in his hand then leaned down and kissed me, slow and deep, as my arms went around his neck.

When Abbie cleared her throat, he moaned softly, breaking the kiss, then laid his forehead on mine. "I'll really miss you," he whispered.

"Same goes for me. Come back to me. Be safe."

"Here you go, Josh." Abbie handed him Viola's shawl which she'd folded into a neat square. "Her dress is inside and I put a comb in there for her. You be careful now, you hear? Tell Viola we'll be prayin for a safe trip."

He turned, smiling as he took the bundle. "I promise I

won't take any unnecessary chances, Abbie." His eyes shifted to me. "I'll come by when I get back and let you know how things went. See you both soon."

After he was gone, I looked at Abbie. "I know you said Viola wouldn't make it but he'll be safe, won't he?"

"Far as I know. It's a little hard for me to see when it comes to Josh. I'm too close to him since we practically grew up in each other's pockets and he's always been like a brother to me. But I ain't gettin any bad feelings about him, just Viola."

I rubbed my stomach as I dropped into my customary rocking chair in front of the fireplace. "I guess that'll have to do then. I keep telling myself that at least she'll be a free woman whenever it happens but that doesn't seem to make me feel much better."

Abbie went over to take the shrilling kettle off the hook. "I'm going to make you some milk thistle seed and mint tea. That should calm your stomach and then we'll talk about what happened tonight."

I lay my head against the back of the rocker. "Remember when I told you about my favorite book, 'To Kill a Mockingbird'? Every time I think about Viola now, that book goes through my mind."

"Why is that?" Abbie asked as she measured herbs into the teapot.

"Remember the old woman, the one who made Jem come to her house and read to her every afternoon after he smashed her prize camellia bushes with Scout's baton?"

"Don't remember her name but I remember her. Why?"

"She was dying and hooked on, um, addicted to morphine and was determined to kick the habit before she died. That's why she would start drooling before she let Jem stop. She told Atticus she didn't want to die beholden to anybody or anything, including the morphine. She wanted to die free and she did. I tell myself that's exactly how Viola would look on it if she knew she wouldn't ever make it up north."

Abbie considered this a moment then turned and smiled at me. "I think that's just the way Viola would see it. She's wanted to be free for as long as I've known her and now she is. It's a nice way to look at it, Lizzie."

"Maybe so but why doesn't it make me feel any better?"

"I don't reckon I know the answer to that. Mayhap because you love her and you'll miss her."

"I guess."

As Abbie poured water into the pot, the sweet, somehow cheerful smell of mint wafted into the air, settling me a bit. Leaving the tea to steep, she walked over to the bed and picked up the small quilt she insisted on draping over the footboard. Old and as soft as a baby's cheek, I knew her mother had pieced and hand-stitched it while she was pregnant with Abbie, an act of love that her youngest daughter cherished. I sometimes teased her about it, but in truth, I envied her that treasure and often wished I had something of my own mother. Abbie usually scoffed at the idea when I said the buttery-soft, pastel quilt was her security blanket. Whenever she needed comforting or felt sad, she would always sit in one of the rocking chairs with the quilt in her lap, running her fingers over the silky trim around the edges.

I smiled when she draped it over my lap, knowing that was a gift of love too. Abbie brushed her hand over my cheek then went back to the table, pouring the tea into the cups then drizzling honey into the fragrant liquid.

She picked up the cups and handed me one before sitting in the other rocker. "Reckon we've stalled enough. Can you tell me what happened tonight, Lizzie?"

"I've already told you most of it. It's, it's just ... it makes me sick to think about it."

"Maybe so but it'll do you good to talk about it," Abbie said softly.

I cleared my throat, took a deep breath then blurted it out, hoping the telling would be easier if I got it all said at once. "I think, oh, God, Abbie, I think he would have raped me if the light hadn't come along. I know he would have beat me senseless. He said some awful, hateful things that scared me. I knew I had to get away from him and I did but he caught me ..." I stopped, remembering how powerless I had felt against him.

Abbie leaned forward and put her hand on my knee. The understanding in her eyes had my own filling and I didn't try to stop the tears from falling. "All right, Lizzie. You go on and get it out. Tell me what he said. You'll feel better when you do."

"I don't know if I remember his exact words but it was something about him wanting to do this since the day he met me and we'd see how I talked to him once he got finished with me. Then he punched me in the stomach, twice, and I don't remember if he said anything else. I was too busy trying not to throw up. I got away from him but, like I said, he caught me."

I tried to smile but don't think I quite pulled it off. Remembering what I'd done to Jackson, that he was gone, helped. "Anyway, like I told you, when he was trying to pull me into the light with him, I kicked him and broke his kneecap and he lost his hold on me. I handled myself, Abbie. I was scared spitless but I handled it."

And that, just that, knowing I'd saved myself, dissolved the tears and brought the smile back to my face.

Chapter Two

Late Spring 1861

Good Times Bad Times

Despite Abbie's soothing tea, it took a long time for me to fall asleep that night. Between worrying for Josh and Viola and my nerves still jumping after my encounter with Constable Jackson, I couldn't seem to get my mind to shut down. It didn't help that my sore scalp and tender stomach were constant reminders of what happened.

My thoughts kept dwelling on Jackson, wondering where and when he ended up and what would happen to him when he got there. I knew his knee wouldn't allow him to go far wherever the light dumped him. Would he be foolish enough to lie there yelling for help, take his chances on who or what might show up if he did? Or would he have the good sense to stay silent until he knew more about his surroundings? I was sure he wouldn't have any idea that he'd traveled to another time and prayed it would take him a while to figure that one out. I hoped with all my heart he would be as disoriented as I'd been when the light first released me after transporting me over a hundred years in the past. More important, that he wouldn't be able to figure it out in time to step back into the light before it disappeared. I tried to remember how long it had taken me to come to my senses but could only recall I'd been pretty stunned and when I finally looked the light had been nowhere around. To my way of thinking, that was a good thing. The longer Jackson stayed where he was, the better.

At least as far as Abbie and I—and okay, Sarie, Maggie and I guess Amanda May, too—were concerned.

I consoled myself by thinking about how long Abbie and I had been searching for the same light. Over a year and a half now without any luck, except for the one time the constable had ruined it for me. Surely it would take Jackson at least that long.

My tired eyes drooped. I needed sleep or I would be of no help to Abbie with the chores tomorrow. Telling my brain to shut down, I had almost drifted off when another thought had my eyes popping open again. What if the loathed Constable Jackson had ended up in 1969, in my time? If I went back, would he be there waiting for me?

On the heels of that came an even more horrifying one. What if the light had simply moved him to another part of Brown Mountain? Would he show up here tomorrow or the next day or even a week from now with a warrant for our arrest?

Worrying over that kept me awake for a long time.

When I finally drifted off sometime in the early morning hours, I kept waking at the least little sound; the soft "hoo, hoo" of an owl as it soared over the trees searching the forest floor for food, minutes later the high-pitched squeal when it found and captured its prey, a short yap from either Billy or Bob as they chased a rabbit in their dreams. Finally, the wind sifting through the pine trees along with the musical whining of their dancing branches soothed my mind enough to send me into a deep slumber.

Thankfully, Abbie took care of the morning's chores by herself so I could sleep later than usual. After I finally dragged myself out of bed and got dressed, I found her in the barn with Jonah, her cheek pressed against his, murmuring quietly to him.

"Is he sick or hurt?" I cleared my throat when my voice came out sounding like a frog. Apparently all that screaming

17

last night had left me hoarse. I walked over to stroke Josh's horse, Boomer. Josh had left him with us while he took Viola on the first leg of her journey, crossing terrain too harsh and at times narrow for a horse to traverse.

Abbie turned and smiled at me. "No, he's fine, just a little restless this morning is all. Probably the storm last night or maybe we're goin to have another one later today." She ran her hand down his soft cheek as she shrugged."Somethin's makin him a might skittish but he'll be all right. Won't you, boy?"

Leading Jonah, she walked out of the barn, headed for our small, fenced-in pasture. I put a lead rope around Boomer and followed. "Sorry I slept so late. I just couldn't fall asleep last night."

"I know," Abbie said over her shoulder. "You tossed and turned most of the night. Too much excitement, I 'spect. Takes a while for it to run its course afore it settles down enough and lets you rest."

I had to smile at the easy way she read my feelings. "For sure."

"Once you wore down, you seemed to sleep well enough. Any nightmares?" Opening the gate, she tapped Jonah's flank to get him inside. "Go on, boy. I'll come back and check on you in a bit."

I shook my head as I slipped the rope off Boomer and watched him follow Jonah. "No, thank goodness. I woke up quite a few times, jumping at every little sound. But when I finally did fall asleep, I think my brain was just too worn out to let anything through."

"Reckon you can eat some breakfast? Sarie sent Amanda May over with some eggs this mornin. And she told her to tell us she has some new hatchlings, five or six of em, if we're interested. Said she'll bring em over this afternoon or we can go by and pick em up ourselves. Shouldn't be too long before we'll have plenty of fresh eggs again. I reckon our girls are gettin too old to lay many anymore."

I had no idea how long Luther, the cabin's previous owner, had had the chickens before he died and was equally in the dark as to how long the ornery animals lived or how long they could keep laying, for that matter.

Before I could ask, Abbie went on, "Have to add on to the chicken coop, a'course." She grinned wickedly. "Won't be long afore you'll get to put those famous egg-gatherin skills to use again."

I groaned as I walked over to pet Jonah, who remained by the gate. Abbie had been nice enough to take over that chore for me. I didn't relish the fact that I'd have to go back to it again. "I don't even want to think about that."

Abbie laughed. "That mean you don't want them hatchlings?"

"No, not exactly. It's the smart thing to do but I really do not want to think about doing battle with those fiendish hens again. I still have the scars from before." When I held out my right hand to show her, I noticed the bruises circling my wrist. I couldn't stop the shudder, remembering what caused them.

"Oh, Lizzie." Abbie took my hand, turning it over to examine the damage Jackson had done. "I bet that hurts somethin awful." She ran gentle fingers over my wrist. "You come on in the house. I'll make you a comfrey poultice to put on those bruises and leave it to set while I see to breakfast. Then I'll put another layer on and let it dry while we eat. After breakfast, we can wash it off and you should feel a little better." Keeping my hand in hers, she checked the gate to make sure it was secure then turned for the cabin. "I'm pretty sure we have a few pieces of that last loaf of sour dough to toast. I need to feed the starter today or tomorrow anyway so we can make a new loaf."

My mouth watered at the thought of Abbie's sour dough bread. "Do we have any peach jam left?"

She slung her arm around my shoulders. "We sure do. And I'll make you some honey tea to soothe that poor throat. Sounds like it's painin you some too."

After breakfast, we worked most of the morning on the barn and were on our way back to the house to wash up when Josh stepped out of the trees.

I ran toward him, smiling, anxious to hear how Viola had done on the first leg of her journey. "You made good time. I

19

didn't expect you back so soon. How did Viola do?"

I stopped short when I noticed he had Viola's neatly folded shawl tucked under his arm. It felt like my heart turned in a nasty somersault in my chest then jumped to lodge at the base of my throat, thrumming there in a jerky rhythm. I swallowed but it didn't help. "Oh, no. Oh, no, Josh. She didn't make it, did she?"

He shook his head as Abbie walked up to us. "What happened, Mr. Josh?"

"When I got to Pokni's last night, Viola was already gone. I'm not sure what happened but Pokni said she thought her heart just gave out on her as they were getting ready to eat dinner. She said Viola was so excited she couldn't talk about anything else all day except how she would soon be a free woman. Pokni was dishing out the rabbit stew she'd made when Viola suddenly went quiet. She looked over and saw her crumpled on the ground and said by the time she got to her, she was already gone."

I covered my mouth with my hand, swallowing hard to hold back the sob which managed to get past my heart. "She was already free. At least there's that, she died a free woman," I whispered.

Abbie slipped an arm around my waist. "That's all you can ask for. Ain't that right, Lizzie, ain't that what you said?" She turned to Josh. "Did Pokni stay with her till you got there, Josh?"

"After she dragged Viola over to the pallet in the corner where she'd been sleeping at night, she sat with her, holding her hand until I got there. She wanted you to know that, Abbie. She said something about hearing the Raven Mocker outside a few minutes after it happened and to tell you she didn't leave Viola alone for even a minute in order to protect her. When I asked what she meant, she said I should ask you, that you'd be able to tell me."

Abbie nodded. "It's the most feared spirit of the Cherokee. Although Pokni's Catawba, she believes in the Raven Mocker like a lot of people around here do, those that have heard the stories, anyway. It flies through the sky in the shape of a fiery bird and its call sounds like a raven. When it finds somebody who's just died or is about to die, it tries to steal their heart. That's why the People have someone sit up all night with the person who's passed on. You can't leave them alone or the Raven Mocker will take their heart. Pokni saved Viola from that."

I stood there, tears running down my face, disturbed and yet somehow comforted by Abbie's tale. "I hate that Viola's dead but I'm glad she wasn't alone when she died and that Pokni kept her safe until you got there, Josh. Did both of you sit up with her all night?"

Josh nodded then held out the bundled shawl to me. "Pokni said y'all might want to have this to remember her by. Abbie's comb is in there, along with Viola's other dress. If you don't want that, I'll take it home with me and give it to Tillie. I'm sure she'll know what to do with it or if someone can use it."

I took the shawl, crushed it to my heart.

"I'm sorry, Lizzie," he said and laid his hand on my back, rubbing gently.

"Thank you, Josh, and thank you for what you tried to do for her. I know it made her happy."

Abbie wiped her eyes with her apron. "Did you bury her, Mr. Josh?"

He nodded. "Dug the grave this morning near Pokni's place, under a wild dogwood tree beside some Mountain Laurel bushes. Pokni said she thought Viola would rest peaceful there. I wanted to build a small cairn over it to keep the animals away but Pokni wouldn't let me. She didn't want anyone wondering who lay beneath it so we left it bare."

I nodded. "Viola would prefer being buried there, I'm sure of it, rather than a slave's graveyard. You'll need to tell Tillie and Samuel where she's buried, set their minds to rest. They loved her so much."

Josh nodded. "I'll tell them as soon as I get back home." He ran his hand over his face. "I just wish I could have done more for her."

I hated to see him hurting and took his hand. "You did all you could, much more than anyone else did. Isn't that right, Abbie?"

"He surely—" Abbie looked away, narrowing her eyes.

I turned in the direction she was facing, wondering what she was staring at.

Holding hands, Maggie and Randall stepped, with obvious hesitation, out of the trees. Maggie had a dreamy smile on her face, the one she always had after a rendezvous with Randall. Anyone who looked at the two of them together could see they were deeply in love.

Josh and I stared as Abbie frowned slightly then her lips turned up into a beaming smile. Her next words echoed my thoughts. "Good thing Sarie ain't here. Why, she'd have a dyin duck fit, sure as I'm born."

"Oh, hang Sarie." I laughed as the two made their way to us. "Don't they make a pretty picture, Abbie?"

She shrugged. "I reckon they do at that, but if'n I know Sarie, she'll put a stop to it quicker'n two shakes of a sheep's tail."

I had my doubts about that. This had been going on for as long as I'd been on the mountain and Sarie had yet to see it. I suspected Maggie, though normally soft-spoken and pliable to Sarie, had an inner core of steel, one that could not be bent where Randall was concerned. If she loved him the way I thought she did, she wouldn't allow anyone to come between them, not even her older sister.

When they got to us, Maggie dropped Randall's hand then leaned in to hug Abbie and give her a kiss on the cheek. She did the same with me before nodding at Josh as she stepped back. When her hand immediately clutched Randall's again, I saw the glint of gold on her left ring finger.

Maggie turned to Abbie, and when she noticed her sister's tear-stained cheeks, her expression changed to one of concern. "What's wrong? Are you all right? Are you hurt?" She reached out with her free hand to run it up and down her sister's arm, her eyes roaming Abbie's body in search of injuries. "What is it, Abbie, what happened?"

"I'm all right, Maggie, just sad. Mr. Josh here brought us some bad news, is all. He just told us Viola's passed on."

"Oh, how awful." Maggie turned to Josh. "I'm sorry, Mr. Josh. She was a good woman. I know she'll be missed by everyone at your place."

"She will. The news is going to break my mama's heart."

"I know it will. Mrs. Hampton's had Viola for an awful long time, before she married your papa even. She told me she brought her with her from her home up in Madison County." She looked back at her sister. "Abbie, we need to make sure to send Mr. Josh home with some Saint John's wort to help Mrs. Hampton get through this."

I frowned, wanting so badly to say Mrs. Hampton may have "had" Viola since before she was married, but Viola had died a free woman. I held my tongue though. I wasn't acquainted with Randall well enough to know how he felt about people owning other people, although his father had several slaves. For all I knew, he could be like Josh or a rabid anti-abolitionist.

Abbie nodded. "I'll give him some afore he leaves." I smiled as Abbie gave Randall a curious look. I suspected Maggie and Randall's reason for being here but Abbie apparently hadn't figured it out yet.

Randall touched the brim of his hat as he nodded at each of us in turn. "Miss Abbie, Miss Lizzie." Without addressing us further, he turned to look at Josh, idly scratching his chin, as if he had other things on his mind at the present. "I reckon you heard the news already, Josh."

Josh shook his head. "I've been busy. What news?"

I expected Randall to say something about Constable Jackson being gone even though I was sure it was too early for anyone to have noticed his disappearance. I did my best to look concerned as I wondered if Sheriff Brittain was even now on his way to question Abbie and me.

"Well, as I reckon you know, since North Carolina seceded from the Union last month, the town's been in an uproar. There's been some high talk about volunteering, and people are taking sides and fighting over who's right, the Confederacy or the Union."

I released the breath that had backed up in my lungs, grabbing Josh's arm as if to keep him from going right that minute to join in the fighting.

Josh merely shrugged. "That was bound to happen

sooner or later. Look at the Walker brothers. Hell ... pardon me ladies ... if two brothers can kill each other over this blamed dispute between the states, I reckon anybody can."

I looked down at the ground, remembering that awful day when Fleming and Carter Walker had come to blows over their different opinions about the upcoming war, at a church picnic, no less. That disagreement had ended with one brother dead, the other one facing murder charges. What Randall said next made my blood run like ice water through my veins.

Randall grimaced. "Yep, but some of the ones siding with the Confederacy are threatening to go ahead and take care of the problem by lynching any slaves they can get their hands on and every abolitionist they can scare up. Said if they're not on the same side, killing them would be an act of war against an enemy and that ain't no sin in their eyes and it ain't against the law so the sheriff couldn't arrest them." He shoved his hat back on his forehead. "They're talking about setting up an unofficial Rebel detachment which they think will give them the right to do whatever they want. I'm not sure if they'll actually do it," he went on, "but you know how these boys can get each other het up, so you might want to set up some kind of guard at your place until this settles down some. I'm gonna tell my pa he needs to do the same thing at our farm. We ain't got as many slaves as you do but our people are awful important to us."

Josh shook his head in disgust. "What good would killing the slaves do them? That will only enrage the slave owners since they won't have anyone to do the work. Not to mention, that'll get the Union sympathizers all fired up. They'll figure they have to retaliate in some way."

"Ain't sure what exactly they're hoping to accomplish. Could be they think if the slaves are dead, the Union soldiers wouldn't have any reason to fight."

"I reckon with those boys, most any reason will do, but it's a mistake to think like that. Some of them are sure to end up dead or injured, but sounds like they're too bloodthirsty to worry about that."

"Happens I agree with you but there ain't a lot we can

do. Still, a guard at your place can't hurt."

Josh nodded. "It's worth thinking about. No reason to take any chances. I'll talk to Papa about it when I get home and we'll do whatever we can to make sure our people are safe and stay that way. Have you heard any other news?"

"No. That seems to be all everybody's talking about. How about you?"

Josh shook his head. "I haven't heard anything. Of course, I haven't been in town for awhile." He turned to me and took my hand. "I need to get on home, Lizzie, and talk to Papa. Would you walk with me for a minute?"

Abbie snorted. "Ain't no need for that, Mr. Josh," she said brightly. "Just go ahead and kiss her here while I fetch the St. John's wort." She winked at Maggie. "I've seen it before, and from the sight of you two, I reckon you and Mr. Randall won't be offended none."

Josh grinned. "Well, since I have your permission, Miss Abbie, I reckon I'll do just that." He bent down, brushed his lips softly against mine, whispering, "I'll come back when I'm able. If you and Abbie decide to visit Viola's grave, Pokni can show you where it is."

I went up on my tiptoes to kiss his cheek. "Thank you, Josh, for taking care of her."

He smiled. "It was the proper thing to do." He looked around at everyone. "Y'all take care of yourselves."

"I hope we'll get a chance to talk later," I called after him as he walked off toward the pasture where Boomer and Jonah were grazing side by side. I watched him lead Boomer back to the barn and saddle him. After he was mounted, he disappeared into the trees with a wave in our direction. As always, I hated to see him go.

Abbie drew my attention back to her as she demanded, "All right, what the heck is goin on with you two?"

Randall looked into Maggie's eyes. "Do you want me to tell her, Maggie?"

"No, I can do it." She cleared her throat. "Randall and I need your help, Abbie."

"What with?" Abbie asked, obviously confused. She pinned Randall with a glare.

Her puzzlement brought a smile to my lips. Apparently Abbie still hadn't caught sight of the thin gold band Maggie now wore on the ring finger of her left hand. Unless I missed my guess, they wanted Abbie to help break the news to Sarie that they were married, maybe even help smooth the path a bit for the two newlyweds.

Randall opened his mouth but, seeing Abbie's look, seemed to go blank. He turned helplessly to Maggie, waving his hand in a circle as if that would jumpstart the words or force them out of his mouth somehow.

"Well, Randall and I went to the church this morning ..." Maggie started then faltered, looking beseechingly at her sweetheart.

Randall cleared his throat. "What Maggie's trying to tell you is we had Preacher Hennessy marry us. Miss Freda acted as witness." He broke off to smile at his wife. "We're married and we're going to move in with my parents until I finish the cabin I'm building out near Morgan and Connie's place. That way, Maggie will be close to her family and so will I."

Maggie's imploring look turned into a dreamy smile. She leaned against Randall before looking back at Abbie, whose mouth hung open.

I grinned, tapping a finger under her chin. "Close your mouth, Abbie, before you catch flies."

Abbie's teeth clicked together but she remained silent.

I held out my hands to Maggie and Randall. "While Abbie catches her breath, I'll say congratulations to you both."

They each took a hand. "Thank you, Lizzie," Maggie said as she pulled me into a hug.

Randall nodded his agreement. "Yes, Miss Lizzie, thank you."

"You're both more than welcome. I'll wish you many years of happiness." And peace, I silently added but without much hope of that happening. After all, though we may have only been a month or so into it, we were involved in what would be known in my time as the bloodiest war in the history of this country, even into the next century. I knew that the years after the war were hard ones for the South but had no idea how the mountaineers fared.

I looked at Abbie, rubbing my hand over her back then patting it. "How are you doing there, Abbie?"

She shook her head, a smile appearing on her mouth before she stopped, grabbed Maggie, pulled her into her arms and bounced her up and down. "You're married," she whispered, as though it was still a secret. Then, a few seconds later, she laughed. "You're married! That's wonderful, Maggie." She held out a hand to Randall who took it. "And yes, congratulations to both of you. You'll take good care of my sister, won't you, Mr. Randall? If not, I'm goin to want to know the reason why."

"We'll take care of each other, Abbie," Maggie said before looking up at Randall again with both eyebrows raised in question.

He smiled at her. "Oh, right. I'm sorry, Maggie. Actually, we need to talk to you, both of you, about something else."

"What's that?" I asked.

"Well, it's more Miss Abbie we need, but you might be able to help some too, Miss Lizzie." He paused, cleared his throat. "Fact is, we're hoping you can help us tell Miss Sarie and convince her to give us her blessing. She's the head of the family, with Maggie's ma and pa both gone, and it, well, it'd mean the world to me if ..."

I couldn't hold back the snort. "Good luck with that. And believe me, you don't want my help. Sarie hates me and would just as soon see me covered in honey and staked out on an anthill as to go along with anything I say."

Abbie made a shushing gesture. "Oh, hush up now, Lizzie. Sarie don't hate you. She's just not quite sure of you yet. And she's not that bad. I think she might be agreeable if she knew for sure Maggie was happy. All a person has to do is look at the two of em. Why, even a blind pig could see they're in love, they're glowin like one of them lights up here on the mountain." She grinned at them. "I swan, it makes me happy just lookin at you two."

Maggie and Randall smiled.

"Does that mean you'll help us?" Maggie asked.

"A-course we will. When did you want to tell her?"

With obvious reluctance, Randall said, "I reckon now's as good a time as any. Get it over with and all. The sooner we do that, the sooner we can start our married life."

"I reckon that's a good idea," Abbie said. "But first have y'all had lunch yet?"

Randall shook his head. "Miss Freda served us coffee and blueberry muffins after we said our words then Maggie wanted to come tell you right away." He looked at Maggie, who shook her head, before saying, "We ain't really hungry at the moment."

Abbie nodded. "We had sort of a late breakfast so I ain't hungry. Can you wait a while, Lizzie?"

"Of course. I'm so full of joy that I may never be hungry again. Let's go conquer the raging beast."

Abbie nodded. "All right, that's what we'll do then. I'll go in and get my basket in case we see something we can gather on the way."

She turned to go just as movement in the trees behind Maggie and Randall caught my eye. "Abbie, when did you say Sarie was going to bring those chicks over?"

"She said she might be here this afternoon—" She broke off as Sarie and Amanda May, carrying a small wooden crate, stepped out of the woods. "Oh, no. Give me a minute with her, Maggie."

Abbie stepped around Randall and went to greet her older sister. Maggie turned, caught sight of Sarie, and dropped Randall's hand like it was a hot potato, hiding her own left hand in the folds of her skirt.

When Randall saw Sarie, he winced then turned and took Maggie by the arm, sliding his hand down and linking fingers. She tried to shake him off but he held tight, raising her fingers to his lips to kiss them softly. He gave her an encouraging smile even as Maggie's cheeks pinked with color. "It's all right, Maggie. We'll handle this together," he whispered.

Abbie was talking to Sarie, gesturing wildly, but Sarie only had eyes for Maggie and Randall.

She shushed Abbie with a slash of her hand then

marched over toward us, cutting furious eyes at Randall before focusing on Maggie. "What's goin on here, Maggie?"

Maggie straightened her shoulders, bracing herself for her sister's wrath, I'm sure. It might have worked, but when she opened her mouth, nothing came out. She turned to look at Randall beseechingly.

"It's a pleasure to see you, Miss Sarie," he began. "You're looking right well today."

Sarie only spared him a quick glare. "I ain't talkin to you, Mr. Randall." She pointed her finger at Maggie. "I asked you what's goin on."

Maggie swallowed audibly then somehow found her courage. "Randall and I went to the church this morning and had Preacher Hennessy marry us. I know ..."

Sarie's face grew red. "You did what?"

Randall drew closer to Maggie as if protecting her. "We got married, Miss Sarie. We're hoping you'll give us your blessing."

Sarie's response was to turn around and stalk away from us. Abbie rushed after her, catching her just as she was about to enter the woods. She took Sarie's arm, saying something in a voice too low for us to hear. Amanda May looked on in confusion as if she didn't know whether to follow Sarie or stay where she was.

"I think it might be a good idea to go inside and let Abbie handle this for now. She's better with Sarie than anybody I know. Amanda May," I called out then motioned her over. "Let's go in and see what we can scare up for lunch." I pointed at the crate. "What have you got there?"

She blushed as she always seemed to do when addressed directly but answered the question readily enough. "These are the hatchlings I told Abbie about this morning. I can put them in the chicken coop if you want." She glanced nervously at Randall.

I smiled. "Bring them on inside. We'll let Abbie decide what to do with them. Have you met Mr. Randall?"

Her cheeks turned a brighter red when she looked at Randall. "I reckon I've seen him in church but we ain't been properly introduced." She nodded in Randall's direction then with a glance at Maggie, said, "I sure have heard a bunch about him though."

"Miss Amanda May," Randall said, "Maggie's told me a lot about you too. How are you liking our mountain? Maggie says you're settling in fine."

"It's nice," she muttered then shot Randall a worried look before turning back to Maggie. "Did ya do it?"

"We did." Maggie held out her left hand to show off her wedding ring.

Amanda May smiled at it then threw another concerned look in Randall's direction. Before I could assure her there was nothing to worry about, Maggie spoke up. "It's all right, Amanda May. Mr. Randall's family now."

Amanda May's silvery blue eyes shot up to Randall. "Pleased to meet ya," she said, almost whispering the words.

"Here, let me get that for you," Randall said, reaching for the crate then turning to me. "Where do you want it, Miss Lizzie? Chicken coop or inside?"

I could hear the cheeps coming from inside the wooden box. "They sound like they're awful young yet, so I guess we'll need to keep them in the cabin where they'll be warm. Wouldn't you say, Maggie?"

Maggie peeked in the crate and smiled. "They need to get some age on em before I'd trust em in the coop. You'll need to watch the other hens around em for a bit. They might peck at em until they get used to sharing their home."

"Inside it is, then," I started to go up the steps but stopped when Sarie called out to Maggie.

Turning, I watched with the others as Sarie and Abbie walked back to us. Braced for an angry tirade, it was my mouth that fell open this time when Sarie gave Maggie a tight smile before holding out her right hand to Randall. "I can't say I like how you went about it, Mr. Randall, but I welcome you into our family."

Maggie pulled Sarie into a tight hug. "Oh, Sarie, thank you, thank you."

"I want to thank you, too, Miss Sarie," Randall said with a smile. "I promise you I'll take real good care of your sister."

"You better if'n you know what's good for you."

Abbie stepped up beside me, tapped her fingers under my chin. "Close your mouth, Lizzie, afore you catch flies."

Abbie and I threw together a quick celebratory lunch for Maggie and Randall, who left shortly afterwards to share the news with his parents. Sarie and Amanda May followed a bit later, intending to check on a family suffering from abdominal cramps and diarrhea. "I s'pect they didn't cook their chicken well enough," Sarie said sagely as they left.

As Abbie and I were clearing the table, my mind turned to Jackson and with a start I remembered his beautiful black horse. "Abbie, Jackson had to have ridden his horse up here. Do you think he's here on the mountain somewhere, wandering around? I didn't see him last night."

Abbie gave me a look. "Knowing the constable, he's either tied to a tree or hobbled and can't break free."

Without speaking, we rushed out the door.

We searched the perimeter of our cabin then alongside the trail where I had met Constable Jackson, breaking off to go into the woods, listening for sounds of a large animal nearby. I didn't know what Jackson called his horse so instead made clucking sounds as I wandered around. I heard Abbie's voice in the distance and ran that way, coming upon her in a small clearing, trying to free the horse. Jackson had tied him to a tree, high enough that he couldn't move his head down to the ground to graze or even back away a foot or two from his tether.

When she saw me, she hollered, "You got your knife with you?"

I felt in my apron, nodding when my hand touched it. Since the start of the war, Sarie had insisted we all carry knives with us for protection. I hurried over to Abbie and sawed through the rope, cursing the knot Jackson had tied, which had tightened as the horse struggled to free itself.

Once the rope loosened, the horse immediately lowered his head to the ground, as if greatly relieved. After a moment, he began to graze on the grass at the base of the tree.

I stooped down to remove his halter so he could feed more freely. "What kind of an idiot was that man?" I raved.

"The poor horse couldn't graze, get water. And what if a bear or mountain lion found him? They'd have killed him."

Abbie gave me a look. "I reckon the constable didn't think he'd end up stepping into a light and disappearing."

I couldn't help but laugh at her expression. After a moment, I said, "What should we do?"

She shrugged. "I reckon we can take him into town or have Josh do it."

I shook my head as an idea occurred to me. "Let's keep him."

Abbie's eyes widened.

I hurried on, hoping to convince her. "Jackson didn't have any family, Abbie. And if anyone says anything, we can just tell them we found him wandering the mountain and were taking care of him while we were waiting for Jackson to come claim him."

Abbie thought about that for a bit.

"Please, Abbie. I don't want him to go to another person who will mistreat him the way the constable did. You saw how brutal he was with him."

She finally shrugged. "I reckon I'll leave it up to you, Lizzie. Asides, we ain't lyin other than to say he was wanderin when he was actually tied up. And we did find him. I reckon Jonah will be happy for the company," she went on, rubbing her palm up beneath the horse's mane.

I smiled at her, thrilled at the thought of showing this gorgeous animal that life for him would now be a happy, safe one. At least, as long as I had him. As if sensing my thoughts, he raised his velvety nose and placed it against my neck, snuffing, his breath warm against my skin. "We'll call him Beauty," I said, kissing him between the ears.

CHAPTER THREE

Late Spring 1861

You Upset the Grace of Living When You Lie

Although we kept anticipating his arrival, close to a week passed before Sheriff Brittain came by to question us about Constable Jackson. Abbie and I had just finished breakfast and were walking outside to let Jonah and Beauty out of the barn when we heard the jangling of a harness in the trees nearby. As we stood still, waiting for the rider to reveal himself, I thought what a beautiful morning it was, the trees and foliage around us seeming to shine in varying shades of green, colorful wildflowers blooming in the meadow, with a faint, warm breeze carrying the verdant odor of growing plants reaching for the sun mixed with the faint, musky tang of horse manure from the barn and pasture. We tensed when Sheriff Brittain came into view, tilting his hat at us before reining in his horse and dismounting. Abbie and I gave each other a wary glance before forcing smiles on our faces and going to greet him. We had discussed what we would say when someone came looking for the constable but I feared my acting skills did not match up to Abbie's and I would give us away.

"Good mornin, Sheriff," Abbie said, grabbing his horse's halter.

"Morning to you both." Sheriff Brittain took off his hat and beat it against the side of his leg. Watching dust motes dance in the air around him, I stepped back before they landed on me. I was having a hard enough time dealing with pollen as it was.

Ignoring this, Abbie said, "We just finished breakfast, Sheriff. You hungry or perchance thirsty? We got some coffee left, I reckon."

"I thank you kindly, Miss Abbie, but I ate before I rode up here." He looked from Abbie to me, his gaze lingering on me.

Growing nervous from his stare, I burst out, "We're glad to see you, Sheriff. Abbie and I have been meaning to come into town to see Constable Jackson but we've been so busy doing chores and tending to the sick, we never got the chance."

His eyes narrowed slightly. "That right? What were you needing to see Jackson about?"

"We found his horse wandering around a few days back but no Constable Jackson. We figured the horse must have got lost so were planning to return him to the constable."

"Is that right?" He drew back, studying both of us with open interest. "Fact is, I come to talk to you about Jackson. Seems the man's disappeared."

I made my eyes go wide while putting my hand to my chest, trying to act surprised. I didn't dare look at Abbie to see how she showed her faux shock at this news, afraid I'd burst out laughing from nerves and the sheriff would know we were lying. He watched us both and I could only pray we were convincing.

"Well, we ain't seen him on the mountain in a good bit," Abbie said. "Used to, why, he'd show up ever other day, seemed like, wanting to question us about this or that."

The sheriff spat out tobacco juice. "Well, Jackson had his suspicions about y'all, that's for sure. Was convinced you were helping runaway slaves get up north."

Abbie snorted with derision. "Like we ain't got enough to keep us busy tendin to the sick on the mountain and down in Morganton. If you want to know the truth of it, Sheriff, he was mad 'cause Sarie rebuffed him sometime back. Couldn't seem to get over that and took it out on us ever chance he got. We told you about him before but you didn't want to get involved, told us it'd work itself out. I'm sorry the man's gone missin but not sorry we don't have to put up with him accusin us of ever'thing under the sun all the time. I ain't gonna lie to you when I tell you it's a bit of a relief."

"Well, I figured he'd eventually give up and move onto something else," Sheriff Brittain said, looking defensive. "Didn't know he would hold a grudge for so long. But that ain't why I'm here. I've come to ask if you've seen him in the last week."

Abbie and I shook our heads.

"Ain't seen hide nor hair," Abbie said. "Like Lizzie said, we found his horse wandering the mountain a little under a week ago. We brung him here and've been feedin and waterin him, thinking the constable would show up to claim him afore we got a chance to go down to Morganton to seek him out." She glanced at me. "I wonder where in the world the man could have got to."

I shrugged, trying my best to continue to look shocked at the news of the constable missing.

"A-course, we ain't the only ones the constable give a hard time," Abbie continued. "Have you talked to anybody else to see if they know where he might have gone?"

Sheriff Brittain nodded. "Been all over this mountain but no one claims to've seen him. I ain't seen Sarie or Maggie yet, figured I'd go on over there after I talked to y'all."

"I reckon that's a good idea. He always found a reason to seek Sarie out, so maybe she's seen him. But you best look for Maggie at Randall's folks' place. They got hitched, you know."

Sheriff Brittain nodded. "I heard the good news. I'll be sure to wish her well when I see her."

Abbie frowned as if thinking. "You reckon the constable's got family somewhere else he's gone to see?"

Sheriff Brittain shifted the wad of tobacco from one side of his mouth to the other. "Don't think so. He never talked about having family. Didn't have many friends, but the ones I've talked to ain't seen him neither." He hesitated. "To tell

35

the truth, the man wasn't well liked around these parts. Seems they's quite a few people won't be missing him."

Hoping to distract him from suspicion of us, I said, "What about the lights?" Ignoring Abbie's gasp, I continued, "I've heard they take people from time to time. Remember Mr. Westscott and his slaves? A lot of people said the lights took them and they still haven't been found. You reckon that could have happened to Constable Jackson?"

Sheriff Brittain shook his head, his lips in a thin line. "That's all just talk, has been for years. As for Westscott and them two boys, if you ask me, them slaves ran away and Westscott got lost or snake bit or something. He's probably at the bottom of a ravine somewhere. Other than that, ain't nobody disappeared off this mountain in a good while, not since Abbie's pa." He paused, studying her. "How long ago has that been, you reckon?"

Abbie shrugged. "A good many years. If'n you ask me, Pa got drunk and wasn't watchin where he was goin and fell off a cliff or met up with a hungry bear. He was a mean drunk, as I'm sure you'll recall. Why he'd just as soon shoot you as look at you even when he wasn't drinkin. Wouldn't surprise me at all he got hisself all liquored up and tried to take on a bear instead of run from one."

Sheriff Brittain nodded, his eyes on the forest behind us. "I don't reckon many looked too hard for the man. He was a mean son of a ..." Seeming to remember he was talking to the daughter of the very man he was belittling, he glanced at Abbie and sighed. "Begging your pardon, Miss Abbie." He waited for her nod before he went on. "Well, I reckon I'll head on over and talk to Sarie and Maggie. If'n Jackson shows up to collect his horse, be sure and tell him I'm looking for him. He's left us a man short and we need all the help we can get, what with this war raging and everybody in an uproar over which side to fight for."

"What about his horse, Sheriff?" I asked, hoping we could keep him. He was a gorgeous animal, solid black and well-muscled, with a gentle temperament, which I found surprising, having witnessed the harsh treatment he received from Constable Jackson. Although it was too late, Abbie constantly cautioned me not to get too attached. Every time she said this, I couldn't help but reply, "That horse has already left the barn, Abbie." When I explained what I meant, she frowned at me, not appreciating the humor. "I mean to keep him if I can," I told her. I wasn't sure how but I intended to do everything I could to make sure such a beautiful, sweet animal stayed with someone who loved him and didn't end up with a man as brutal as Jackson had been.

Sheriff Brittain sighed as if aggravated. "Ain't nobody I know to give him to till Jackson shows up. I shore don't want to pay the stable fee for him. I reckon you can keep him with you, if you've a mind to."

I smiled at that. "We'd love to. He's no problem at all."

"I can't pay you for his care," Sheriff Brittain said, his brow furrowed.

"Oh, don't worry about that. We have pasture and water, he'll be fine." I squeezed Abbie's hand, happy at this.

"You be sure and let me know if you see Jackson," Sheriff Brittain said, putting one foot in the stirrup and swinging up onto the saddle.

"We will, Sheriff. Good luck finding him. Hopefully he'll turn up soon."

"He better or he ain't gonna have a job." He doffed his hat and nodded at us before riding away.

We waited until he was well out of earshot before speaking. "You think he believed us, Abbie?"

She stared after the sheriff with a worried look. "I ain't for sure. He's a smart man, Lizzie, smarter than he acts." She sighed. "Ain't no use to worry about it now. We'll find out sooner or later if'n he doesn't."

As we made our way to the barn, I couldn't help but again wonder where the light had taken Jackson and what his life was like at this point. Would it be as hard for him as it had been for me? Would he be accepted or rejected, believed or disbelieved? As much as I disliked the man, I couldn't squelch the pity I felt for him, knowing how traumatic it was to travel from one time and place to another. I could only pray he never found his light and made it back to this time and place, because if he did, he would make our lives hell on earth if he didn't kill us as soon as he saw us.

That afternoon, we decided to hike up to Pokni's place to visit Viola's burial site. We found Pokni placing wildflowers on the still-fresh grave resting beneath a wild dogwood tree, the wind causing the shadows of the leaves above to dance over the dark earth as if celebrating the body beneath. Josh told us Pokni insisted no marker be placed in case anyone got suspicious as to who lay beneath the earth but I thought there couldn't have been a better one than the beautiful tree she rested beneath, especially when it flowered in the spring. After we knelt in the cool breeze beside the grave and said a prayer for Viola's spirit, we all walked back to Pokni's small hut, where we sat outside, Pokni and I sharing one of her handmade cigarettes while Abbie played with Pokni's wolf pup Nashoba.

"He's going to be huge," I observed as I took a puff and handed the cigarette back to Pokni.

Pokni nodded, a proud smile on her face. "Did I tell you the story of Hatakachafa, the hunting god who met the very first wolf and taught him to howl?"

I smiled. I so loved hearing these legends. "No, but you know I can't resist one of your stories, Pokni."

Abbie joined us, saying, "Me too, Pokni."

Pokni took her last puff of the cigarette before burying the stub in the dirt at her feet. I caught Nashoba as he darted by, pulled him to me and kissed his furry face. He licked me before squirming to be put down and darted off, chasing a leaf scurrying over the ground.

Pokni looked into the dark forest, smiling a bit as she always did when relaying these legends. I often wondered if she saw images there of her people, or perhaps was remembering the story being told to her as a child. "Hatakachafa means Nameless One. Some say Nameless Man or One Man Alone. Hatakachafa was the only son of Eyasho, the war chief of the Choctaw village. He was known for his handsomeness, great courage, and hunting skills. Although he had outgrown his boyhood name, he had not

38

been given his adult name because he had yet to kill an enemy of the Choctaw in wartime. Hatakachafa was in love with Imma, the most beautiful maiden of the time, and always placed large amounts of game at the door of her family's lodge, but the two could not marry until he won his adult name in battle. He finally got his chance when the Choctaw made plans to war against the Osages. He said goodbye to his lover atop a hill filled with pine trees and with four hundred other braves left to face the enemy.

"Days later, the party he was leading sought shelter for the night in a huge cave in Osage country. Overnight, Osage warriors killed the sentries and started a smoky fire, using the fumes to suffocate the Choctaw war party, killing with arrows those who emerged from the cave coughing and choking. Hatakachafa went deeper into the cave to escape the smoke and wound up wandering for many days before emerging into a strange part of the world no Choctaw had ever seen before. He encountered a horse-sized white wolf, the very first wolf on Earth. The two began to fight but were so impressed with each other's battle skills that they became loyal companions and the wolf let Hatakachafa ride him like a horse as they traveled along. Armed with a blowgun and bow and arrow, Hatakachafa and his wolf had many adventures together, slaying many monsters. They spent twelve turns of the moon trying to find the way home, and when Hatakachafa finally returned, he learned that his beloved Imma, thinking him dead, had grieved herself to death atop the hill where the two lovers said goodbye. Hatakachafa and his giant wolf went there, where he knelt down and let out long, mournful howls over and over again before falling down dead. The wolf, in sadness, imitated the howls of Hatakachafa before leaving to mate with dogs and spawn all the smaller wolves in the world, teaching them the howl of his late Choctaw friend. It is said that for many years after, even the pine trees atop the hill where the two lovers died would howl like wolves to honor them. Nanishta welcomed Hatakachafa to the underlife and elevated him to godhood, and many Choctaw pray to him for success in hunting. Imma became the beautiful idol of warriors, whose successes are dedicated to her."

"It's a lovely story, Pokni," I said, as I once again caught the pup as he ran by.

Abbie wiped tears from her eyes. "It's so sad she died grieving him afore she could learn he was still alive."

I nodded, making a mental note to tell Abbie the story of Romeo and Juliet.

"But they came together in the after," Pokni said, her eyes distant. "Just as I will with my warrior."

Abbie and I smiled at one another. Pokni didn't often talk about her dead husband, but when she did, it was obvious the love she had for him still flamed bright.

Abbie and I began to talk about inconsequential things, giving Pokni time with her memories. When I noticed Pokni watching us, I told her about what happened with Constable Jackson and the sheriff's subsequent visit. When I finished, I said, "I think we convinced him we didn't know what happened to the constable, but I'm not sure."

Pokni shrugged. "He has no proof you were near the man the night he went through the light, so there is nothing he can do."

I looked at her. "I wonder sometimes where he went, Pokni."

"There is no need to wonder about something you have no way to know. He is where he is and on his own journey."

"I just pray he doesn't find that light and come back here."

"There is no need to worry about that, Daughter, until it happens. I doubt he will understand he has to come through the same light that carried him to wherever he is. He will probably stay or end up in another time and place."

"Well, I can't say I'm sorry it happened to him," Abbie said, getting to her feet in preparation to leave. "All I know is our lives will be a lot easier around here without him."

I joined her, bending down and kissing Pokni on the cheek. "We'll see you soon," I told her, waiting as Abbie kissed her goodbye. I turned back before we entered the forest to wave bye but Pokni was staring off into the distance again, no doubt returning to her memories of her beloved warrior.

Chapter Four

Early Fall 1862

Find the Cost of Freedom

Before I knew it, well over a year had passed on Brown Mountain with no luck finding my light, but then again, I rarely had a chance to search for it. The sisters and I stayed busy tending the sick due to an influenza outbreak that started in the early fall and lasted through the winter, some cases leading to pneumonia, others to death. When we weren't treating the infirm, we stayed busy finding and fixing hidey holes for our animals and food in case of raids. Sarie knew of the perfect hiding place for our horses, mule, goats, milk cows, chickens and food. It stood in a hollow between two ridges, both of which were heavily wooded and hard to transgress unless one knew about the hidden trail we had made. With Josh's and Randall's help, we built pens for the livestock and hid food in the weeds and grass, piling hay on top so it looked like stacks of hay in a meadow to anyone passing by. We did this at night so no one would see us then created a false hidey hole a couple of miles away the raiders could easily find, which we hoped would stop them from exploring further. It seemed we were gone from sunup to well after sundown, with rarely any time for respite or simply to sit and enjoy time alone.

Constable Jackson's disappearance caused a small stir of interest on the mountain but most seemed relieved he was gone. I noted no one made an attempt to really find the man, other than Sheriff Brittain, who quickly gave up. After a couple of months, I rarely heard Jackson mentioned, and only then in a negative context. Sarie never talked about him but, like us, I'm sure his absence was a welcome one.

During this time, Josh became our source for information about the war, other than rumors that bounded about like flies on rotted meat. Josh occasionally received outdated copies of the *New York Times*, smuggled to him from the news reporter he spied for, and although the news he relayed was delayed, we were all eager to learn how the war fared and if it presented any threat to Brown Mountain from the North. I was surprised when Josh said at the start of the war, the Confederacy called for 100,000 volunteers, and so many men stepped up, 1/3 had to be sent home. At that time, there were 21 million northerners and 9 million confederates, 4 million of which were slaves. I told Josh this must have contributed in some way to the fact that the South lost, with such a vast difference in the number of soldiers each side would have. The South cheered when Robert E. Lee declined President Abraham Lincoln's offer to be field commander of the Union due to his loyalty to his home state of Virginia, which had seceded.

At the beginning, both sides somewhat optimistically thought this would be a 90-day war. I hadn't been aware that Lincoln insisted he was making war on secession not slavery and initially ordered escaping slaves be returned to their owners. Congress eventually interceded and the slaves were used as labor in the Union Army.

The South cheered its victory at the first major battle of the Civil War, the First Battle of Bull Run, also called the First Battle of Manassas, which was fought on July 21, 1861, just 25 miles distant from Washington, DC. This was the war where General Thomas J. Jackson received his famous nickname Stonewall due to his stubbornness in standing his ground and not retreating. I couldn't believe it when Josh told us that civilians rode out to picnic while watching the battle, apparently their confidence in the Union overriding their commonsense. The Union seemed to be winning until Confederate reinforcements arrived to save the day. As the Union troops began to withdraw under fire, many panicked, turning their retreat into a disorganized rout, frantically running in the direction of Washington, DC and getting tangled together with the civilians, who were also fleeing. It became known as the Great Skedaddle with close to 5,000 Union casualties. This battle brought home to the North that this war was not going to be a short-lived one to be watched from afar and commented on but rather a longer, bloody one.

The same reality came to the South with the Battle of Shiloh, fought in April, 1862, when Union General Ulysses S. Grant's Army met Confederate forces under the command of General Albert Sidney Johnston at Shiloh, Tennessee. This was a brutal, bloody battle involving close to 100,000 troops, resulting in thousands of fatalities and tens of thousands casualties. I found it somewhat ironic when Josh told me that Shiloh meant place of peace. The North's victory proved to the South that Lincoln was serious about maintaining the Union, which seemed to make the Confederacy dig in their heels, determined more than ever to win the war, no matter how long it might take.

But on Brown Mountain, we saw no action nor heard of battles nearby and began to hope we were insular and would not be drawn into this war. Although we were aware a Confederacy training camp had been established near Morganton, we had never actually seen it and didn't know much about it other than it was called Camp Vance after former Congressman, Civil War hero and now governor, Zebulon Vance. But one Sunday after church services when I spied a young man in a gray uniform stepping out of the forest, glancing around, as Josh and I were standing outside talking with Abbie and Amanda May, I suspected we would know much more before too long. Josh, following my gaze, squeezed my hand before moving away to greet the stranger. They spoke for a few moments, Josh gesturing our way, then began walking toward us.

Once they reached us, Josh said, "Lizzie, Miss Abbie, Miss Amanda May, this here's Thomas Crowley, a Confederate soldier from over in Camp Vance."

Without thinking about it, I held out my hand before remembering women in this day and age rarely shook hands with anyone. To cover my gaffe, I quickly raised it to brush at my hair, saying, "It's nice to meet you, Mr. Crowley."

"Ma'am," he said, his Adam's apple bobbing up and down. I studied him for a moment, noting he wore a uniform more resembling that of the Southern militia than the Confederacy. Although he didn't look old enough to shave, he was a handsome devil in that uniform, his body lean and strong, with dark blond hair, pale blue eyes and a square jaw.

"Is that the training camp for the rebels we're hearin so much about?" Abbie asked, looking interested. I vaguely wondered at the cause, the camp or this young soldier standing before us.

"Yes, ma'am, it's a training base for the state troops, of which I'm proud to say I'm part of, and a stopping ground for Union prisoners on their way to Salisbury Prison Camp."

"Where exactly is the camp?" I asked.

"Oh, I reckon it's roughly three, four miles outside of Morganton, right near the end of the Western North Carolina Railroad."

"What brings you to our neck of the woods?" Josh asked, shifting restlessly.

"Well, sir, we got us some recruits out there a-needing some medical tending, I reckon."

Abbie and I perked up at that. Before we could say anything, Josh interjected, "Are you looking for a doctor or anyone in particular?"

"Ain't had no luck in regards to a doctor. I went into town but the doc there said he ain't in no sort of mood to go traipsing out to where we're set up on such a fine Sunday as this, said I might come on up here and fetch the Collins sisters. Said they're healers and could probably help us out."

Abbie smiled. "I reckon he's right. I'm Abbie Collins and this here's my cousin Lizzie Baker and that there's Amanda

45

May, our ..." She squinted her eyes at me. "What's that you call her, Lizzie?"

"Intern."

"Intern. She's stayin with us while we teach her all about healin." She glanced around. "My sisters Maggie and Sarie are around here somewheres."

His eyes brightened with relief. "You reckon you could fetch them, ma'am, and see if they'd be willing to come help us out?"

Abbie shrugged. "Won't hurt to ask. I'll be right back." She turned on her heel and flaunted away. I didn't miss the way the young soldier's eyes followed her, alight with appreciation. Josh and I exchanged an amused glance over Amanda May's head at this.

"Don't you have doctors in camp?" I asked.

"Well, we only got the one for now and he's overwhelmed, what with so many sick and all."

"What's the trouble out there?" Josh asked.

"Got some burned hands, cuts, whatnot." He glanced around as his face reddened, then leaned forward and whispered, "A good many's got the diarrhea awful bad and can't seem to get any relief." He straightened up, saying, "Our commandant, Major McClean, thinks they're spreading it among themselves so ordered me to fetch somebody to come right away to see if they could get it stopped afore everybody caught it and the whole camp went down."

Oh, boy, I thought.

"Well, I don't reckon you could get better healers than the sisters and Lizzie and Amanda May here," Josh said. I threw him a dirty glance, thinking, wait until you have to deal with foul-smelling diarrhea and see how you feel, but Josh blatantly ignored me.

Abbie joined us, towing Sarie and Maggie with her. We listened to the young trooper tell them the camp's woes all over again and all waited tor Sarie, who was definitely our leader, to make the decision.

She gave him a curt nod. "Well, I reckon we ain't got nothin better to do. That is, unless your major ain't willin to pay us for our trouble."

"Oh, no, ma'am, he'll pay."

"Not in any of them Confederate dollars," Sarie said. "It ain't no use around these parts, or anywhere else, from what I'm a-hearing."

Thomas looked embarrassed. "I don't rightly know what he was planning to pay you with, ma'am. I reckon it's best you take that up with him. But if you're willing to at least talk to him afore treating the sick, I'll be happy to take you on over."

"We got to go to our cabin and get our medical bags," Sarie said. "I reckon it'll take us an hour to get there and back."

"I got me a horse and wagon right inside the tree line there," Thomas said, gesturing in that direction.

Sarie nodded. "That'll do." She turned to Abbie. "Y'all brought Jonah and Beauty with you today, didn't you?" At our collective nods, she continued, "Well, it shouldn't take you much longer than us to get up to your cabin and collect your things. We'll meet you down below, on the road to Morganton."

Josh put his hat on his head. "I'll ride along if y'all don't mind." I did not miss the excitement in his eyes, which terrified me. I knew he was thinking he could possibly find out some crucial information to pass on to the New York Times reporter he had agreed to spy for. Josh didn't seem to appreciate how terribly dangerous this could be, and no matter what I said, I couldn't make him understand. Or he simply chose not to.

"You can help empty the chamber pots," I said, giving him as bright a smile as I could manage.

His enthusiasm faltered a bit at that but he quickly regained it. "Of course, Lizzie, I'll be glad to help in any way I can."

As Abbie and I rode back to our cabin, I tried to remember what I had learned about the Civil War and illnesses suffered by soldiers. I must have been paying attention that day in school because some facts seemed to have taken hold in my mind. After Abbie and I retrieved our medical bags and were making the return trip down the mountain, I told her what I remembered. "If I'm correct, two out of three soldiers didn't die from battle but from illness. Of the over 600,000 soldiers who died, more than 400,000 succumbed to sickness. Diarrhea and dysentery were the leading causes, I think."

"What's dysentery?" Abbie asked.

"Like diarrhea but with bloody stools."

"Fancy word for flux," she said with a grin.

"They also suffered from pneumonia, typhoid fever, rheumatic fever, measles, mumps, small pox, a whole host of diseases."

"Why do you reckon they got so sick?"

"Well, probably because a lot of the soldiers lived in smaller communities or were pretty isolated on farms, so they didn't experience the common, contagious diseases of childhood which made them more susceptible as adults."

Abbie was silent for a moment before saying, "I shore hope we don't have to deal with small pox again, Lizzie. But if we do, I'm glad we have you to help with it."

We rode past the church and onto the road leading to Morganton, where we found Sarie, Maggie and Amanda May standing at the wagon with Thomas, waiting for us. Josh stood aside talking to Maggie's husband Randall, who had brought her on horseback. Abbie and I remained on our steeds while Sarie hoisted herself onto Buck's back. Maggie gave her husband Randall a quick kiss, then she and Amanda May, aided by Josh, stepped up into the bed of the wagon and settled themselves. As Randall, who was helping the pastor do some sort of repair to the church, assured Maggie he would wait for her, I couldn't help but smile at the loving looks they gave each other. After Josh mounted his horse, we all set off at a quick pace.

It didn't take long to go the four miles or so, according to Thomas, to where the railroad tracks ended. Not far from there, we found the camp, set in a forest clearing, the soldiers living in primitive log huts and tents. Men strolled about in everything from snappy gray wool uniforms to pieced-together garb, trying to look soldierly, as we rode by. I was appalled at the condition of the camp, which smelled like a cess pit. Spoiled foods and refuse were thrown on the ground, among what looked like heaps of feces and wads of spat-out tobacco. Flies were everywhere, so thick in places, you couldn't tell what lay beneath.

We followed Thomas's wagon to a tent larger than most and waited outside while he led Sarie inside. The nod Sarie gave us when she exited a few minutes later told us Major McClean had apparently agreed to better compensation than the dreaded Confederate currency. Josh, Abbie and I dismounted while Maggie and Amanda May climbed out of the wagon. After assuring us our horses would be tended to, we followed the major toward a tent bearing a yellow flag which we were told was the infirmary. As we walked along, Major McClean told us the camp covered about five acres and had been established as a training facility by the state government with the majority of its occupants being volunteers, about 400 from Burke County alone.

Shaking my head in dismay at the unsanitary conditions of the camp, I stepped into the tent, immediately pulling my kerchief out of my apron and putting it over my nose to try to filter the smell, which was atrocious; a horrid mixture of feces, vomit, blood and body odor. Noting somewhat ironically that the major hadn't followed us inside, I nudged Abbie, pointing at my covered face. When she saw my nose and mouth hidden, she did the same, touching each of her sisters and Amanda May on the shoulder to alert them. All four looked at me, identical expectant expressions on their faces.

"This could be just a bad case of diarrhea being passed around or dysentery, which is contagious," I explained. "Keep your nose and mouth covered and be sure to wash your hands after you examine each person."

Sarie nodded. "I reckon the best thing to give those with such ailments is a tea of Turk's cap lily or raspberry leaf. Sassafras bark works pretty good too. I reckon I got plenty of raspberry leaf and sassafras bark in my bag if'n y'all need any."

As Sarie dug in her medical satchel for the herbs, we were joined by a man, tall and angular, with thick dark hair and eyes, who introduced himself as Dr. Glover. "I'm very pleased you were able to come," he said, gesturing at the inhabitants of the tent. "I only have three medics to assist and it's become a bit overwhelming."

Sarie gave him a curt nod. "We're right pleased to help." She turned to Amanda May, saying, "Amanda May, you stay close to me." Then she gestured toward the left side of the tent. "Lizzie, you and Abbie take that side of the room and Maggie and me will take this one." She marched off to help an ailing soldier, tying her kerchief over her face as she went.

Dr. Glover, who hadn't taken his eyes off Sarie, hurried after her.

I noticed a young man sitting on a cot nearby holding his hand, wrapped in a white rag. I crossed over to him and introduced myself. "Did you hurt your hand?"

"I reckon I burned it purty bad," he said.

I knelt beside him and began to unwrap the bandage, inwardly wincing when it revealed a bright red, blistered palm. "How'd you burn it?"

"On my ole muzzle loader." I gave him a questioning look. "The barrel gets awful hot after you shoot it a couple of times and if'n you don't wrap a rag around your hand, it'll burn you. I didn't have one with me and figured I could stand it but it's a-paining me somethin awful. I tried putting it in the creek out yonder like my ma says is best to do with a burn but the water ain't cold enough to draw out the fire."

"I'm sure it's terribly painful." I smiled at him as I unlatched my medical bag. "But I have something that will help you, I think." As I applied lavender ointment to his palm, I heard the man in the next bed moaning. I looked at him, vaguely wondering if he was even old enough to enlist, as I noted the bloody rag he held to his mouth. I turned back to my patient. "Did he get hit in the mouth?"

He snickered. "By hisself."

I raised my eyebrows.

"According to the Confederacy, you got to have an upper tooth and lower tooth that meet and he made sure his don't."

"Why do your teeth need to meet?"

"So you can bite the top off the powder cartridge." At my confused expression, he went on, "You see, the powder and shot come put together in little paper pokes they call cartridges which we're supposed to tear open with our teeth when we're a-loadin our guns."

"And he tried to remove his teeth?" I asked, shocked.

"Shore did. Figgered if he busted every one of em out, none would mash together so they'd send him home. Didn't count on it hurtin so much."

"Is there a dentist in camp?"

"No but the doctor's sent for one." He shook his head with disdain. "If'n you ask me, the feller deserves that pain, tryin to do something so foolish."

"Do you see that a lot, soldiers trying to find ways to get out of serving?"

He nodded. "They come here expectin all the glory of battle, not to find theyselves so homesick and livin in such poor conditions while learnin to be a soldier." I couldn't help but nod at this. The conditions, indeed, were horrid. "Ever once in awhile some fool might get the idea to shoot theyselves in the foot or arm just so they can go home. I reckon he's the first what tried to remove all his teeth."

I studied the young man with the bloody rag to his face. "He looks too young to be serving in an army."

"I reckon he ain't but 18 or so. Old enough, according to the Confederacy." He leaned forward conspiratorially. "That's the official enlistment age but we occasionally get young'uns in here tryin to pass for 18." He tilted his head toward the boy. "Could be, he's a bit younger."

I shook my head, feeling sorry for the soldier. He must miss his family something awful to do so much damage to his teeth. After I tended to the burn, I sought out an infirmary volunteer and asked him to make a tea of the powdered roots of Rattlesnake Plantain I handed him. While he tended to this, I checked the young man's mouth, wincing at the broken teeth jutting from his red, swollen gums. Waving at flies lighting on the bloody rag, I said, "You'll probably have to have these pulled." He only shook his head with misery. "I have a tea coming which should help with the pain until a dentist gets here. Hold it in your mouth as long as you can." He nodded before putting the rag back to his mouth, moaning in pain. I then moved on to my next patient, a young man suffering diarrhea.

The afternoon passed quickly as we treated the men in the tent, which became stifling as the day wore on. I went outside at one point to get some fresh air, irritated at the necessity to watch where I stepped, and saw Josh nearby engaged in conversation with the major. It was a warm day, the sun beating down without a cloud in the sky to offer respite, and I suspected the temperature in the tent had risen to at least 90 degrees. The bodice of my gown was soaked with sweat and clung to my breasts and back. Even though the apron I wore made the heat worse, I was glad of it, as I'm sure if I hadn't, I might resemble a young woman from my time in a very wet, very thin top. I smiled at that, thinking of the looks of shock that would bring about. When I joined Josh and the major, they cut off their discussion, turning to me with curiosity. "Major McClean, if I might have a word," I said.

He tilted his head. "Certainly, ma'am."

"The reason your men are so ill lies with the state of this encampment and there are things you can do to make it better so that more men won't come down with the same diseases."

He raised his eyebrows. When he glanced at Josh, Josh said, "Lizzie knows what she's talking about, sir. I reckon it'd be best if you listen to what she has to say."

It annoyed me a man had to speak up for me but this was the 19th century and there was nothing I could do about it so I squelched that feeling. "Where is your latrine?"

His eyes widened with shock at this question.

"If it's above the camp or near the camp, which I certainly feel it is because of the strong odor, you need to move it away and down from the camp so that rain won't cause any runoff to stream down among the huts and tents. I've seen dung heaps all over this camp and they're loaded with bacteria, which is sure to cause disease. The latrine trenches also need to be at least five feet deep and covered with dirt, or better yet, lime, every day."

He nodded. "We need to move the latrine. I reckon that's easy enough."

"Yes, and I notice you have horses and mules corralled nearby. Are you having their manure removed every day?"

He shook his head.

"You need to. Also, all the refuse and spoiled food and wads of tobacco all over the ground need to be taken away and burned. Clean this camp up, have the men wash their hands after they use the latrine and before they eat and you'll see a remarkable improvement." I looked around. "Where do you get your water?"

"We have to carry it from a pair of springs nearby."

"Don't let your men use one of the springs if they want to bathe or wash up and don't let the animals drink from it, so at least the water in one will be clear and clean. Also, in the hospital, have the men's cots placed head to toe so that they're not facing one another and can breathe or cough in each other's faces, passing contagion."

It vexed me he had to think about this but finally he nodded. "I'll see to it right away." He started to move off but then returned. "Would you mind speaking with my staff and our hospital workers and telling them what you've told me?"

I hesitated. I hated the idea of public speaking but figured the need was dire enough it had to be done. "Not at all."

"I'll call a meeting before you leave today."

After he walked off, I turned to Josh, swiping the back of my hand over my perspiring forehead. "Did you find out anything of value?"

He shook his head. "Nah, all he wanted to talk about was his home and how much he missed it and couldn't wait to get back." His eyes lingered on me. "You sure are a sight, Lizzie. Not many women would stand up to a major of the Confederate Army, telling him what he needs to do."

"Only after you vetted me, Josh. In my time, it's not like that usually."

He reached out, squeezed my hand. "I'm getting more and more curious about your time, Lizzie, simply because you're so wondrous. I pray we get there one day."

I squeezed back before recovering my face and returning to the hospital.

As I went about my duties, I noticed women lingering outside the tent, some of whom looked haggard and filthy. At one point, I looked up to see a young woman standing beside me. I smiled at her, thinking of the term "cute as a speckled pup", the freckles dotted across her nose and cheeks and her large brown eyes bringing this to mind.

She gave me a lopsided grin. "My name's Sally, and I come to see if I could help y'all with anything."

I straightened up, using my apron to wipe my hands while I studied her. She looked young and healthy and relatively clean, not as worn down as some of the other women loitering nearby. "We can use all the help we can get. Would it be too upsetting to you to empty the buckets?" I motioned to several standing beside the bunks, which the men with diarrhea and dysentery had been using and which Josh had been busily emptying. She wrinkled her nose but nodded and went to help Josh, after I instructed her to empty them far away from the camp and to be sure to wash her hands after each trip.

Sally worked as hard as any of us and I found myself talking to her as she came and went. I learned her husband was a soldier in training and she had come from home to be with him. "We ain't been married but a couple of months and I got awful lonesome without him so I figured I'd come on down and stay with him till they send him off. It's been a relief he ain't had to go nowhere just yet."

"Is he sick?"

"Oh, no'm, he's just fine. I told him what my mama always told me, wash your hands ever chance you get, especially if'n you come up against somebody sick, and I reckon it's workin, 'cause he ain't got sick yet."

"Smart advice," I told her, smiling at her look of pride. "Where will you go when he leaves?"

"I'll go on back home and stay with my folks. I'm their only young'un and they thought I was too young to marry, so they'll be glad to have me back till Billy comes home."

"I bet they will." I glanced outside. "What about those women standing around outside the tent? Are they wives too?"

Sally made a face followed by a sound of disgust. "They call themselves laundresses but they're actually whores." She nodded at my look of shock. "Some call em camp followers. They follow the men, trying to get em to pay for their carnal lusts."

"They don't do laundry, then?"

"Shoot, they don't do nothin but lay on their back and collect money." She leaned close and whispered. "They ain't too healthy neither and pass the pox to the soldiers. I told my Billy if I ever caught him with one, he wouldn't be welcome in my bed again. I don't want no sores all over my body."

The word "pox" sent a chill through my veins, thinking she meant small pox, until I remembered gonorrhea and syphilis were often referred to in that way during this time. Then I wondered what was utilized to treat the two because antibiotics hadn't been invented yet. I vaguely recollected something about mercury being used but couldn't recall what the treatment was. I shrugged inwardly, glad to leave that to the doctor.

Abbie and I finished with our side of the tent late afternoon. Since it appeared Sarie and Maggie were nearing their end, we stepped outside for a breath of air, tainted as it was by the condition of the camp. The women I had noticed earlier were still standing around, eyeing us curiously, and I wondered if they needed our help. I approached the one who appeared to be the oldest of the group, offering a smile and saying, "Is there anything we can do for you?"

She straightened slightly, her gaze bordering on hostile. "We was wondering if you'uns was the healers we heared about?"

"Yes, we're healers." I turned to get Abbie's attention. "Do you need our help?"

"We're laundresses." She gave me a look as if expecting me to challenge what she said. When I simply nodded, she continued. "Some of us is in need of some medicine, I reckon."

"We'll be glad to help," Abbie said, as she joined us. She looked at the other women, four in all. "Is there anybody else needs tending?"

The older woman nodded. "I can take you to a tent you can use." She turned on her heel and stalked away, the others following behind.

She led us to a midsize tent that had clearly seen better days. When I stepped inside, the scent of mold and smoke was strong. The space was relatively bare save two cots, one on each side of the tent, with threadbare blankets and no pillows.

The older woman turned toward Abbie and me. "My name's Liza, by the way, and I share this tent with Diane." She waved her hand at a woman who had followed us into the tent. "I reckon you can use this tent to tend to the girls." She craned her neck around us, searching, before hollering, "You can come on in if you've a mind to. I reckon they won't bite."

Abbie and I watched as two other women came into the tent. A third stood just outside the opening, watching us with interest.

I smiled at the women in turn. "It's nice to meet you all. I'm Lizzie and this is Abbie. We're happy to assist you with whatever issues you're dealing with."

The women eyed one another, as if unsure what to do.

"Why don't we do it this way," I said. "We'll go two at a time, starting with Liza and Diane. The rest of you can wait outside until we're finished with them, then we'll move on to the next two."

When Diane and Liza were alone with us, Abbie said, "I'll tend to Diane, I reckon, and Lizzie can tend to you, Liza." She placed her hand on Diane's arm. "Why don't we go to this cot over here and you can tell me what's ailing you."

I gestured for Liza to go to the other cot then asked her if she was feeling ill, although quite clearly she was not in the best of health. Her coloring was very pale, she had deep circles under her hazel-colored eyes and her brown hair looked like it was thinning. She glanced away from me, shaking her head a little. "I reckon I got the pox," she said in a harsh voice.

I studied her face then picked up each hand and looked it over. "I take it you're not talking about small pox or chicken pox."

"No'm." She sighed. "I'm sure you heard talk about us already so you know what we do here. I seen this afore on others and, well, I been told it needs to be treated."

"Do you have a lesion anywhere or rash I can look at?"

Without hesitation, she unbuttoned her blouse and pulled it open, pointing to a rash on her torso. "It's on the bottom of my feet too," she said. I resisted the urge to draw away, reminding myself this was not contagious to me. "Any sores in your mouth or on any other parts of your body?"

She opened her mouth and pointed. Her teeth were yellowed and several were missing. "Had one inside my mouth but it's gone now." That would be stage one, I thought. She lifted up an arm and pointed to a large, white lesion. I checked her lymph glands under her arms and on her neck, all swollen. Stage two. "Are you feeling fatigued ... um, tired?"

"I am. Gotten to where it's hard to get out of bed anymore."

"Syphilis," I said, more to myself than her.

"I reckon I know what that is," she said, in a sad voice. "You got any of that mercury that cures it?"

I shook my head. "You'll need to see the doctor for that." I hesitated before speaking again. "I know this is how you make your living, but for now, as long as you're infected, you shouldn't have sex, uh, lie with another person, of any sort. You're contagious and can pass it on to them, and they could pass it right back to one of the other women."

"If I got it, I reckon they do too." She buttoned her blouse, glancing at the women standing outside the tent.

"Once you're treated and no longer contagious, it would be a good idea to wash yourself and have the man wash himself before and after you, well, lie together. If you see that they have a rash or lesion or anything that looks suspicious, don't continue on with them, don't even kiss them."

She made a face. "I never kiss em, don't you worry about that."

I thought she must since she had a sore in her mouth but then remembered there was another way she could have gotten that. "Right now, you're in the secondary stage. If this isn't treated, you'll go into what's called latent syphilis where the disease lies dormant in your body for years but it can progress to the tertiary stage, where it can damage your brain, heart or other organs. It's very serious."

She nodded before turning away, saying dismissively, "I thank you for your attention." She walked away from me and stepped outside the tent, gesturing for another woman to enter.

I looked over at Abbie, wondering if she knew about syphilis. She and Diane were watching me. "Do you need help, Abbie?"

"I reckon Diane's suffering from the same illness Liza is. We heared what you said to her, and Diane says she understands well enough." She turned to Diane. "Is there anything else we can help you with today?"

Diane shook her head, a look of annoyance on her face. "If I'da known we was passing it to one another through them men, I'da done something." She started toward the tent flap but stopped when she neared me. "What about giving em my hand?"

I drew back, unsure what she meant. "Your hand?"

"You know, helpin em out with my hand?" She made a rude motion to clarify.

I glanced at Abbie, who looked just as surprised as I felt by the question. "Um, well, I'm not sure. As long as you don't exchange body fluids, I guess you'd be all right."

"What's body fluids?"

"Saliva or spit, a man's ..." I stopped, embarrassed.

She gave me a curt nod. "Well, then, I guess we'll stay in business." She flounced out of the tent.

Abbie stepped closer to me. "I've heared of Sarie talking about syphilis only once afore but ain't never seen it."

"It's a terrible disease, Abbie." We looked outside to see if anyone else was waiting to see us but the women had disappeared. "I guess we're not needed," I said, adding as we walked outside, "I hope they do what I suggested once they're cured, make sure to keep themselves clean and check the men first to ascertain they're not diseased."

Abbie sighed. "I can't imagine a worse way to try to make a living."

I nodded. "From what I remember reading about the treatment, it's pretty hard to go through. In my time, it's simply a matter of taking penicillin."

"What's that?"

"A strong antibiotic."

We saw Sarie and Maggie standing in front of the hospital tent looking around. When we joined them, Sarie said, "The major's been looking for you. He wants you to talk to the boys about things they can do to stop the spread of diarrhea and such."

"Where is he?"

"He's gone off somewheres. He told the boys inside you'd be a-speaking to them, so I reckon we'll need to go back in."

During the afternoon, we had asked the volunteers to air the tent out as much as they could. When we went inside, although a strong odor still lingered, it wasn't as harsh as when we first came and the cross ventilation from each end of the tent had cooled the air considerably. I found Dr. Glover, who expressed his appreciation for our help before shushing the men and telling them the major had ordered them to listen to my instructions. And so I repeated for the sick and medical staff the same things I'd told the captain. I asked the staff to pass along these instructions to the men who were well so that they would know how to try to keep themselves from falling ill. I also made it a point to tell them that the camp followers who called themselves laundresses were suffering from syphilis which they could pass on to any man who used their services. I didn't fail to notice more than a few panicked faces at this news.

As we left, I saw several troops scattered about, shovels in hand, clearing away the garbage and detritus on the ground. In the distance, I could see men digging a new latrine. I was relieved they seemed to be following the proper protocol but didn't know how long it would stay in place. Once the men were well enough to travel and had been trained, they would be on their way to other encampments and battlefields, and I was fairly sure conditions there would be as bad if not worse. No wonder so many soldiers died from disease, I thought, as I mounted Beauty and rode home.

Chapter Five

Early Fall 1862

I Live One Day at a Time

On April 16, 1862, President Jefferson Davis signed into law a bill called the Conscription Act requiring all able-bodied white men between the ages of 18 and 35 serve at least three years in the Confederate military. I vaguely remembered studying in my high school history class that this was the first national draft in American history and, as always, felt a bit disoriented when I realized that what I had studied 110 years in the future, I was now living.

There were several factors behind this conscription. Federal forces were closing in on Richmond, Virginia, New Orleans and at vital points along the Atlantic coast and Mississippi River, and the Confederacy had suffered thousands of deaths and casualties in the Battle of Shiloh, the largest battle ever fought in America up to that time. Plus many men who had enlisted in the Confederate Army for 12 months at the beginning of the war were about to be released and would be headed home. Under this bill, draftees were given 30 days to volunteer instead of being conscripted and men could pay a $500.00 commutation fee to evade the draft, this being applied specifically to pacifists such as Quakers and Mennonites as well as skilled laborers and the wealthy, who it was felt could serve the Confederacy in other, nonmilitary capacities.

One provision that proved to cause conflict and resentment was that allowing men to hire substitutes to serve in their place, including persons outside the specified age range, or even foreigners. From what Josh told me, substitute brokers became a very lucrative profession as a result of this provision. However, it was eventually repealed because it caused much widespread resentment among those not wealthy enough to hire a substitute.

Other than these two commutations, the original Act offered no exemptions and I feared Josh would be required to go to war. But the Confederate Congress, concerned that conscription could deplete the Southern workforce, enacted an amendment five days later that included exemptions for such professionals as government workers and laborers in certain industries as well as telegraph operators, hospital employees, apothecaries, river ferrymen and pilots, printers, clergymen, and educators.

But more importantly to me, in my selfish heart, was the "Twenty Negro Law", which exempted from the draft men who owned 20 or more slaves so that they could continue to supervise farm production and also defend against potential slave uprisings. Josh's father immediately deeded his plantation over to Josh so that this law would apply to his eldest son. This surprised me somewhat as I knew Mr. Hampton was a strong supporter of the Confederacy. But poor health had tempered his passion for war somewhat, and always a man more interested in monetary gain than most other things, I suspected he was well aware that without Josh, who had been taking care of his father's financial dealings for years, the plantation would suffer greatly in his absence.

I knew Josh felt conflicted by this. On the one hand, he was responsible for the plantation and its slaves, but on the other wanted to do more in the fight against slavery and felt constrained by having to remain on Brown Mountain. He continued to place his life in danger by helping slaves escape via the Underground Railroad and from time to time sending coded missives to his journalist friend in New York. I told him countless times the contribution he was making was important and helpful, but Josh didn't see it that way. I had begun to realize my love was more of an adventurer, maybe even a warrior at heart, and prayed his joining the war effort would never come to pass.

Freda Hennesy, our preacher's wife, having come to the conclusion that I had some culture about me—I presume after learning my father was a doctor—had begun giving me well-read though outdated copies of the *Asheville News* and other small community newspapers, perhaps as a way to nudge me back to my hometown, Knoxville, Tennessee, and away from the more primitive habitat I currently occupied on Brown Mountain. Evenings, Abbie and I would pour over these newspapers, reading the articles aloud to one another, Abbie more out of curiosity about events of the world but me as a way to involve myself in current history.

During the late summer of 1862, I read with interest an article reprinted from *The New York Times* about the United States Sanitary Commission. I was surprised a newspaper from the South would pass on an article from the North but suspected this was a subtle nudge to the Confederate Congress that perhaps the South should be doing something along the same lines. In any event, the United States Sanitary Commission was a private relief agency created under federal legislation on the 18th of June, 1861, to support sick and wounded soldiers of the Union Army. The article linked its origin to a meeting of women held in New York on April 25, 1861, from which the Women's Central Association of Relief was formed, which seemed to stall due to no formal plan until Dr. Henry W. Bellows, pastor of the All Souls Unitarian Church in New York, advised the group to first find out what the government could and would do and then do only those things the government itself felt unable to. It all boiled down to a relief agency to help staff field hospitals, raise money, provide supplies and educate the military encampments on matters of health and sanitation.

I glanced up at Abbie, feeling a thrill of excitement as I re-read parts of the article to her. "It doesn't say anything about the South having this kind of help but we're already doing some of this at Camp Vance. Maybe we should try to put together our own organization in Burke County to help the soldiers."

Abbie tilted her head, considering. "Who would we get to help us, Lizzie?"

"Sarie and Maggie and Amanda May, of course. And I don't know, maybe we could enlist the aid of other women on the mountain and in Morganton. Although you and I and more than a few others don't support the South in this war, Abbie, a lot of these soldiers are having to fight under the Conscription Law, whether they want to or not, and I'd like to be able to help them since so many are going to die due to unsanitary conditions at their camps."

Abbie nodded.

"But I feel we should help any soldier, Union or Confederate. We should stay as neutral as possible, don't you think?"

She shrugged. "This is a Rebel state, Lizzie. We might get in some kind of trouble if'n we help Yankees." As I thought about that, she said, "Don't you reckon we ought to have a meeting place of some sort?"

"Definitely. We can't have it here, our cabin's way too small. In fact, the only place I know that would work would be the church."

Our eyes met. Nothing at the church happened unless Freda gave her official okay.

Abbie shook her head, as if reading my thoughts. "You know how Miss Freda is, has to have her nose stuck in ever little thing what's going on. She won't like it less'n we talk to her first."

This was no embellishment. Freda made it a point to know all the goings-on in the community, let alone the business of each and every congregant of her husband's church. I tended to avoid her whenever I spied her nearby, due to her inclination to interrogate me to the point of exhaustion. It was not lost on me that many others did the same. I nodded my agreement. "Can't see any way around it. We'll have to talk to her first."

Abbie snorted. "Only way to get Miss Freda involved is to let her think she's the one a-running it. Ain't no other way to get her on our side."

I nodded, inwardly sighing. "Nothing will make Freda happier than thinking she has the authority to boss everybody around. We'll just have to find a way to work around her, I guess. Let's talk to Freda after church this Sunday."

Abbie's lip twitched. "I reckon I'll leave that up to you."

And so, after the next Sunday's church service, I sought our preacher's wife out, something I had never done. I found her beneath a large oak tree outside the church, where she had cornered Amanda May, of all people. Amanda May was by nature a shy, reserved young woman with a timid disposition who mostly kept to herself, although many young men were beginning to seek her out due to her exotic beauty. When Amanda May saw me, she did not bother to hide her sense of relief as her shoulders lifted and a smile touched her lips. I leaned in to kiss her cheek while squeezing her hand and saying, "Amanda May, I have something I need to discuss with Miss Freda. Would you mind if I interrupt for a bit?"

Amanda May simply shook her head, sidled around Freda, and scampered away.

Freda watched her, a frown creasing her forehead. "That young woman has a most quiet nature." She glanced at me. "As you know, Lizzie, I make it a point to know each and every person who is a member of this church but I have yet to find out anything about her. She answers any question I ask with a shrug or simply ignores it. Is she such a mystery to you?"

"It's just her way, Freda. She's an introvert, not an extrovert like you."

She looked as if she thought I'd called her something highly offensive, a line forming between her brows and her mouth setting in a firm, prim line.

"I mean," I said, "she's very private, likes to be by herself, keep her thoughts to herself, whereas you are very outgoing and friendly and like to interact with others."

Her expression relaxed into one of pride, as if I had paid her a great compliment. "Well, as you know, Lizzie, I have been blessed with a personality that draws people to me. Why, in no time at all, I can learn a person's history, without any sort of inquiry. I look upon it as a gift from the good Lord."

I smiled at Freda, thinking she had just contradicted herself in regard to querying people. "Oh, no doubt," I said, stroking her ego. "No one on this mountain knows more about its people than you do, Freda."

She literally puffed up at this compliment.

Going in for the kill, I said, "Actually, Freda, I have something I wish to discuss with you, something we can do for the war effort, I believe."

Her eyes lit with interest. "Well, as you know, I didn't support our great state's secession but what is one to do? We are in the war and must do whatever we can to support our troops, don't you think so?"

"That's exactly what I wanted to talk to you about." I went on to explain the Sanitary Commission and my thought that it would be a good idea for the women of our community to form a Relief Agency. "Although we have been blessed so far in that the war hasn't touched us geographically," I went on, "there are things we can do, such as send food and supplies to the soldiers, sew or mend uniforms, provide medical care for those who are wounded and returning home."

Freda clapped her hands together with glee. "Of course. Lizzie, what a wonderful idea. And I'll be more than happy to organize it. I'm quite adept at that sort of thing, you know." And went on to tell me all the things she had done for the church, most of which I was sure had been either at the behest or hands of her husband.

When she finally wound down, I said, "Do you think we can do it here at the church, Freda? We'll need a large space to store and put together supplies for the soldiers as well as use it as a medical clinic to treat those who have been injured and returned home."

"Well, of course, I see no problem with that." She hesitated. "I will have to confer with my husband, the pastor, you know. But I'm sure I can persuade him to allow it. After all, it is the Christian thing to do."

"Of course."

She patted my arm. "After which, I'll speak to the other women of the church and community and get things started." With a final squeeze of my arm, she flitted off, a spring in her step.

Abbie appeared beside me, her head popping into view. I jumped, putting my hand to my throat. "You scared me."

She smiled. "I was behind the tree, a-listenin to you. Good job, Lizzie. I reckon we'll get that Relief Agency, though I doubt you'll be the one takin credit for it."

"Oh, I'm sure, Abbie, but at least we've got something started, yes?"

She nodded.

True to her word, Freda managed to get enough women to form what she called the Brown Mountain Relief Agency, some of whom I am sure she had to browbeat to gain their participation. But Freda was an expert at this technique and I imagined drew some sort of pleasure in doing so. Although a lot of the women on the mountain didn't have much to contribute by way of supplies, they could sew and offered their services making and/or patching uniforms for the soldiers. Women from the plantations and the town of Morganton who were more financially able provided foods from their larders and materials for bandages, handkerchiefs and small garments. Twice a week, the sisters, Amanda May and I would visit the church, where we would set up our clinic, more often than not, treating wounded or ill parishioners rather than soldiers, but I enjoyed this, seeing it as a way to expand my expertise with medicine, primitive as it was at the time. We began to talk about continuing the clinic after the war, since so many sought us out there, I'm sure more for the convenience than anything else.

On one such visit, a young mother came to the clinic, her son in tow. She pushed him in front of me, saying, "He got into the poison ivy and won't stop scratching. I put some bear grease on him, thinkin it might help, but it ain't done a thing but make it worse."

I drew back from the odor emanating from the boy, wondering why in the world she thought bear grease might work. As if reading my mind, she said, "My mama used it on ever'thing, called it a miracle cure, but it sure ain't cured this."

"Have you tried anything else?" I asked, bending down to peer at the red spots just barely visible through the globs of grease.

"Tried the dogwood tea but it didn't help much. Told him to pee on it but that didn't stop the itch at all."

I raised my eyebrows at that, making a mental note to ask Abbie about that later. I had never heard of urinating on poison ivy as a cure.

She sighed with frustration as she swatted her son's hand away from his face. "He won't stop scratching."

I nodded as I picked up a rag and wiped a small area of bear grease off his arm, peering closer at what looked to be dozens of tiny red spots in the shape of teardrops. I straightened up, addressing his mother. "Where else does he have it?"

She shrugged. "Pert near all over his arms and legs, on his chest. Even got it on his head and ears." She glared at her son. "Had to have been rolling in it to get it all over him like that."

I ignored this. "Has he had a sore throat recently? Respiratory infection, anything of that sort?"

She shrugged. "I ain't sure what you mean by respiratory infection but he claimed he had a sore throat a week back. He seemed to get over it pretty quick, I reckon. Leastwise, he ain't complained about it lately."

I smiled at the boy, who seemed embarrassed by all this attention. "Can you open your mouth for me and stick out your tongue?"

He glanced at his mother, who nudged him, saying, "Go on, do what she says."

I peered down his throat, noting enlarged tonsils and a reddened throat. Although I had never seen this condition, I had certainly studied it and felt a thrill of excitement at being able to make the diagnosis. I straightened up, patting him on the head. "He doesn't have poison ivy, Mrs. ..."

She seemed startled by this, saying, "Oh, I don't reckon I told you my name. It's Selma, Selma Alfred, and this here's my boy Alfred."

Alfred Alfred, I thought with some amusement. Someone in that family either had a wry sense of humor or no imagination at all. "It appears Alfred has guttate psoriasis, Mrs. Alfred."

Her forehead furrowed. "What in tarnation's that?"

"It's a form of psoriasis. A skin condition," I went on, seeing her confused expression. "Named for the Latin word guttate, which means drop." I raised her son's arm. "You can see these red scaly patches look like teardrops or raindrops."

She made a sound in her throat. "Well, what can you do for it?" she said after a bit of further study.

"First thing is give him a bath and get that bear grease off of him." After her nod of confirmation, I went on. "We need to control the itching as much as we can or else he'll develop a skin infection." I dug through my medical satchel as I continued to talk. "I've got some witch hazel salve which we'll try first. Just smooth it on over the red spots and see if that helps with the discomfort and itch."

She nodded as she took the tin from me. "What do you reckon caused it?"

"The sore throat could have been caused by strep throat which could lead to this kind of an outbreak. But I noticed his tonsils are swollen, so it looks like he has tonsillitis which would give him a sore throat and cause this condition. In any event, unlike plaque psoriasis, this should clear up and hopefully he won't have any more outbreaks. Just keep bear grease off of it, it won't help at all. Oh, and definitely don't have him pee on it, he could cause more damage than good from that."

"I thankee," she said, with relief.

"Also, if you have any slippery elm, you might want to give him that for his throat. It will help with the soreness."

"I do and thankee."

"And a tincture of Echinacea should also help his throat."

She frowned at me. "Echi ... what?"

"Coneflower. It works as an antibiotic."

She looked even more confused. I sighed inwardly. "His throat is still red and his tonsils swollen, meaning there's an infection. The coneflower will help fight the infection, the tonsillitis."

"I reckon they's enough coneflower on the mountain, I shouldn't have no problem gettin some."

"Let me know if you need any."

She gave me a curt nod before turning and glaring at Alfred.

He finally got her message and hung his head, muttering, "Thank you, ma'am."

"You're both more than welcome," I said, adding, "Come back if the witch hazel doesn't work. We'll try aloe vera next."

Mrs. Alfred nodded then guided her son out the door, everyone stepping away from them, looking as if they were resisting pinching their noses closed against the odor hovering around young Alfred like a swarm of bees.

It seemed a great deal of our practice involved children. One of the more frightening cases to me was when a matronly woman brought in a girl of about ten or so who was having trouble breathing. The woman herself was so agitated, she became quite short of breath as she tried to explain to me about the girl, who turned out to be her granddaughter. When I finally got her calmed down enough to talk, she told me that her granddaughter had had bouts like this on and off all her life. "They usually don't last but a short while but this one has been going on longer than normal," she said. Her vernacular told me she was either a plantation owner's wife or from the town of Morganton.

I nodded. "What's her name?"

"Esmeralda," she said, putting her hand to her chest and patting it.

I became alarmed that she might be having a heart attack. "Are you all right? Does your chest hurt, is it hard to breathe?"

"No, no, I'm fine," she said, waving in her granddaughter's direction. "Or will be when she can breathe again."

I guided Esmeralda to a chair, watching her labored breaths. I noted a blue tinge to her lips and fingertips, a sign she was not getting enough oxygen. "Has she been diagnosed with asthma?" I asked the grandmother.

"No, but we've never taken her to see a doctor about this before. All her other spells were so short-lived and her breathing never this bad." She stopped and took a deep breath. "I hoped to take her into town to the doctor but the church was so much closer and I've heard what good healers y'all are." She looked at her granddaughter with such loving concern, my heart twisted. Lowering her voice, she added, "I didn't know if we'd have time."

Not for the first time I wished for a stethoscope so I could listen to the girl's lungs. I put my ear to her chest and could clearly hear her breath whistling in and out. "Does your chest feel tight?" I asked her. She nodded, her eyes big and round. I patted her hand, sensing she was very close to all-out panic. "Don't worry, Esmeralda, we'll have you breathing normally real soon."

I glanced around for Abbie, who was helping fold linen for bandages. As if she sensed my gaze, she looked up at me. I gestured for her to come help. When she reached me, I said in a low voice. "What do you do for asthma?"

Abbie studied Esmeralda, watching her breathe. "Pokni told me the Catawba smoke the dried leaves of jimsonweed. Ain't never tried it but that girl's in trouble." Her eyes returned to me. "We make a tea of hyssop for mild cases. I reckon we can try both."

"I've got hyssop but no jimsonweed. Do you have any?"

She thought for a moment then her eyes lightened. "I think Pokni give me some last time I went to visit. I'll go check." She turned to leave then hesitated, digging through my satchel for the hyssop, saying, "I'll get Amanda May to making that hyssop tea for you."

I nodded, thinking frantically, then remembered that caffeine is a drug similar to theophylline, a bronchodilator drug taken in my time to open up the airways in the lungs and relieve the symptoms of asthma. Touching the grandmother on the arm to get her attention, I said, "I'll be right back. Watch her, and if she looks to be getting worse, yell as loud as you can." With that, I hurried to the small kitchen at the back of the church, where Freda usually kept a pot of coffee going for her husband. I smiled at Amanda May, busy heating water for the tea, as I checked the coffee pot, relieved at the sound of liquid sloshing around inside. As I poured a cup, I noted the dark color, thinking it must be pretty strong. All the better. After adding a bit of sugar to the cup, I returned to Esmeralda's side. "Drink this, sweetie. Don't gulp, just sip, but try to get as much down you as you can." Esmeralda made a face after that first sip but doggedly continued to drink the coffee, even though I knew it must be hot and bitter. I watched her drink, hoping the caffeine in the coffee would indeed act as a bronchodilator. When she finished, I noted the color in her face was better and her breathing had begun to ease.

Abbie returned with a bowl filled with dried leaves of the jimsonweed, which were smoldering from the small fire she had started within. She put this under Esmeralda's nose after I placed a blanket over her head and around her shoulders, and we encouraged her to breathe in. By this time, quite a crowd had gathered around us, watching with curiosity as we worked to get the little girl to breathe normally. Amanda May shoved her way through the gathered group, teakettle in one hand and china cup in the other. I didn't know if the hyssop would react to the caffeine but felt it was worth the risk as I once more encouraged Esmeralda to drink. After what seemed hours but actually couldn't have more than half an hour, she straightened a bit and looked at me. I noted she did not seem to be as panicked as I put my ear to her chest again, saying a silent prayer of thanks when I heard her take in and release what seemed to be deeper breaths. I smiled at her as I removed the blanket. "I think you're going to be fine, sweetie. I'll tell your grandmother what to do for you if this happens again, all right?" She nodded at me as she relaxed back against the chair, looking tired and haggard.

The crowd, seeming satisfied there was not going to be anything as horrific as a death in their midst, started to drift away as I explained to Esmeralda's grandmother that her granddaughter would probably be very tired and groggy the rest of the day and instructed her on what steps to take when the next asthmatic attack occurred, assuring her there would be more attacks in the future. I studied the grandmother as I talked to her, hoping her earlier breathlessness wasn't an indication of an impending heart attack, but her color seemed good and she didn't sound out of breath. She assured me she would watch her granddaughter like a hawk and immediately begin treating her if this happened again. If, I thought to myself, knowing it would only be a matter of time but hoping it would be a long time, as I saw them off.

We treated a lot of toothaches, at least a couple a day, it seemed. It was an irritant to me that toothbrushes were not in use during this time and the only thing at hand was feathered twigs, which I used continually, paranoid as I was about tooth decay. But a good many mountaineers didn't do this so were missing teeth or what few they had were rotten or decaying. There was a dentist in town but most mountaineers couldn't afford him so would either pull the tooth themselves or have a family member do it. Some would resort to us, hoping if we could heal a bleeding wound, we could heal a toothache. The only remedies we could offer were willow or lavender teas, or in severe cases, the tea of root of rattlesnake weed, which Pokni assured us would decay the tooth to the root, preventing more toothache, which did indeed seem to offer relief.

There were always the grieving families, those who lost brothers or sons or fathers to the war and came to us, hoping we could give them something to help alleviate their pain. All we could offer them was St. John's wort or lavender tea, which at best treated mild depression, and a shoulder to cry on, which I never felt was enough. But then, I would tell myself, remembering my grief over my mother's death, there was nothing that could heal this sort of pain, not even time, which would only alter it or tamp it a bit.

When called upon, we would travel to Camp Vance to treat soldiers there for training or occasionally prisoners awaiting their deportation to the prison camp in Salisbury. Most suffered from mild illnesses such as colds and flu, dysentery, athlete's foot, with an occasional case of measles or mumps thrown in, along with those who were so anxious to exit this war that they wounded themselves. At the clinic, the returning veterans who sought us out for follow-up treatment were usually missing a limb, which always seemed to bother them with phantom pain, and I was appalled at the brutal amputation methods that were utilized in field hospitals, as explained to us by the soldiers. We did what we could for them, which wasn't much more than making sure infection didn't take hold and reassuring them that they could live a relatively normal life.

Chapter Six

Fall 1862

I Wondered Where You Be

I recalled from my high school history class that there were close to 10,000 battles during the Civil War, many of them skirmishes among small groups, and many which we never heard about on Brown Mountain. But we did learn of the major battles through newspaper reports and first-hand and second-hand accounts. In September, 1862, Confederate General Lee, hoping that a Confederate victory in Maryland would convince the state legislature to secede, pushed into the border states, meeting Union General George McClellan's troops at the Battle of Antietam, resulting in more than 23,000 casualties, which to that point became the bloodiest single day of battle of the war and another Union victory when Lee was forced to retreat back to Confederate territory.

After this battle, President Lincoln issued the Emancipation Proclamation, freeing all slaves in the Confederacy although limiting its effects to the secessionist states, not the border states of Missouri, Kentucky, Maryland, Delaware and West Virginia, which Lincoln did not want to provoke into secession. This, however, proved to be relatively unenforceable as the Confederacy did not consider

Lincoln their president.

But during all this, life in Morganton and on Brown Mountain went on as usual except for the continuing controversy over which side was right in this war and the Conscription Act, which was bitterly resented in our state and turned many residents against the war, resulting in increasing numbers of deserters and draft dodgers. These men were called outliers, or bushwhackers in the mountains and buffaloes on the coast. In September of 1862, Zebulon Vance, the governor of North Carolina, issued orders to deal with the deserters and draft dodgers, vowing to hunt them down and prosecute all. This only served to make the outliers more ruthless, and they began to carry out armed raids on towns and houses and even shot at the Confederate Army. A secret society was formed, calling itself the Heroes of America, its purpose to organize support for the outliers by finding safe hiding places, providing food and supplies, and warning if Confederate troops were nearby.

Abbie and I were mucking out the barn one day when someone spoke behind us, causing both of us to startle and make little squeaking noises.

Abbie turned around, pitchfork in hand, scowling. "What in tarnation are you doin sneakin up on us?" she demanded. I couldn't see whom she was speaking to so made my way to the barn door to see who had come to call. A matronly woman stood in the yard, looking agitated. From her manner of dress, I surmised she must be from town. She looked familiar but I couldn't place her right off.

"Why, I came to see you," she said in a lilting, melodic voice, and I remembered this was the wife of the owner of the town's mercantile. It appeared as if someone stood behind her, but due to her bulk, I couldn't tell who was back there. I spied a horse and buggy in the yard and was curious at the nature of her visit. Surely she didn't need medical attention. Most of the town folk saw the doctor in Morganton.

"Good afternoon, Mrs. Cowell," I said as I stepped out of the barn.

Abbie propped the pitchfork against the inner barn wall and when she spoke her voice was contrite. "I apologize, Mrs. Cowell. You startled me and then the sun blinded me for a moment so I didn't know it was you I was a-speakin to. What can we do for you? Are you a-ailing or needin some medicine?"

Mrs. Cowell moved aside and we stared at a short, wiry young man with flaxen hair, a matching moustache struggling to find purchase on his upper lip. "I've brought my son Evan." Mrs. Cowell motioned for her son to step up beside her. I noticed his wince when he put his left foot on the ground and tried to walk but quickly gave up and lifted it in the air, appearing to be a human stork. "I'm afraid he's done something to his ankle. Not sure if it's broken, but I was hoping you ladies could take a look at it and help him."

"Very nice to meet you, Evan," I said, smiling as I approached. "Let's go in the cabin where we can all be more comfortable. Here, lean your weight against me and I'll help you in." He put his arm around my shoulder as I put mine around his waist and with some effort got him into the cabin and settled in a chair in front of the table.

Mrs. Cowell and Abbie followed us in, and I listened as Abbie inquired why she hadn't gone to the doctor in town with her son. When Mrs. Cowell remained silent, Abbie and I darted glances at one another. Uh-oh, I thought, this could be trouble.

"You might as well tell them the truth of the matter, Mother," Evan spoke. Due to his height and build, I was surprised at his voice, a deep bass and quite beautiful, thinking to myself he'd make the perfect disc jockey 100 years in the future.

"It's all right, you can tell us," Abbie said. "We don't judge and, as Lizzie is always sayin, whatever is spoke between a patient and his doctor is confidential. We couldn't tell even if we wanted to."

Mrs. Cowell's face relaxed into one of great relief as she gave us a smile of thanks. "Well, I'm sure you've heard of the Conscription Act," she began.

We both nodded.

"My Evan here just turned 18 and by law is required to go to Asheville to sign up for the Confederacy."

Oh, boy, I thought.

She grimaced before continuing. "We're abolitionists, don't believe in slavery or this war, for that matter, and Evan can't in good conscience fight for a cause he ... we don't believe in."

I nodded. "And you're afraid if you take him to the doctor, he'll report Evan."

"Yes. When he didn't report like he was instructed to, some men came around asking about him. They claimed they were appointed by the governor to round up deserters. I told them I hadn't seen him and thought he was in Asheville. They're relentless, have been everywhere looking for Evan, but so far we've managed to hide him until last night." She turned and gave her son a disgruntled look. "He was running from them and his foot got twisted and I fear he's broken his ankle."

I knelt by Evan's foot and began untying his boot. Abbie and I had a devil of a time getting that boot off due to swelling and I feared we were going to have to cut it off but, with a lot of tugging and yelps of pain from Evan, managed to free his foot. I pulled off his sock and felt the skin, which was hot and red. The ankle was puffy and bruised, and I watched his face as I manipulated it. By the time I finished my examination, his complexion was pale and sweat beaded on his brow. I got to my feet, saying, "I don't think it's broken. Could be a torn ligament or tendon, which sometimes is worse than a break. We'll need to bind it and keep him off it for awhile."

Mrs. Cowell began twisting her fingers in her voluminous skirt. "But that won't do. He needs to be able to get away from here before they catch up to him. I've been hiding him in our cellar, but if he has to stay in one place for long, I fear they'll eventually find him."

I wondered if Josh would be able to take Evan up north through the Underground Railroad. "We may know a way to get him up north but I can't promise."

Abbie gave me a shocked look. "Lizzie, that might not be

a good idea."

"I know, but do you want those men appointed by the governor to get him?" Abbie and I had heard stories of men being hanged for deserting but I didn't want to say this in front of Mrs. Cowell.

As if on cue, we heard horses neighing and men's voices calling to one another. Abbie and I rushed to the window and looked toward the forest, watching a quartet of men ride into the yard.

"If those are the ones looking for him," Abbie said, her voice a hiss, "they'll hang us right alongside him if they find him in here."

I was very close to panic as I hurried over and bolted the door. "Where can we hide him? There's no place in here except under the bed and you know they'll look there."

Mrs. Cowell moved closer to her son, saying in a voice shaking with fright, "Get under my skirt. Hurry, now."

Abbie and I watched in awe as Evan scurried under his mother's roomy skirt and crinolines. We quickly began to settle the heavy material around her, trying to hide any evidence that a young man hid there.

"Stay here," I said before opening the door and walking out onto the porch followed by Abbie.

Abbie and I stood waiting as the men dismounted. "Can I help you?" I said, stepping forward. "You got anyone injured or sick needs tending to?"

The shortest of the group walked toward me, sweeping his hat off his head. "No'm, not that. We been trackin a boy and looks like that buggy there belongs to his mama." He nodded at the horse and buggy standing in the yard.

I tensed, reaching behind me for the back of the rocker, wondering why Abbie was so silent. "Who are you?"

"Why, we're here on official business for Governor Vance. It's our duty under the Conscription Act to round up deserters, fellers what don't want to enlist and are hiding out, escaped prisoners of war and such, and bring em to justice."

"And you're looking for someone, you said?"

"Boy goes by the name of Evan Cowell. You had any visitors lately? Got anybody hiding out in that cabin we don't know about?"

Abbie moved to stand beside me. "What in tarnation are you doin tracking people, Brett Galloway?" she said, ignoring his question.

He gave her a slow grin. "Miss Abbie, you was so quiet, I weren't sure that was you."

She put her hands on her hips, waiting for an answer.

He finally shrugged. "Too old to fight in the war so figured I'd help in other ways." He straightened with a proud look. "They hired me right off."

Abbie made a snorting sound. "Why you ain't barely past 35, if my memory serves me right, and you look well enough to fight."

He scowled at her before saying, "According to the Conscription Act, 35's the cutoff." He twitched his shoulders. "Asides, that ain't why we're here. Like I said, we're following a trail leads right to this cabin."

"Mrs. Cowell's here," Abbie said in a calm voice, "but we ain't seen hide nor hair of her son Evan."

Brett stepped closer. "That might be but I reckon I'm gonna need to have a look inside that cabin, see for myself."

I moved to block his way. "What for?"

"Make sure you ain't hiding a deserter in there."

I didn't move, simply stared at him.

He narrowed his eyes at me. "By law, I got the right. Now either you step aside and let me by or I'll have to move you and bash that door in."

"Well, then, I reckon you best go on inside and have a look around," Abbie said, drawing me away.

Brett stepped around us and opened the door. I expected his companions to follow him, but they stayed behind, close to their horses. Abbie and I followed him inside the cabin, watching as he gave an evil grin at the sight of Mrs. Cowell. "We been looking all over this mountain for you," he said to her.

She gave him an innocent look. "Why, I've been right here all afternoon."

His eyes narrowed with suspicion. "You ailing? Come to these here ladies for some herbs or somethin?"

Oh, God, I thought. What reason could we give him for her being here? But Abbie, as always, came to our defense, saying, "Not at all, Brett. Mrs. Cowell heared what a fine seamstress I am after what I done to Lizzie's dress last year and she's come to hire me to sew her a dress just like it."

I forced myself not to look at Abbie, afraid nerves would get the best of me and I'd begin to laugh hysterically. Instead, I clenched my hands in my skirt, trying to force myself to stop shaking.

Brett looked at Abbie, then Mrs. Cowell, then me. I nodded as if in agreement with Abbie. When his eyes returned to Mrs. Cowell, he said, "That right?"

She gave him a curt nod. "It's one of those artistic dresses." Was she at that dinner, I wondered, as she continued, "They're all the rage and Abbie did such a wondrous job with Lizzie's dress, I thought instead of sending off to New York for one, why, I'd just hire our sweet Abbie to do it." She turned to Abbie. "The bodice was just beautiful, Abbie, and I'd like you to embroider mine in the same way. But perhaps with a lighter green thread. Now, don't you worry about a thing, I'll get all the materials for you. The only thing I require from you is your talented hands."

"Why, thank you, Mrs. Cowell," Abbie said, with a wide smile. "I was right happy with the way Lizzie's dress turned out. I wasn't there, a-course, but I imagine she was the most beautiful woman present that night."

"Oh, she was," Mrs. Cowell crowed.

I watched these two in awe, wondering why in the world I couldn't be a natural liar as each was. Well, I came from a different time, I consoled myself, where the most I ever told was a white lie.

Brett shifted restlessly but they ignored him for a moment longer as they discussed the design of the dress. Then, as if remembering him, Mrs. Cowell returned her gaze to him. "I assume you've yet to find my son, Mr. Galloway."

Brett narrowed his eyes again. "You know I ain't. Thought we had him last night but the lad got away from us."

"I don't see how that's possible. He's down in Asheville hoping to join up with the North Carolina State Troops."

"Like I told you, he never showed up. He's on this mountain, hiding, I just know he is, and when I find him, well, let's just say he'll get our form of justice. He's a deserter, plain as can be."

"How can he be a deserter if he hasn't even enlisted yet?" I asked.

The look he gave me reminded me of the one Constable Jackson used to bestow on me, one filled with much malevolence. "He ain't showed up like he was told to, which tells me he ain't gonna sign up and is tryin to hide out."

"Well, that seems a little ridiculous to me." I ignored his frown. "He could have met up with an accident on the way to Asheville." I turned to Mrs. Cowell. "I don't want to alarm you, Mrs. Cowell, but perhaps you should send someone along the same path he took to Asheville just to make sure?" I thought about mentioning the people who had disappeared mysteriously on the mountain, Abbie's father, Mr. Westcott and his men, but held my tongue.

She gave me a shocked look. If I didn't know it was a faux one, I would have believed her expression was true. "Of course. I never thought of that. Thank you, Lizzie, I'll have my husband send someone after him." She dramatically put her hands to her cheeks as if a thought had just occurred to her. "You don't think something terrible has befallen him?" Tears filled her eyes and I stared in awe. "Oh, Lord help me, I can't stand the thought."

Abbie patted her arm, making comforting noises. She turned and glared at Brett. "Look what you done now, Brett Galloway. Upsetting this nice woman for no reason." She jutted her chin in a defiant way. "I think you best leave before you make things worse."

I watched emotions range across Brett's face, from anger to confusion to chastisement then back to anger. "I ain't searched this house yet and I'm a-gonna do that afore I take my leave."

I waved my arm around the room. "Take a look. As you can see, there's no place for him to hide except under the bed."

With a glare my way, he crossed over to the bed and

knelt down to look under it.

"Only thing you'll find under there is dust balls," Abbie said.

When Brett turned around, I moved in back of Mrs. Cowell, hoping to hide the rather obvious bulge. He stared at me for a long moment then I remembered Viola being in the privy when Constable Jackson came here searching for her after she escaped from the Hampton plantation. "Have you checked the outhouse or the barn?"

His eyes seemed to light with anticipation. "No, but I planned to do that on my way out." He headed for the door and I suppose wanted to leave us with a dramatic warning, as when he reached the threshold, he paused and said, "I find that buggar, you'll all be swingin right along with him."

Abbie snorted with derision. "I can't see Governor Vance givin you the right to hang a person, Brett Galloway. Seems to me that's a waste of a life, when all you need to do is take him on down to Asheville and see he joins up. Way I understand it, the Confederacy needs every man it can get. That's the reason for conscription, ain't it?"

Brett ignored this and, with a final scowl her way, stomped onto the porch and up the path toward the privy. Abbie closed and bolted the door behind him, then leaned against it as if for support.

I immediately raised Mrs. Cowell's skirt, concerned for Evan, as it was a warm day and those skirts were heavy. He tumbled out, sweating profusely. Abbie, seeing this, went to the window to close the curtains tighter so no one could see in.

We waited until the horses rode away before we spoke. "What are we gonna do?" Abbie said.

"Well, he can't walk. I suppose we can send word to Josh and when he comes talk it over with him. He should know what to do." I turned to Mrs. Cowell. "You should go on back home or it will look suspicious."

"But I can't leave him here," she said. "I'll do what I did when I came up here, hide him in the floor of my buggy."

"What if you meet up with those men?" Abbie said.

"The floor of the buggy has a false bottom." She

hesitated, looking embarrassed. "My husband, in his younger days, engaged in a bit of, er, smuggling, you might say." I immediately thought moonshine. She shrugged as if it had nothing to do with her. "I'll take him home with me and hide him in our cellar again, there's a hidden room there, until you speak to Josh. You can have him contact me about what should be done."

"If you had him hidden, how come those men were trailing him?" I asked as she made movements to leave.

She gave an exasperated sigh. "He lit out yesterday evening, hoping to go see a certain young lady friend." She turned and frowned at her son who looked chagrined. "Which he won't do in the future."

"Well, he can't." I turned to Evan. "You need to stay off that foot as much as you can until it heals."

"Yes, ma'am, I will do that," he said with an emphatic nod of his head.

Abbie looked out the window. "Might be best if y'all wait until after dark to leave. That way, if the Home Guard is nearby, they can't see us load him in that buggy."

Mrs. Cowell smiled widely. "That will be lovely, Abbie. We can make plans for that dress, yes? And I'm sure you'll need to take measurements and such."

I grinned at Abbie's look of despair as I got things together to bind Evan's ankle. Looked like she had a dress to make.

Chapter Seven

Late Winter 1863

Evil Ways

On July 7th of 1863, the North Carolina General Assembly passed legislation to create an organization called the Home Guard to act as an emergency police force due to the large sections of western North Carolina openly opposed to the Confederate government and the administration of Governor Vance as well as the Conscription Act and heavy taxes levied to pay for the war effort. Men between the ages of 18 and 50 exempted from the conscription laws were automatically enrolled in these units, their duties to replace the militia in catching deserters, breaking up armed gangs of deserters that were plaguing areas, aid in repelling Union invasions of the state, and to guard supply depots, bridges and other strategic points. However, many times these policing forces were as ruthless as the men they were trying to catch.

Burke County created its own Home Guard, of which Brett Galloway was now a member. He reveled in this role and was becoming known for the cruel and unjust ways he and his men had of dealing with those they caught when not under supervision of their superiors. Brett would occasionally show up at my cabin, inquiring after this or that person, and I was beginning to think he had replaced Constable Jackson, as he seemed to look upon Abbie and me with deep suspicion.

Abbie had been called out by a family nearby to help doctor one of their horses, bloated from getting into the oat bin. Taking a respite from chores, I decided to sit on the front porch and read for a bit, a rarity and luxury for me, but found myself dwelling on my time on Brown Mountain. I had been here around three and a half years now and with each passing day was becoming more and more resigned to living the rest of my life in these primitive, harsh conditions. Would I ever find my light, I wondered with despair. If not, I thought with resignation, at least I had Josh and Abbie, who helped make things better. Hearing a horse's harness jangling, I rose to my feet, glad for the distraction. I smiled when I recognized Maggie's husband Randall, on temporary leave from the Army, along with his brother Martin, to attend their mother's funeral.

In my eyes, Maggie couldn't have chosen a better mate. With dark hair and eyes, Randall was a complete contrast to fair-headed, blue-eyed Maggie, and I thought them an awfully handsome couple. Randall was an amiable sort of fellow, friendly to everyone and always willing to help when asked or even when not. He had a way about him that would allow even the most prideful mountaineer to accept his assistance without feeling obligated or offended. The fact that he had managed to befriend Sarie, who held men in great disdain, spoke volumes for the sort of man he was.

I grew concerned when he drew close enough I could see his usually upturned mouth set in a hard, determined line. I ran to meet him, alarm prickling at my spine. Grabbing hold of the horse's halter, I said, "What happened? Is it Maggie? Is she all right?"

Randall shook his head. "Ain't Maggie but Connie, my brother's wife." I well remembered Connie, the young woman whose twins I had helped birth with Maggie. She had a sweet disposition but strong will and loved her husband enough to ignore her parents' efforts to dissuade her from marrying him. "What happened?"

"Bushwhackers raided their farm. They ..." He stopped, looking away, and I realized without the words being spoken what he didn't want to say. Anger pricked at my mind. Why Connie, I wondered, why someone as sweet and loving as her? I forced myself to focus on Randall. "I'll get my satchel and collect Beauty and meet you there."

"I'm going to collect Maggie, she's over at Sarie's," he called over his shoulder as he rode off.

Not bothering to take the time to saddle Beauty, I put on his halter, mounted and left. When I arrived at Connie's and Martin's homestead, I found Martin standing just inside the open cabin door, watching his wife across the room, sitting with her head on her knees which were drawn to her chest, rocking back and forth. Their small cabin was in disarray, the table and chairs overturned, the rocking chair she used to rock her babies broken and shattered, a quilt from the bed crumpled on the floor, bits of food and broken plates scattered everywhere.

Martin looked at me, tears in his eyes. "She won't let me touch her, won't let me comfort her, won't let me do anything for her."

I squeezed his shoulder before crossing the room to Connie. Kneeling beside her, I put my hand on her forearm. Without looking at me, she hunched her shoulders and drew away. "It's me, Connie, it's Lizzie. I've come to help."

She ignored me as she continued to rock back and forth. I glanced around the room and out the door. "Where are the twins?"

"My pa took em to his place," Randall answered. "They were here when we got back from cutting timber, playing on the front porch."

Our eyes met and the fear I saw in his reflected my own, as I prayed they hadn't witnessed the assault on their mother. I turned back to Connie, looking her over as best I could, noting the torn sleeve on her dress, the bruise beginning to form on her left cheek. And the blood on her skirt. I could smell whoever had assaulted her, his acrid body odor, the faint, bitter scent of tobacco, tang of musty clothing. "Connie, honey, it's me Lizzie. I'm here for you. I can help you feel better if you'd let me." I reached out to her.

"Don't touch me," she screamed, raising her head and glaring at me. I drew back in shock. One eye was swollen closed, her lip split and bleeding. Her dress had been torn down the front, and above the swell of one breast I saw what looked to be bite marks. "Who was the bastard that did this to you?" I asked before I could stop myself.

"Bushwhackers," she spat out. She looked at Martin and started crying. "I'm no good to you anymore, Martin. They damaged me. You won't look at me the same way anymore and I can't bear the thought of it."

He approached her, holding out his hands in front of him, speaking in low tones, much as someone would to a skittish horse. "No, honey, that ain't true. You'll always be my sweetheart. It don't matter to me what they did, don't matter one bit. Why, we'll just forget about it and go on like nothing happened."

"You won't forget," she said, swiping at her eyes. "I won't forget. How could we?"

"Connie, you might not forget but you can put it behind you," I said. "This shouldn't have happened to you but please don't let this define your life. It isn't fair to you or Martin or your babies."

I heard movement behind me and looked up to see Maggie and Sarie coming through the door. Maggie rushed over and knelt beside Connie. Without saying a word, she took her in her arms and began to speak to her in soothing tones as Connie sobbed.

Sarie touched Martin's arm to gain his attention. When he looked at her, she tilted her head in the direction of the door. He walked outside after Sarie, me following behind.

Sarie closed the door behind us. "Who was it?" she said, facing Martin.

"Only thing she said was bushwhackers. Never named anybody."

Sarie looked away. "They been breaking into homes all over this mountain, stealing food and livestock. Never hurt nobody before, only threatened them with guns." She looked at me, her eyes hard and determined. "This can't lie."

I nodded. "I agree."

She glanced around. "Where's Abbie, Lizzie?"

"She went to the Flemings' cabin to help with one of their horses that got into the oats."

Sarie looked off into the woods. "Ain't your cabin the closest one to Martin's?"

"On the south side, yes."

"Did you see anybody when you was coming here?"

"I didn't see anyone." I turned to Martin. "Has anyone gone for the sheriff or the Home Guard?" I hoped Brett Galloway was the one who would deal with these bushwhackers. They deserved his form of justice.

"Randall said he'd fetch em after he found Maggie," Martin said.

Sarie straightened. "Them bushwhackers are still on the mountain, no telling where they'll go next." She turned to me and for the first time I saw panic in Sarie's eyes. My stomach clenched in response. "I got a bad feeling about Abbie, Lizzie. I think we need to go on over to your cabin and see if she's there. If she ain't, we need to go find her."

"I brought Beauty, he can get us there quick."

She nodded. "I'll leave Buck for Maggie."

I mounted Beauty with the aid of Martin then helped Sarie up. We were back at my cabin within minutes and rode into the clearing to a scene that scared me so much I almost fell off the horse. Three men were in the yard, one of whom had Abbie by the hair and was dragging her toward the cabin. Without thinking, I kicked my heels into Beauty's side and went straight for the man. His two companions jumped out of the way, yelling out in alarm. The man turned and, seeing my muscular horse bearing down on him, shoved Abbie in front of him. I immediately reined up. Before Beauty came to a full stop, both Sarie and I slid off and ran for the man. He pulled a gun, put it to Abbie's temple. That stopped us.

I looked at Abbie, at her eyes pleading with us to help her. I nodded, trying to tell her, we'll save you, we won't let him hurt you.

The man chortled as if happy at this turn of events. I stared at him, thinking he couldn't be much beyond teenage years. His dark-blond hair was matted and dirty, his beard splotchy and uneven. He had a stocky build, his muscular arms bulging against his filthy, tattered shirt. I glanced at the other two men, thinking they had to be brothers or twins, both of the same height with shaggy red hair, their faces and hands covered with freckles. Their clothes were as dirty and ragged as their partner and, like him, each had a gun.

"You must be the outliers," Sarie said, her voice cold and hard.

"I reckon I prefer the term bushwhacker," he said in a mocking tone.

"You the one that beat and raped that girl back there?" Sarie tilted her head in the direction of Martin's cabin.

He grinned. "I'm a pillager and a plunderer and I reckon I pillaged and plundered her right well." He glanced at the two others, who were sniggering. "Ain't that right, boys?"

They nudged each other and laughed.

"Now if'n you'll excuse me," he continued, "I got me another woman I mean to pillage and plunder." Abbie shrieked when he yanked at her hair.

"You'll be dead afore you do," Sarie said, her voice cold.

His lips turned up in a snarl. "Looks to me like I'm the one a-holdin the gun." He made it a point to look her over from head to toe. "I don't see one in your hands. Don't see a weapon of no kind."

Sarie smiled back at him. "That's 'cause you ain't lookin close enough."

His smile faltered. He stared at her for a long moment as if searching for a gun or knife. Without taking his eyes off Sarie, he said, "Boys, go on over there and tie these two up. Save em for me for later. I'll get around to em after I'm done with this one."

I clenched my fists, resolved they would hurt no other woman while I lived. "I don't think so," I said as the two young men moved closer. I was a bit shocked to find myself more relieved they had guns than if they had not. If only Sarie and I could get those guns away from them, we had a better chance of saving Abbie.

He snorted. "Looks like we got us two feisty fillies here, boys. Since they's one for each of you, I think I might just go ahead and let you two have em and I'll take the dregs."

Sarie moved so fast, I barely noticed. She turned, plucked the gun out of the hand of the man nearest her and without blinking shot him in the leg. With a loud shriek, he collapsed. This shocked the other one so much he froze, staring at his brother, writhing on the ground, screaming in pain. Before he could react, I hiked up my skirts, kicked the hand holding his gun then followed the gun as it spun on the ground. I snatched it up, got to my feet, all the while keeping my gun trained on the one holding Abbie. I was a bit surprised he hadn't reacted by shooting one of us, but Abbie had distracted him by struggling with him, trying to get away. Almost casually, Sarie shot the other brother in the arm. He screamed, grabbing his arm, but didn't go down. We all watched as he seemed to panic, realizing he and his brother were defenseless, reached down and yanked his brother up. Both took off into the woods, the one with the shot arm half-dragging the one with the shot leg. Although time slowed down for me during all this, I doubt ten seconds passed from the first shot to the time they left.

I waited for Sarie to halt their progress into the woods by shooting them again, but she ignored them as she turned and smiled at the one remaining man, who had managed to gain control of Abbie. "Looks like things are a bit more even now, Bushwhacker," saying this word in a mocking tone. "Turn her loose."

He pressed the gun into Abbie's temple. "Ain't gonna happen. I do that, you're liable to shoot me too."

"Oh, I ain't gonna shoot you, I'm gonna kill you," Sarie said in a low, flat voice.

Goosebumps rose on my arms when I realized she was serious.

"You raped a woman, beat her, bit her," she went on, her words cold and dead. "Way I see it, that's a crime deserves killing."

Sweat broke out on his brow and he shifted to move behind Abbie. "I was just a-foolin with you, I didn't hurt nobody," he said, his words sounding weak and unsure.

"Way I see it, you got two choices," Sarie went on as if he hadn't spoken. "You let her go and I kill you, or we wait here for Brett and his boys with the Home Guard and let em hang you after they teach you a lesson."

I could see the panic in his eyes as he looked toward the woods then back at her. He glanced around, seeming to be trying to come up with a solution. I noticed the hand holding the gun to Abbie's temple had begun to shake. Sarie moved away from him, in the opposite direction of me. He followed her with his eyes then began to turn to keep her in sight. Remembering me, he glanced back at me, saying, "Get over there with her."

I looked at Sarie, who barely nodded at me, darting her eyes to him then me. Understanding what she wanted, I began to move in that direction but closer to him. I waited for his gaze to shift to Sarie, and when it did, I moved closer and used the handle of my gun to hit him over the head, hard enough to cause him to stumble and drop his weapon. Reaching out with my other hand, I pulled Abbie out of his arms then kicked his gun out of reach.

Sarie kept her gun trained on him, waiting patiently for him to gain control of his feet. "Abbie," she said once he had, "go fetch Brett and the Home Guard. They're probably at Martin's cabin by now."

Abbie's gaze turned to me. "Go," I said.

Without a word or backward glance, she jumped on Beauty's back and rode off.

When she was out of sight, Sarie shot the man in the groin. Screaming in agony, he immediately dropped to the ground, holding his hands between his legs. Sarie looked at me, her eyebrows raised. "You reckon that'll hold him?"

"I reckon it might kill him if we don't treat him," I answered, surprised that I had no compassion to spare for this man.

Sarie shrugged. "You can try to save him if you want. I won't stop you."

I looked at the man, writhing in pain, his blood seeping into the ground. "He beat and raped Connie and was going to do the same to Abbie. He doesn't deserve to live." I walked over to where his gun lay on the ground, picked it up, and stood with my back to him, deliberately ignoring the noises he made while staring at the beauty of the clear blue sky overhead as I tried to identify a bird calling out in the woods.

When all grew quiet behind me, Sarie simply said, "It's done."

I returned to her, trying not to look at the body. "Brett will be here any minute."

"Go on and tell him I killed that boy, Lizzie. Killed him in cold blood but he deserved it."

I watched her for a moment, could clearly see the pain in her eyes, and before I could stop myself said, "Sarie, did you kill your pa?"

Her head snapped up and she glared at me but didn't answer.

"Maggie told me he gave you to Constable Jackson." I shook my head. "It's hard for me to believe a father would just give his daughter to another man. She said it was to pay a debt but still …"

Sarie nodded as she looked away. "He was mean and cruel, even when he weren't drunk." She glanced at me then toward the forest, as if watching for the Home Guard. After a long moment, she continued. "I made a deal with him after our ma disappeared, told him if he'd leave Maggie and Abbie alone, he could do what he wanted with me and I wouldn't stop him or tell nobody."

"You mean he …" I couldn't say the word.

"Said it was a girl's duty, to take care of the man of the house."

"Oh, Sarie, I'm so sorry."

When her eyes turned back to me, they were hard and sullen. "I don't need your pity. I did what I could to keep him away from Maggie and Abbie, so ain't no need to feel sorry about it."

"You're right. You're a great sister, Sarie. They both know that."

She ignored me as she continued. "I endured my pa's wrath in every way possible. Tried to protect Maggie and Abbie as best I could. When he give me to Constable Jackson, I knew once I was gone, he'd turn to them to meet his needs. So after he told me what he'd done and that I was gonna marry Jackson whether I wanted to or not, I followed him to where I knew he stashed his liquor." She bit her lip. "Oh, we got into a fierce argument up there in them woods. It's a wonder the whole mountain didn't hear us." She stopped and turned to me. "He told me if I didn't do what he said, I was as like to disappear as our ma did. Maggie and Abbie and me'd always thought she run off to get away from him. And let me tell you, Lizzie, that hurt somethin awful, thinkin she'd leave us alone with him. She loved us somethin fierce and we couldn't understand why she'd just abandon us. But when he said that word disappear? Why, I knew he'd done somethin to her. So I asked him what he'd done, and he spat at the ground and said he'd beat her till she fell unconscious then threw her off a cliff for the bears to eat. I went for him, then, couldn't stop myself, started hittin him and clawin at his face, and next thing I know, he's got his knife out, threatenin to kill me. Well, he was an old man and a drunk at that, and I was young and strong, and it didn't take much of an effort to get that knife away from him and sink it in his scrawny neck." She sat down hard as if the effort of standing was too much for her. "And oncet it was done, I dragged his vile body to a cliff and threw him off for the bears to eat just like he did Ma." Her gaze returned to me. "I'm a murderer, Lizzie, I done killed two men now. I won't hold it against you if you tell them it was me what done it and him without a weapon to defend himself."

I crossed over to the dead man, put his gun on the ground next to him, then returned to Sarie and sat on the grass beside her. I took her hand, surprised she didn't rebuff me like she usually did. "Sarie, I can't fault you for what you did, with either one of those vile men. They both deserved it, in my eyes. But you need to know something, Sarie. It wasn't your fault, what your pa did to you, how he treated you. I hope you know that."

She made a snorting noise and opened her mouth to speak, but before she could, we heard horses coming our way. Sarie gave me a grim look as she got to her feet, pulling me up with her.

We waited for Brett and his Home Guard to dismount. Brett strode over to us, his eyes on the body on the ground. "That the one?" he said to Sarie.

"He claimed he was. Seemed awful proud of it."

"You kill him?"

"I reckon I did."

I stepped toward Brett. "It was self-defense, Brett. I saw the whole thing."

Brett studied me for a moment then shrugged. "Way I see it, Sarie saved me the trouble of having to hang him ..." his eyes went back to the body "... or worse." He moved closer to peer at the man's face. "Don't reckon I ever seen him afore." He turned back to Sarie. "How about you? He live on the mountain?"

She shook her head.

Brett glanced around. "Anybody else with him?"

I nodded. "Two others."

"They nearby or they take off?"

"We got their guns away from em," Sarie said. As she and I handed the guns over to Brett, she continued, "I reckon I managed to shoot em both before they took off."

"They hurt bad?"

Sarie shook her head. "Not enough to kill em but enough to slow em down a bit, I suspect."

"You ever seen em before?"

"Here and there. They's brothers, go by the name of Waverly, live close to the top of the mountain."

"I reckon I know who you're talking about, got red hair, the both of em, with freckles all over their faces?"

"That's them," I said.

Brett turned to one of his men. "Collect the body, take it into town for me. I reckon we'll make an example out of this one, show them bushwhackers we ain't gonna tolerate them hurtin our women." He turned back to us, tilted his hat. "Ladies, I reckon I got business to attend to."

We watched as he mounted, motioning for his men to join him, then stood by while the man left behind lifted the dead man's body up as if it were a child's, threw it over his horse's back, then mounted and rode away. Once they were out of sight, Sarie went to the patch of dirt soaked in blood and began to scoop more dirt over it. I knelt beside her to help.

"We can't let Abbie see this," she said, in a whisper. "She's been traumatized enough."

"What will we tell her, Sarie?"

"We'll just say Brett and the Home Guard took care of him. That's all she needs to know."

"All right."

She stopped, turned to me. "About my pa."

"I won't tell her. I won't tell anyone, Sarie. It was justified, in my opinion."

As I helped Sarie cover the bloodied ground, I realized with a bit of a shock how much I had changed from the person who came through the light, one who led a sheltered, protected life, naïve to the realities of a harsh world such as this. I had begun to adapt, it seemed, to harden internally and externally. How would I adapt if and/or when I went back? Would that life soften me again, make me inured to the injustices of the world, or would I be one who would seek to rectify them? Hide bloody secrets from the innocent as I participated in my own or others' perceived justice? I had no answer.

Chapter Eight

Summer 1863

Bad Moon Rising

More than a year after the Conscription Act had passed, as Josh and I walked home from church service, holding hands, my thoughts lingered on Connie. I think most everyone's biggest fear for her after being raped was an unwanted pregnancy but mine veered more along her mental state. The pregnancy didn't happen but the assault affected her to the point that she went into a deep depression. The sisters and I visited her often, trying different herbs to help her mood, hoping to engage her in conversation or social events, anything that would bring life back into her eyes, but Connie would only sit in a chair, staring into space, ignoring everyone and everything around her. Sarie and I quickly came to the conclusion that the two things Connie needed most were time and her husband Martin. Although Martin should have been serving in the Confederate Army, Sarie convinced Dr. Glover to provide a medical excuse that would keep him home, which proved to be a godsend. Martin stood by Connie faithfully, taking over the chores she normally would do and patiently watching after their twins while carefully tending his fragile wife.

I was thrilled when that morning, for the first time in months, Connie attended church with Martin and the twins. After hugging her hello, I stood back, covertly looking her over, hoping the depression had lifted at least a little. Noting her rosy glow, the flare of life in her eyes, I smiled at her as I leaned close and whispered, "Are you?"

She smiled back, her face flushing slightly as she spoke into my ear. "Martin doesn't know yet, so let's keep it a secret until I tell him."

I smiled to myself as I walked along with Josh, so glad to have this sweet, young woman back with us, but lost that good feeling when my thoughts turned to Abbie, who had been manhandled by one of the bushwhackers but who didn't seem to have suffered any ill-effects. I often wondered if Abbie simply accepted his assault as the way of some men due to how she and her sisters had been treated by their father when she was younger.

Josh cleared his throat, bringing me back to the moment. I glanced at him, unsure what to say, dreading what he wanted to tell me. He had been preternaturally silent and distracted, a sign to me something was amiss. I finally stopped walking and turned to him. "What?"

He sighed as he squeezed my hand, reaching for the other one. "I have something to tell you, Lizzie, and I know it's not going to make you happy at all to hear it."

"You're going away."

He nodded. "We knew this day would come."

"I thought it was taken care of, Josh. Your father's in poor health and has deeded the plantation to you, so you're exempt under the Conscription Law."

He shook his head. "That's all well and good, but he has Eustus overseeing the plantation."

I glared at him. "And we all know how horrible Eustus treats the slaves."

"Not anymore. I won't let him, and I've convinced my mother if she doesn't want a revolt on her hands while I'm gone, she best see to it that Eustus minds his ways." He looked at me intently. "I have to do something, Lizzie. I can't stand not contributing in some way."

I shook my head with frustration.

"I have a plan, Lizzie, and even though I don't want to fight for the Confederacy, there may be a way around it. You know my good friends Isaac and Alphonso Avery."

I nodded. The sisters and I treated the slaves of the Swan Ponds Plantation from time to time. The Averys were a well-established, well-respected family in Morganton with much influence in all aspects of the community, most notably in law, education and politics, on local and state levels. The oldest son, William Waightstill Avery, had gained notoriety when he killed in cold blood a man who had flogged him in public. It was bad enough he shot the man before eyewitnesses, but he picked one of the most public places of all, the courthouse in Morganton, to do so. Even so, the jury found him innocent and he was set free, although when one looked at him, it was obvious he had created his own prison for himself. His younger brother Isaac, named for their father, managed one of the family's plantations in Yancey County until the Western North Carolina Railroad was chartered in 1854, when he partnered with Charles F. Fisher and Samuel McDowell Tate as contractors in building the railroad from Salisbury to Morganton and eventually to Asheville. But that had been interrupted by the war and the railroad had only been completed to within a few miles of Morganton.

"Well," Josh went on, "as you know, Isaac and Alphonso raised Company E of the 6th North Carolina Infantry which then became part of the Sixth North Carolina State Troops, with Isaac being appointed captain. He recently sent word that he's been temporarily assigned command of the 6th North Carolina State Troops after Brigadier General Robert Hoke was wounded at the Battle of Chancellorsville, and he's asked me to join them."

"Isn't that the battle where Stonewall Jackson died?"

He nodded.

"They can't even keep a general safe, Josh."

"It's war, Lizzie."

At my look, he held up his hand. "Let me explain what Isaac's offered. The brothers understand my feelings about this war but they look upon it as being one about states' rights as well, feeling that we should be able to abolish federal laws we don't support." He shrugged. "I can actually see their point about federal authority, Lizzie. Anyway, Isaac has offered me a position as his courier and aide. All I'll be required to do is carry messages back and forth from him to other regiments. I may occasionally be on the battlefield but that's doubtful." He smiled. "Don't you see, Lizzie, it's a way for me to pass on information to my informant in New York."

I stepped away from him, anger flaring in my brain like a raging fire. "You could be killed, Josh. You know the Confederacy won't win this war and will suffer more fatalities than the Union. There's no need for you to do anything. You could die from illness— that's what the majority will die from, by the way—simply by being exposed to it in the camps."

He reached out and took my hands but I grabbed them back. "I want to go, Lizzie. I have to go. I have to contribute in some way, and this is the safest way, the surest way I know that almost guarantees I'll come back to you."

"You already contribute, Josh, with the Underground Railroad. Look at the good you're doing there."

"I want to be involved in the war effort, Lizzie. It's a way to gather more information than I'll ever be able to here." His face clouded. "But it's not only that. If I'm to be a respected member of this community, I have to play my part. I'm sure others see me as a coward for hiding behind that exemption from the Conscription Act. Better men than me are fighting this war, whether they believe in it or not. This is the safest way for me to participate."

I looked away from him, thinking, trying to accept his decision. "When will you leave?"

"Tomorrow. Isaac sent word that they're marching to catch up with Lee, who's decided to lead a second excursion into enemy territory north of the Potomac River. It's his strategy to strike a war-winning blow against the Union, which is closing in on Vicksburg, Mississippi under General Ulysses S. Grant. Vicksburg's a strategic strongpoint for the Confederacy, and if it falls, that will give complete control of the Mississippi to the Union. Since Lee's too far away and can't help Vicksburg directly, he's decided to do so in another manner by diverting the Union troops north. Isaac says he also hopes to gain recognition of the Confederacy by France and Britain and to strengthen the cause of the northern Copperheads who favor peace." The Copperheads were secret organizations, such as the Knights of the Golden Circle and Sons of Liberty, formed to end the war. They gained their names from the snipped heads of liberty from copper pennies they wore on their lapels.

Fear tore through me when I remembered it was near the end of June, and from July 1st through the 3rd was ... "Josh, this will come to be called the Battle of Gettysburg, the bloodiest battle of the war with over 50,000 casualties. It will last for three days and the Confederates will lose. It will be known as the turning point in the War Between the States." Tears flooded my eyes. "This may be the last time I see you, Josh, if you go."

He cupped my cheek with his hand. "Then let's spend the day together, Lizzie, as much time as we can. Let's make it count."

I put my hand over his, an overwhelming sense of loss falling over me like a lead blanket, but then, I thought, I don't have to stay here. "I'm going with you," I said with resolve.

He stepped back from me, a stunned look on his face. "I can't place you in danger, Lizzie. Besides, what about your light?"

"I don't want to go back without you. I can be of help, work as a nurse in the field hospital, help treat the injured and sick."

"Lizzie, please, I fear for you."

"As I do you." I stepped closer to him. "Together forever. You said it, Josh. I can't stand the thought of staying here, worrying and wondering every minute of the day if you're safe."

He studied my face for a long time before sighing with resignation. "If there's anything I've learned about you, Lizzie Baker, it's that when you get that look in your eyes, there's no use talking to you. Just promise you'll stay off the battlefield. Please, promise me that."

"Of course." We began to walk toward home, but very shortly, I stopped. "Josh, I need to go visit Pokni. I don't want to leave without telling her goodbye."

"I can go with you."

"I want to spend time with her alone. She's become like a grandmother to me. I cherish her and need to tell her my own way in case we, well, don't make it back."

"Of course, I understand." He pulled me to him, kissed me fiercely. "Meet me at the church tomorrow morning at dawn," he whispered. "I'll arrange the transportation."

I nodded. "If you have it in mind to leave without me, just to keep me here, think again, bucko. I'm coming with you."

He gave me a smile, both sad and happy. "Never," he said, before walking away, leading his horse by the reins.

Pokni and I sat outside her small hut watching the sun begin its slow descent behind the mountain, painting the sky a beautiful pale pink. I smiled at her as I sat beside her, watching silently, feeling content and at peace for the moment. I had come to tell her I was leaving but kept putting it off, wanting to savor my time with Pokni without any emotionality, which I knew would happen once the words were out of my mouth. As we spent the afternoon gathering jimsonweed I planned to leave behind for Sarie in case Esmeralda had anymore flareups, I would at times find myself tearing up. I had grown close to Pokni during my time here and looked upon her as a beloved family member.

Pokni finally turned to me. "Have I told you about Hashtali, the sun god of our People?"

"No," I said, intrigued.

She nodded. "Hashtali rides his giant buzzard across the sky each day, but because his brightness is so much more intense than that of his wife, the moon goddess Hvashi, our eyes are too weak to behold even an outline of him at the center of his brilliant light. In the before, dead bodies were laid out in the sun, where Hashtali's fierce heat and his buzzards would nibble away at their earthly remains. This was to help the spirit's journey to the afterlife, leaving it with no body to return home to even if it wanted. After Ucta, the spider god, stole flames from the sun to provide our People with fire, each fire was considered still faithful to Hashtali and reported to him all they witnessed so that he was aware of everything that happened in the world. Our chiefs would only conduct councils on sunny days because cloudy days were Hashtali's sign that he did not want them to converse."

She looked up at the sky, making a sweeping gesture with her hand. "All the stars in the sky are daughters of Hashtali and his wife Hvashi. When there is no moon, Hvashi is with her husband in his home in the west. When there is no sun during the day ..."

She looked at me questioningly.

"You mean an eclipse?"

"Yes. This is when Hashtali's greatest enemy, the giant black squirrel, is trying to devour him and the giant buzzard he rides. When I was a child, my mother would tell me to make as much noise as I could during these eclipses ..." she raised a questioning eyebrow at me and after I nodded continued, "... to help Hashtali drive away his monstrous enemy." I watched as she reached into her pocket for one of her hand-rolled cigarettes, hoping there would be more to the story. She glanced at the sky, even more beautiful than a few moments before, now a rose color tinged with pale orange, fading to a soft salmon. "Do you know, Daughter, why the sky is red at sunrise and sunset?"

"No," I said, smiling widely as she lit her cigarette from a glowing ember in the fire, took a puff, then handed it to me.

"Tashka and Walo were two Choctaw braves who volunteered to follow Hashtali to find out what happened to the sun god at the end of his daily journey. They left from Nanih Waiya and spent long years following Hashtali by day and sleeping at night. They were very old men by the time they reached the waters in the west which Hashtali and his giant buzzard would dive into each night. During their journey, the brothers had learned much magic and were able to walk across the waters until they reached the entrance to Hashtali's home, which was a doorway floating on the waters. They climbed down through this door which was in the roof of Hashtali's home. It was a moonless night, so inside, they encountered Hasthali and his wife Hvashi, who were startled because no human had ever reached their home. After they questioned the two brothers about their journey and why they had come, Hashtali decided to test their worthiness so had his wife boil a huge pot of water and submerge the men into it. But they survived being boiled so Hashtali rubbed their skin until it was red and chafed and even then they did not cry out. This decided Hashtali that they were worthy, so he welcomed them to spend the night and presented them to each of his daughters. When morning came, he invited Tashka and Walo to ride with him on his great buzzard and they flew out of the other doorway in Hashtali's home, the one that opened to the waters in the east.

"As they flew along, Hashtali told the brothers that he would deliver them to the Choctaw people's home near Nanih Waiya but warned them they would die if they told anyone about what they had witnessed in Hashtali's home. Tashka and Walo were welcomed back by their people, but when they learned that those they had known and loved had died during their journey to the house of the sun god, they decided they did not want to live.

"At the huge feast for the brothers that night, they told the Choctaw all about everything they had seen and promptly died. Afterward, Hashtali welcomed them into his celestial home to marry some of his daughters, and they came to be worshipped by our People, one as the god of the dawn and the other as the god of dusk, to herald Hashtali's emergence in the morning and to welcome him home in the evening. Their skin was forever reddened by being boiled and scraped, and that is why the sky is often red near sunrise and sunset."

I smiled as I leaned against her. "What a beautiful story."

She returned my smile then took my hand. "What is it you came to tell me, Daughter?"

I blinked my eyes against the nascent tears. "I'm leaving, Pokni."

She nodded, as if she had been expecting this.

"Josh has joined Company E of the 6th North Carolina Infantry and I have decided to go with him. I want to work as a nurse in the field hospital, helping injured or sick soldiers."

Pokni looked away, silent for a long time. She finally turned to me. "I do not know if I will be here when you return, Daughter, but whether I am on this Earth or with my fierce warrior standing beside our Creator, I will watch out for you."

I grew alarmed. "Are you ill, Pokni?"

"No, child, not ill, but I am old, I have lived on this Earth for a long time and my body is telling me my time here is limited." She touched my cheek. "Don't despair, Daughter. I am ready to go. I have been for a long time."

I swiped at the tears falling down my face. "I pray you're here when I come back, Pokni. If it weren't for you and Abbie and Josh, I don't think I could have stayed here as long as I have."

Her smile was tender and full of love. "You have your own fierce warrior now, Daughter. I see the fire that burns when you look at him. And he at you. He will protect you and see you return to your time, if that's what you want."

"Oh, I wish you could go to that time with us, Pokni. Things would be so much easier for you."

"I only wish to join my warrior," she said, staring at the darkening sky. "He waits for me and calls me when I sleep."

I watched her, wondering if the love I had for Josh would last as long as Pokni's had for her husband. Would our fire grow stronger as we aged or perhaps become a steady, constant flame instead of the raging heat it was now, or over time become weaker and finally sputter out, as I had seen so many others do. Time would only tell.

Near midnight, I crept back into our cabin, fearful of waking Abbie. But she was waiting on me.

"I heared the news about Josh," she said as I undressed.

I nodded, blinking my eyes. It would be hardest of all leaving Abbie, but I was tired of crying.

"What are you gonna do?" she asked as I slid under the quilt.

I hesitated, unsure how to tell my sweet friend. "I'm going with him, Abbie."

She gave me a look.

"Not as one of those camp followers, looked upon as prostitutes. I figured I'd work in the hospital as a nurse." I grasped her hand. "But I don't want to leave you here by yourself and I'm worried for you."

Abbie's mouth twitched. "I figured you'd want to go with him, thought maybe I'd go with you, Lizzie."

I squealed with delight, reaching out and hugging her, then drew back with concern. "It could be dangerous, Abbie. I wouldn't want you in harm's way."

Abbie only smiled. "Probably so, Lizzie, but it seems to me it would be a great adventure."

I resolved to myself I would be Abbie's protector, make sure no harm came to her. Then remembered what Josh had said, that this would take me away from my light, delay my going back to my time. But I didn't want to go there without Josh, and he wouldn't be here with me to search for the light anyway. And what about Abbie, my inner voice whispered. Can you stand to leave her behind when you go through the light? No, I thought. I can't.

Chapter Nine

Summer 1863

Going Up the Country

Abbie and I spent most of the night making plans and rose well before dawn. There were many things to do before we left, most of which involved seeing to the care of our animals. We had decided not to take Jonah or Beauty, fearing the Confederacy would claim them for their own, and hoped Sarie would take them while we were gone. After banking the fire in the hearth and neatening up, we rode to Sarie's cabin where we endured some intense questioning from her followed by loudly voicing her objections and railing at Abbie, who stuck to her guns about leaving. Once Sarie realized Abbie wasn't going to give into her demands, she agreed to stable Jonah and Beauty with Buck, promising me that if the mountain was raided, she would take them away to the safe place we had found for them, an area well hidden and one the raiders would discover too hard to maneuver. Abbie seemed to be having almost as hard a time leaving her two precious dogs as she did her sisters and Amanda May, and I was just as relieved as she was when Amanda May told her she would take care of Billy and Bob, whom we had also brought with us.

As we made preparations to depart, when Abbie's back was turned, Sarie pulled me aside and swore to me she'd see me dead if I let anything happen to her sweet sister. "And I would gladly let you do it," I told her, watching the shocked expression on her face. "I love her as you do, Sarie," I said, pulling her into a hug, surprised when she accepted my embrace. "I would die for her," I whispered before turning and leaving.

We found Maggie at her cabin, making breakfast. Upon hearing the news, Maggie wept openly while Abbie reassured her all would be fine. Maggie promised to look after my homestead, along with her husband Randall until he left to rejoin his unit, which left me feeling more secure knowing our chickens, barn cats and goats, as well as my home, would be cared for in my absence. I had fallen in love with my cabin and our animals and was saddened to leave them behind. Randall offered us the use of Maggie's horse, telling Maggie he would accompany us on his own horse to meet Josh. After many hugs and tears, we finally secured our packs and medical satchels to the horses and rode to the church, where Josh waited on us. When I saw he had brought along steeds for each of us from his father's stables, I looked at him.

He shrugged. "I figured where you went, Abbie would too, so brought an extra horse."

I smiled at this. Although I had assumed we would travel by train for at least part of the journey, I preferred the scent of a horse over that of numerous unwashed male bodies packed into a train car. We bid goodbye to Randall, and as we mounted and rode away, I felt a small thrill of anticipation about what lay before us, knowing I would be participating in something I had read about during my time. Abbie had referred to it as an adventure and at that point I tended to agree with her.

Josh told us he wasn't sure we would be able to catch up with Colonel Avery's brigade, marching from Harrisburg to meet General Lee, but hoped if we pushed hard enough we might not be too far behind. Although I once more reiterated to Josh my concerns over his participation in the war, this fell on deaf ears. There was an air of excitement about him now, a sense of eagerness to be part of the war effort, and I could only pray he would not be injured or die, either on the battlefield or from illness.

As we rode along, I told Josh and Abbie the Union and Confederacy would meet at the crossroads village of Gettysburg, which wasn't a planned battle but began as more of a sudden skirmish between General George Meade's Army of the Potomac and General Lee's Army of Northern Virginia. Other than that and the fact that the Confederacy suffered a terrible loss during the Battle of Gettysburg, there was little more I could convey to them. History had not been one of my favorite subjects in school, something which I now regretted very much, so all I could do was share with them what little I remembered about the battle, which left much speculation on their part as to what brought about the defeat of the Confederacy.

The ride was, for the most part, uneventful. We had over 400 miles to go and Josh estimated we could be there in 10 days if we rode steadily. Days passed in a fugue of heat and humidity, swatting at flies and mosquitoes, while trying to stay hydrated. Although Abbie and I had made a tincture of dandelion leaves and roots which helped keep mosquitoes at bay, we sweated so much, the mixture didn't have much effect. Nights, we would fall into our bedrolls, so exhausted we rarely stirred until daybreak. Josh stubbornly pushed onward, knowing we were behind Avery's brigade and in all likelihood would arrive after the battle had been fought, but thought we might have a chance, as three people on horses could move much faster than a battalion of soldiers. As we made our way into Pennsylvania, I was unsettled at the lack of humanity. Where had they all gone, I wondered, as we rode by farmhouses and settlements that looked to be deserted.

We caught up with Colonel Isaac Avery's brigade on the morning of June 30th. Isaac seemed pleased to see Josh and not at all befuddled at the sight of Abbie and me, feeling haggard and tired from the hardships of our ride north. He assured us we would be a most welcome addition to the medical staff and offered to have one of his men take us straight to the field hospital once we caught up with Lee's troops. As the brigade was preparing to leave, we watched Isaac present Josh with a gift, telling him theirs was the only Confederate outfit to claim ownership of a personalized regimental belt buckle. Abbie and I stepped forward to admire the oval, cast-brass belt plate containing the legend 6th INF – N.C.S.T., which Isaac explained stood for Sixth Infantry – North Carolina State Troops. He told us the belt buckles had been manufactured in 1861 in a small railway shop in Greensboro, personally financed by the regiment's first commander, Colonel Charles F. Fisher, who died at the First Battle of Bull Run from a Yankee bullet through his forehead.

Isaac apologized that we must travel at once, as he planned to join General Lee before the day was out. Josh rode with Isaac at the front of the battalion while Abbie and I were placed near the end with the wagons bearing food and supplies, trailed by the camp followers, consisting of whores and soldiers' wives and those looking to earn money by doing laundry or other chores for the troops. We didn't catch up with Lee that day and only stopped long enough to grab a few hours' sleep then began the journey in the dark. When we arrived at our destination early morning of July 1st, Abbie and I were tired and out of sorts but perked up when we heard popping sounds a distance away. I hoped this was only soldiers target shooting and not the actual battle.

After dismounting, we stayed beside our horses, wondering where to go and what to do. Less than an hour later, a young private approached us, snatching off his cap as he came to a stop. "Ma'am, ma'am," he said, nodding at me, then Abbie.

We both nodded back.

"I'm Private Donald Hughes, and I've been instructed by Colonel Avery to take you two to the field hospital closest to our battalion." He straightened up, a proud look on his face. I figured he felt honored at being singled out by the well-respected colonel.

"Thank you, Private Hughes," Abbie said, retrieving her medical satchel from her horse then handing me mine. She waved a hand in the air. "I reckon we'll just follow you."

As we walked along, I was astounded at how many tents there were in the encampment and all I could think was that many of the men who occupied those tents would no longer be alive by the end of the battle. I noticed the gunfire we heard earlier seemed to be increasing in volume. So it's started, I thought as I touched Private Hughes on the arm. "Is that a battle going on?"

Private Hughes nodded. "We wasn't expecting a battle so soon, but yesterday, one of our Confederate divisions set out toward Gettysburg in search of supplies and spotted Union cavalry heading that way." He grinned. "I reckon we've caught up with Mead." He stopped and pointed to a large barn. "This is the Culp farm and that there's the hospital."

I was a bit shocked at this, as I had been expecting a large canvas tent with a yellow flag flying nearby. I looked up and saw the flag had been nailed to the upper loft window of the barn.

"Colonel Avery sent word ahead that you'uns are a-comin, so I reckon they'll be expecting you. He said to tell you he's secured a room for you in the house there." He pointed toward the Culp home, a large, two-story building sitting placidly nearby.

I smiled at him. "Thank you, Private Hughes. You've been a big help."

He nodded then turned and left at a run. I suspected he was anxious to get in on the fighting.

We stepped inside to turmoil, doctors and nurses rushing around, trying to get everything organized before the wounded began filing in.

A matronly looking nurse stopped, looking us over. "You the two Colonel Avery sent word about?"

"Yes'm," Abbie said.

"Nurses, the both of you?"

"Yes'm."

She nodded toward a corner. "Put your bags over there and follow me. We got a battle a-goin on out there and the wounded will start piling up right quick."

We hadn't gotten far when a young soldier ran into the hospital, shouting his wife needed attention. One of the doctors went up to him and asked if she was hurt. "She's having a baby," he yelled, wringing his hat in his hands, "and she ain't due for another month or so."

The doctor shook his head. "She'll have to handle that on her own, we're getting ready for the wounded."

Abbie and I looked at each other. "We can help," Abbie said, before I could even think about it. She turned to the doctor. "I'm a midwife."

He gestured for us to go.

"It ain't far," the soldier said, hurrying out the door. We ran after him and well before we reached his tent could hear the screams of a woman, which I'm sure frightened those nearby as she sounded as if she were being butchered. Without asking permission, we pushed through the tent flap and stepped inside, where we found the soldier's wife lying on a pallet on the ground, writhing in agony. Abbie and I knelt beside her, waiting for the contraction to end. Once it did, we introduced ourselves and told her we were there to help.

"I ain't due yet," she said, her voice panicked, as I did a quick exam.

"Maybe so, but your babe's decided otherwise." I glanced at her husband, standing over us looking like he wanted to be anywhere but there. I vaguely wondered why he hadn't joined the battle as I said, "We'll need clean rags and hot, boiling water."

He nodded before rushing out.

"I'll go get our medical satchels in case we need em," Abbie said. In our rush to help the mother-to-be, we had left them behind at the hospital, much to our mutual regret.

"You better hurry, Abbie, she's already fully dilated."

She squeezed my shoulder and was gone.

I smoothed hair off the young woman's face. "What's your name?" I asked, hoping to distract her.

"Amelia, Amelia Preston."

She looked like a teenager, with a young girl's slender build, small breasts and hips. I hoped that wouldn't present a problem during the birthing. "How old are you, Amelia?"

"Fifteen," she answered.

There had been a time when that would have shocked me but I was past that now. "How come you to be here in camp? With your time so near, why didn't you stay home with your parents or family?"

She shook her head. "Eddie's all I got. My family's all dead and gone." Tears flooded her eyes. "I didn't have nowhere else to go."

"It's all right," I said, taking her hand. "We're here, we'll help you."

"I'm so scared, Lizzie," she said, her eyes wide.

"Everyone is when they're delivering. But Abbie's birthed many a baby and we'll take real good care of you."

She squeezed her eyes shut and let out a scream that hurt my eardrums. I talked to her as the contraction progressed, encouraging her to breathe in and out, trying to help her relax. She didn't seem predisposed to listen to me but rather to scream as loud as she could.

When the tent flap was jerked back, I looked that way, expecting Abbie, frowning when I noticed a stern-looking soldier with a star on his collar. "Shut her up," he shouted. "She's liable to bring the whole Union Army down on us. She's got the whole camp in a panic."

I ignored him, knowing that for a lie. With tens of thousands of soldiers around us and a battle going on, I doubted her screams would reach even the middle of camp. Besides, I figured the gunfire was ample enough reason for anyone to panic.

The tent flap jerked again and Abbie stepped through. She frowned at the man. "Unless you got some business with this young lady, I suggest you leave," she said in an annoyed tone. "We're about to have a baby here."

"Stuff a rag in her mouth or something," he grumbled. "She's scaring everybody."

Abbie made a shooing gesture with her hand, herding him outside. He went grudgingly. She joined us, kneeling on the other side of Amelia.

"Amelia," I said, "when the next contraction comes, try to breathe through it, it will help with the pain. Watch us and do what we do."

"Yes'm," she said, squeezing my hand so hard, my bones ground together. And within seconds it seemed she let out another bloodcurdling screech, ignoring us altogether.

"Okay, er, all right," I said afterward, glancing up at the sound of movement near the door. Her husband came in carrying a large cauldron of boiling water in one hand, his shoulder dipping toward the ground due to the heaviness of the pot. He clutched a bundle of rags in his other hand.

On his heels followed an older woman with iron-grey hair and a buxom build. "Can I do anything to help?" she asked, peering inside curiously.

"I reckon we can handle it," Abbie said, "but if'n you want, you're more than welcome to stay."

"I've helped birth many babies," she said, coming closer, smiling at Amelia. "My name's Ruth but ever'body calls me Mama Ruth."

Ruth had a comforting air about her and I felt Amelia relax slightly as she smiled back. Ruth crossed over to Eddie, back to wringing his hat while anxiously hovering over us, and maneuvered him away from the action a bit, talking all the while to distract him.

Abbie turned her attention back to our patient. "Amelia, when you feel the need to push, you need to tell us right off."

Amelia nodded then held her breath for a moment before expelling another scream. Thankfully, the next contraction produced the urge to push and it seemed within minutes, with me supporting Amelia and Abbie encouraging her to push, a small infant slid out from between her legs.

I wiped sweat from Amelia's face with a clean rag while talking to her, giving Abbie time to check the baby and remove any breathing obstruction. When I heard a loud wail, I thought things were probably all right. I knew that the lungs were one of the last organs to fully develop and had been worried about that.

Abbie finally looked up, a smile on her face. "You got you a right pretty little girl," she told Amelia, placing her on her chest.

Abbie and I stepped back, watching as Eddie knelt beside his wife, exclaiming over his daughter. She was a tiny thing but looked perfect, her color a healthy pink, all toes and fingers accounted for, her vocalizations sounding as normal as any newborn. Mama Ruth came forward with a soft blanket which she extended to Amelia.

"Let me bathe the baby first," I said. After I had her clean, we wrapped her in the blanket and gave her back to her mother. I thanked Ruth, who smiled at me, joy evident in her eyes.

"All babies are miracles, if'n you ask me," she said.

As we were massaging Amelia's abdomen, helping to pass the afterbirth, a bugle sounded nearby. We all looked toward the outside of the tent.

Eddie kissed his wife and daughter on the cheeks, saying, "They're calling my regiment, sweetheart, I got to go." He donned his hat as he rushed outside. Amelia watched him, a panicked look on her face, but Ruth diverted her attention, encouraging her to try to nurse the baby.

After we had done all we could for Amelia, knowing she didn't have any family, I asked Ruth if she could stay with the young mother and baby for awhile since we had to go to the hospital.

"I reckon I'll stay here as long as she needs me to," she said with a smile at Amelia.

After Abbie and I assured Amelia we'd be back to check on her and the baby later that afternoon, we made our way back to the Culp barn. As we hurried along, I said a silent prayer we wouldn't be overrun by Union soldiers and that Eddie would return to his wife unharmed.

The encampment was in turmoil, soldiers and civilians running here and there, horses and mules milling about restlessly. I searched for Josh but didn't glimpse him anywhere and fought hard not to panic at the thought that I might not see him again. I resisted the urge to put my hands over my ears as sounds of battle nearby grew louder, with gunshots popping and cannons booming, men yelling and screaming in pain accompanied by the shrieks of horses injured or dying. I glanced at Abbie as we neared the hospital. "Are you going to use your gift as a Blood Stopper?"

She hesitated a moment before resuming her fast pace. "I didn't think to bring my Bible with me, Lizzie. Besides, some people look at that as witchcraft." She shrugged. "I don't reckon I'll know what I'll do until I do it."

At the Culp barn, which we were later told was about a mile behind the battle lines, I hesitated outside, staring at a pile of discarded arms and legs that looked to have been thrown out a window.

Abbie, standing beside me, drew in a breath. "Lizzie, do you think those are real?" she whispered, her eyes wide.

Our gazes met but I could not answer. Of course they were.

We stepped inside to chaos. Doctors knelt over patients, operating or bellowing for help from nurses who were scattered throughout the room. Men cried out in agony, some calling for loved ones, others screaming with terror. I noticed a group of men lying against the wall, blood-soaked bandages covering their heads or torsos, and wondered if there was any sort of triage in play. I resisted the urge to pull my apron over my nose. The smell was atrocious, a mixture of vomit, blood, feces, and body sweat cooked to a boil in the heat captured inside the barn.

One doctor near the door looked up, spied Abbie and me, and yelled, "To me, now!" We rushed over without hesitation. Without asking our names or why we were there, he instructed us to hold down the young man on the cot before him. We each put our hands on a shoulder and watched as the doctor washed out a leg wound with a blood-stained cloth, then began to probe it with his finger, the soldier writhing in pain beneath us. I assumed the doctor must be looking for the bullet or perhaps bits of cloth or bone. He glanced at the young man and said, "No help for it, it's gonna have to come off."

The soldier screamed as he struggled against us. His eyes fixed on mine, wide with panic. "Don't let him cut off my leg, please, ma'am, don't let him cut off my leg."

The surgeon, his gaze on the injury, yelled at Abbie and me to continue to hold the soldier down.

I tried saying consoling words to the soldier but he didn't listen, instead continued to scream until the surgeon put a sweet-smelling, cone-shaped towel over his face. I turned my head away, not wanting to breathe in the fumes.

Abbie wrinkled her nose. "What's that smell?"

"Chloroform, an anesthetic. Don't breathe in the fumes, Abbie, it will make you lightheaded or possibly pass out." I glanced at the soldier, whose eyes were now closed, thankful at least the doctor would be using an anesthetic.

Once the young man succumbed, I winced as the surgeon picked up a bloody scalpel. Why in the world didn't he sterilize that first, I thought wildly as I watched him make an incision through skin and muscle to the bone, above and below the knee, leaving a flap of skin on one side. He then picked up an amputation saw, which I later learned was called a bonesaw, leading to the Civil War slang Sawbones for doctor. Working quickly, he sawed through the bone until the leg was severed, then casually tossed it onto the floor. A man whom I assumed to be an orderly picked it up, went to the window and nonchalantly tossed it out. I could feel Abbie looking at me but kept my eyes on the doctor, who was busily tying off the arteries with what looked to be horsehair threads. Afterward, he scraped the end and edges of the bone smooth, I assumed so the bone would not penetrate through the skin. The flap of skin he had left was pulled across the site and sewn closed, leaving a drainage hole. He then covered the stump with isinglass plaster and bandaged it. I was shocked to realize he had accomplished all this within minutes.

The doctor straightened up, glancing at the patient, who was still out of it. I noticed the surgeon's coat was stained with blood and pus and his hands were red. His gaze landed on us. "With me," he said as he walked off. We followed him to another soldier, this one with a bullet wound to the upper arm. Without washing his hands, he bent over the young man and began probing the wound, ignoring the soldier's screams of pain.

During the course of the day, Abbie and I followed this doctor, doing as he instructed. I surmised he was looked upon as an expert at amputation as most of his patients ended up missing limbs. I itched to do something to soothe these poor boys, treat them with kindness and gentleness, but was never allowed to. Although I did not appreciate our doctor's brusque bedside manner, I had to admit he was a good surgeon, although was probably killing, or at the very least making very ill, every person he treated by not washing his hands, sponges or instruments with some form of antiseptic.

Late afternoon, he walked outside for a breath of fresh air, bidding us come with him. We followed him to a mess tent, where, after washing our hands in a bucket of water near the entrance, we all got a bowl of what looked to be vegetable soup and a tin cup of water then retired to a long trestle table to eat.

He finally seemed to notice us. "Julian Blackstone," he said, nodding. "You are?"He lifted one black, bushy eyebrow as he stared at me, then Abbie.

"I'm Lizzie Baker," I said, and this is my cousin Abbie Collins."

"You both did a fine job today. I commend you." He focused on his food but I was more curious than hungry.

"Why so many amputations?" I asked.

He glanced at me. "May I ask why you want to know?"

I shrugged. "It seems to me some of those limbs could have been saved."

He bristled at that. "Are you a doctor?"

Abbie drew herself up. "I reckon Lizzie's more of a doctor than most of the doctors here. She's been to medical school, knows all kinds of doctoring."

His black eyes bore into me. "You've been to medical school," he said in an accusing tone, implying he clearly didn't believe her.

"Yes, I've been to medical school." I resisted the urge to roll my eyes. I hated this century with its bias against women, men being looked upon as superior beings with higher intelligence. I was aware by this point that most medical schools were only two years, some even less. There were no licensing boards, as in my time, and many doctors were political appointments, without any kind of experience or knowledge. I felt I certainly qualified far more than most doctors of that era.

Both eyebrows went up at that. "May I ask where?"

I had attended the University of Tennessee which I knew had originally been known as East Tennessee College. Unsure if the name had changed at this point, I debated a second before answering, "East Tennessee College in Knoxville."

I assumed it was the right answer since he didn't dispute the name as he sat back, his food forgotten. "They allow women in medical school there?" he asked, sounding astounded.

"My father is a well-known doctor, he pulled some strings." I hesitated. Had I just said slang not known at the time?

He considered this for a long moment as he studied me. "And your cousin?" He glanced at Abbie.

"She's a midwife, also a healer." I almost told him she was a Blood Stopper but decided not to because of his attitude toward my medical training. Apparently he was a man of the time who looked upon women as domesticated animals put on Earth to bear babies and do their husband's bidding.

He picked up his spoon and went back to his food.

"I could have helped more today," I couldn't stop myself from saying.

He didn't reply to this.

"So, why so many amputations?" I asked again.

He seemed to debate answering but finally said, "It's because of the Minie ball." He shrugged. "Well, that and cannon balls."

"What's a Minie ball?"

"The soft lead bullet they're using. It's large and heavy, can kill at over 1,000 yards and causes much damage. Leaves large, gaping holes, splinters bone, destroys muscles, arteries and tissue beyond repair. When it hits bone, it expands. Any soldier shot in the head, chest or guts won't live due to the damage it causes."

I nodded, considering this. That explained the soldiers lined up against the wall. "What about infections after the surgery?"

He glanced at me under furrowed brows.

"I noticed you didn't wash your hands or sterilize your instruments. You do realize you're transferring deadly germs from one patient to the other?"

"I know no such thing," he said, sounding defensive.

"Do you have deaths afterwards?" I pressed.

He nodded with reluctance. "We do."

"From?"

"Most often pyemia."

"Blood poisoning?"

"That and tetanus, erysepilas."

"Caused by a bacterial infection," I told Abbie.

"Osteomyelitis."

"Inflammation of the bone."

He ignored me. "And hospital gangrene."

"What's that?"

"A small black spot that appears on the wound and spreads, leading to death."

I considered all this. "If you sterilize your hands and equipment and the wound, you can cut down on the number of post-op deaths."

He stared at me. I knew it wasn't until later that germs and bacteria would be openly acknowledged, antiseptics used to combat them. But perhaps someone would listen to me. Abbie and her sisters had, as well as a few others.

"I know nothing of the kind," he said. Ignoring us, he stood up and left the tent, heading back to the hospital. We hurriedly finished our meal then went to join him.

As large as Lee's Army was and as spread out as they were, we learned that news traveled quickly, the wounded or those bearing them giving us bits and spurts as they came and went. As the day wore on, we heard about the different brigades coming in to join the battle and that General Robert E. Lee arrived around 2:00 pm. Soldiers bearing the news were jubilant that Confederate forces managed to drive the Union defenders to Cemetery Hill, about a half mile south, declaring a win for the Confederacy. General Lee, in an effort to ensure victory, gave orders to attack Cemetery Hill to Richard Ewell, the commander of the Army of Northern Virginia's Second Corps. Whispers ran fierce when he declined to order the attack, his stance being that the Federal position was too strong, some calling him a coward, others comparing him to Stonewall Jackson.

My ears perked up when I heard a nearby soldier who had assisted his wounded friend into the hospital telling others that Colonel Avery's brigade had fought gallantly and driven the enemy back until Union artillery fire from a knoll near Culp's Hill finally halted their advance. When I learned the 6th Brigade would remain on the battlefield overnight, I hoped Josh was off delivering a message to another battalion but feared he more than likely was with his friend Isaac Avery.

Chapter Ten

Summer 1863

It's All Over Now

The second day of battle, the Confederates attacked an area on the battlefield called Big Round Top, and when they charged nearby Little Round Top, so many died, one gravely wounded officer told me, the ground was covered with their bodies and soaked with their blood. At one point, I heard a band playing polkas and waltzes, and when I asked one of the doctors about this, he said it was the Confederate band. I later learned they played all day, which I found a little insane.

This day was filled with chaos, with soldiers flowing into our hospital without respite, the air filled with screams of agony and the coppery scent of blood, along with a sense of near-panic on the part of the doctors and nurses at the number of wounded. Dr. Blackstone allowed Abbie and me to treat those soldiers who were not terminal or did not require amputation or surgery. I wasn't sure if this was due to his confidence in our competence or if he was just too overwhelmed to care. So many injured and dying passed through the hospital's doors, I spared little thought for this as I went from one soldier to another, without time for lunch or even a short break. Time passed quickly, and as I worked, when my mind wasn't occupied with what course of treatment to administer, I would find it turning to Josh and Colonel Avery's Brigade, wondering where they were and if they were engaged in battle.

I had just finished stitching up a laceration from a bayonet wound when I noticed a small person who looked to be more boy than man assisting a soldier into the tent. I went to help, putting my shoulder underneath the wounded man's arm and steadying him. "Over there," I said, pointing to an empty space on the ground.

After we eased him onto the dirt, I checked his pupils then his pulse, listened to his heartbeat, faint and thready. His pants were covered in blood and I ran my hands over the material, checking for a tear or hole where a bullet or bayonet had gone through. I finally found a bullet wound at or near the femoral artery. Alarmed, I ripped the pants open and put my fingers on the closest pressure point, watching with dismay as the blood slowed to a trickle which I feared was not from my actions. I put my head on his chest, listening for the heartbeat, realizing with dismay this man was dying and I could not save him. I looked up at the soldier who had helped him in and shook my head. "I'm so sorry."

The soldier's eyes rolled up in his head and he fell to the ground. I knelt beside him, wondering if he had been injured. There was blood on his shirt but I couldn't tell if it was from the soldier he had brought in or a wound. Without hesitation, I ripped the shirt open, hesitating at the sight of a wide band of material wrapped around the soldier's chest. What in the world? I wondered to myself, as I inspected it for blood or seepage. But there was none. I sat back, studying the band, wondering why anyone would ... and then remembered rumors I had heard of women who disguised themselves as men so they could serve. Concluding that she had simply fainted, I rested the soldier's legs in my lap, waiting for her to come around. When she did, she stared at me with confusion.

"You fainted," I told her.

She sat up, her gaze going to the soldier who had died. "Is he …?" Although she deliberately lowered the tone of her voice, it still sounded very feminine to me.

"I'm sorry."

Tears flooded her eyes. I reached out and held her hand. "Were you close to him?"

"He's my brother," she said. "His name's Truett."

"And your name?"

"Thomas Lowery."

I stared at her, wondering how in the world such a beautiful young woman had managed to pull this off. Her eyes were a beautiful dark gray, encased by long, thick, black lashes. Her cropped, dark-brown hair only seemed to highlight her smooth, flawless skin and dainty, feminine features.

I leaned close to her, whispering, "I know your secret."

She frowned at me.

"Why you bind your chest. You're not the first one to do this."

She swiped at her eyes, speaking in her normal voice. "Well, I guess it doesn't matter now." Her breath hitched. "Truett's dead, no reason for me to fight anymore."

"Is he really your brother?"

She nodded.

"What's your real name?"

"Tavia."

A lovely name for a lovely young woman. "Are you injured, Tavia?"

"No, ma'am." Her face crumpled and she began sobbing. I reached over and hugged her, wishing I could do something to ease her pain.

"I don't know what to do now," she said.

"You can go back home."

"We don't have a home anymore. The bushwhackers burned us out."

"Then you can stay with my cousin Abbie and me until you decide what to do." I stood, helping her to her feet. "We have a room in the farmhouse next door. Do you want to go rest and perhaps clean up a bit?"

She tried to smile through her tears and I knew the effort cost her greatly. I patted her arm. "Just tell Mrs. Culp you'll be staying in Lizzie and Abbie's room. She'll show you to it."

She nodded and turned to leave then hesitated, grabbing my hand. "I can't thank you enough, Lizzie." Her gaze turned to her brother's body. "Can you tell them I claim the body and will see to his burial?"

I squeezed her hand. "I'll let the orderly know." I turned and waved one of the orderlies over and when he joined us told him Tavia's request.

"I'll see to it," he said, with a curt nod at Tavia.

I returned my gaze to her. "I'm just so sorry for your loss, Tavia. Try to get some rest if you can. I'll see you later." I quickly forgot her as I noticed a young man hobbling inside, holding his side, and went to help him.

Late evening, I glanced up and saw Josh hurrying toward me. Blood was smeared on his face and over his uniform but he looked unharmed. Unable to contain myself, I ran toward him, throwing myself into his arms. He smelled of gun smoke, blood and sweat. When he released me, he said, "Lizzie, I need you to come with me."

"Are you hurt?" I asked as he took my elbow and guided me toward the door.

"No, but it's Isaac, he's been shot. They've got him up at the Culp farmhouse." Since we were at the barn, we didn't have far to travel, and as we walked that way, Josh told me what happened. "We've been pinned down all day, sharpshooters all around us. We were finally ordered to storm the heights of Cemetery Hill late this afternoon. The attack commenced a little before dusk and the smoke was so thick you could barely see. Isaac planned to go in on foot but for some ungodly reason changed his mind and led the charge on his horse, a white horse at that, and he was the only one mounted." He shook his head with despair. "Couldn't have given them a better target if he tried! It was growing dark and I lost sight of him. When I found him, he was on the ground, shot." He glanced at me. "He took a bullet at the base of his neck. He's paralyzed and can't talk."

He led me up the wide porch and into the farmhouse. People milled about inside, talking in quiet voices, watching us with interest as we passed. Josh led me to a parlor, where we found his friend lying on a small bed tucked away in the corner. A man hovered over him, as two others whom I recognized as doctors conferred with one another across the room. Josh introduced the man with Isaac as Major Samuel McDowell Tate. He nodded at me, his expression grim. Isaac had his eyes closed and didn't seem to hear us. "Lizzie here's a doctor," Josh explained to Major Tate, who looked stunned at this.

When I touched Isaac's arm, he opened his eyes.

I held his right hand as I knelt by the bed. "Josh tells me you can't speak. Can you blink once for yes and twice for no then?"

He blinked once.

"Are you paralyzed anywhere?"

One blink.

"Both sides?"

Two blinks.

"Right side?"

One blink.

"Are you in pain?"

One blink.

"A lot?"

Two blinks.

I reached for his left hand. "Can you squeeze my hand for me?"

His grip was firm enough but not hard.

"Do you mind if I look at the wound?"

One blink.

I stood and leaned over him, studying the entrance of the bullet wound which was right at the base of the neck on the right side. I thought it had probably penetrated the spinal column. There was no way a doctor of this time could operate on him. By trying to remove the bullet, they could very well kill him. This was tragic. He probably wouldn't live past the morrow.

I smiled at Isaac as I knelt by him again. "Thank you. We'll try to make you as comfortable as possible."

He closed his eyes without responding.

Josh helped me up. Without saying a word, I walked away. When we were near the door, I said, "He won't live, Josh. It's caused spinal damage. I'm surprised he's as alert as he is."

Josh looked stricken. "I need to find Alphonso."

"I'll stay with him if you want."

"Please, Lizzie."

The doctors who had been conferring when we entered the room approached us. I had met them briefly and knew them to be regimental surgeons William L. Reese and John G. Hardy.

Dr. Hardy stared at me for a moment. "Dr. Blackstone tells us you're a doctor. He seems quite impressed."

I nodded.

He glanced at Isaac. "Your opinion?"

"He won't live. Surgery is impossible."

He nodded. "We concur." He drew himself up, glancing at his cohort. "I see no need for all of us to be here."

"I'll stay with him," I volunteered.

Both men nodded. "We need to return to the hospital," Dr. Reese said. "We'll come back from time to time, see how he's doing."

"I'll make him as comfortable as I can," I told them.

After they left, Josh bid me goodbye and hurried out in search of Isaac's brother. I joined Major Tate, who had pulled up two chairs beside the bed. We gave each other a wan smile before settling in for the night.

I had noticed a young black man sitting in the corner when we came in. His gaze always seemed to remain on Isaac and I wondered if they had a connection of some sort. At one point, I approached him and knelt down next to him. "Can I get you some water, perhaps something to eat?"

He glanced at me before returning his eyes to Isaac. "No'm, I thank you."

"Are you with Colonel Avery?"

He nodded. "Been with the Colonel for a good while now. He brought me along to fix his meals and tend to his horse."

"What's your name?"

"Elijah."

"We'll take good care of him, Elijah. If you'd like to go get something to eat, perhaps get some sleep ..."

He shook his head. "I come here to be with Marse Isaac and I ain't leavin him."

I nodded, saying, "Let me know if you need anything," as I rose to my feet.

So, Major Tate, Elijah and I kept vigil that night, bathing Isaac's face with cold cloths. I was unsure if he would be able to swallow due to the paralysis and didn't want to choke him, but when asked, he refused food or water. The wound didn't bleed very much and he slept mostly or just lay very still. The good doctors Reese and Hardy made frequent visits, always leaving with disappointed looks in their eyes. I knew they were trying valiantly to figure out some way to save the colonel but felt that nothing short of a miracle could help this good man. Josh didn't return but I kept telling myself he had only been delayed, nothing had happened to him. When Abbie found me, I explained about Tavia. She promised to look after her for me and left to get some rest while I remained with Isaac.

The next morning, we were joined by a man who introduced himself as Isaac's friend John A. McPherson. When he took the Colonel's hand and asked if he knew him, Isaac pressed back as if he recognized him but for the most part didn't seem interested in what was going on around him. I needed to get a couple of hours sleep before going to the hospital so somewhat reluctantly left Isaac in the care of McPherson, along with Elijah.

I learned later that this day, the third day of battle, brought about the assault called Pickett's charge that would be the culmination of the Battle of Gettysburg, although would not bring about the outcome General Robert E. Lee hoped for. In an effort to force an end to the battle, Lee ordered a last-ditch assault on the Yankee center, to converge on an area surrounding a small cluster of trees just behind the Union line. Lee's contention was that once the Federal line was split, he would be free to march on Washington DC from the rear, ending the war in a matter of days. The assault, led by Major General George Pickett, Brigadier General James Johnston Pettigrew, and Major General Isaac Trimble, consisted of an infantry of approximately 15,000 Confederate soldiers, stretched more than a mile across, attacking Union Major General George Meade's 6,500 troops along Cemetery Ridge. As the line of Confederates advanced, the Union fired 11 cannon and 1700 muskets at once, switching from exploding shells to canister shots, which transformed their cannons into oversized shotguns that could shred whole platoons with a single blast. In less than an hour, half of the Confederate soldiers who had made the charge were dead, wounded or missing. I was told afterward that when Lee realized what had happened, he cried, "It's all my fault." Although he later offered President Jefferson Davis his resignation, this was refused.

During the day, the hospitals were overwhelmed with wounded and dying, so much so that there was no room inside and many were forced to lie on the grass outside awaiting medical attention. Drs. Hardy and Reese and I alternated briefly checking in on the colonel, who held on stubbornly to life. That night, just after dark, I took a break from tending the wounded to see to Isaac. I was so exhausted, I felt as if I were floating on air as I made my way to the Culp home. As I checked his vitals, Isaac seemed to become more alert. He tried to remove something from his pocket and finally produced a piece of blood-soaked scrap paper and what looked to be a stick. He gave the paper to Major Tate, who knelt by his side, holding the paper, and we all watched as he dipped the stick in his own blood and wrote with his left hand, "Major, tell my father I died with my face to the enemy." I put my fist to my mouth, so saddened by this I was afraid I'd sob out loud. Satisfied he had accomplished what he wanted to, Isaac died shortly thereafter.

Elijah seemed to take it the hardest of those gathered in the room. He tried to hold back his feelings but finally succumbed, making a muffled sobbing sound as he fled the room.

McPherson left shortly after him, returning with what looked to be a flag in hand. As he spread it over Isaac's face and upper body, I thought what a beautiful gesture this was. McPherson glanced at me. "Pretty, ain't it?"

"It is." I reached out and touched the blue silk flag, tracing the state seal, representing two women standing by a horn of plenty with the words "To be rather than to seem" written below.

"Those words were our motto. The sister of our first commander, Charles Fisher, gave it to the regiment. We treasure this flag but I reckon it should go with Isaac. He truly earned it."

I swiped at my eyes. "I'm truly sorry for your loss."

He cleared his throat. "Thank you, ma'am. Now, if you'll excuse me, I reckon I need to go see about a coffin for the Colonel."

Word of Colonel Avery's death spread quickly and several of his men came to pay their respects as the evening wore on. Each man spoke of their reverence for their commander and seemed saddened by his passing.

John McPherson returned late that night with an ambulance. He stood over Isaac, telling those of us in the room that he had gone into town and succeeded in finding some lumber after which he had two men detailed from the regiment to finish the coffin. He turned away from his friend's body, saying, "I fear we will be overtaken so have brought the ambulance in case we need to evacuate."

This startled me, although I told myself I should have expected that, knowing that the South would lose this battle. This was confirmed shortly after when we received orders to relocate the hospital farther to the rear. As we made preparations to leave, I listened as John McPherson talked to other men, relaying his last days with his friend, talking about how Colonel Avery rode up and down the lines during the first day of battle, leading and cheering on his men, slept under an apple tree that night and was up early the next day, waiting for orders while evading sharpshooters.

The following morning, the 4th of July, rumors abounded that General Lee had met with General John D. Imboden the previous evening, the decision having been made for the army to withdraw and return to Virginia. Everyone was in poor spirits due to this crushing defeat, word spreading quickly that the Confederacy had lost more than a third of its troops. The wagon train bearing supplies, along with the thousands of wounded, was ordered to leave in advance of the Confederate exodus from Pennsylvania under the protection of General Imboden, accompanied by his artillery battery and five additional batteries borrowed from Lee's infantry corps. The brigades of Brigadier General Fitzhugh Lee and Colonel Laurence S. Baker were ordered to protect the flank and rear of the transport column.

Knowing we would have to leave with the wagon train, Abbie and I were frantic to find Josh, who still hadn't come back. We went around the encampment, asking everyone we came across if they had seen him. We searched the hospitals for him, both now convinced that something had happened. Finally, mid-morning, Abbie and I decided to go onto the battlefield where Isaac had met the bullet that ended his life. Although we were warned Union burial crews would possibly be on-site, this didn't stop us and other medical personnel from searching for the wounded. When I stood on the small rise overlooking the battlefield, I clutched Abbie's hand in despair. It seemed the ground was completely covered with men dead or dying. Red and brown and blue and gray wove together in some sort of weird patchwork quilt, the green of the grass invisible beneath. I noticed there were more than a few doctors, nurses and soldiers on the field, along with a burial detail, helping to identify and remove bodies. Abbie and I picked our way gingerly among the bodies, notifying others when we found someone still alive.

I knelt beside a young soldier, lying on his back, gasping for breath, staring at the sky. When he sensed me leaning over him, his eyes focused on me, and he said, "Mama?"

I smiled at him as I checked his body for wounds, stifling a gasp when I saw the deep gash in his abdomen, blood flowing from an intestinal wound.

"Mama?" he said.

I grasped his hand in mine, smoothing the hair off his forehead. "Shhh, it's all right, we're going to take good care of you, get you home soon."

Tears leaked from his eyes. "I'm scared, Mama. I think I'm dying."

"No, no, you're fine," I lied.

His gave me an intent look as he squeezed my hand. "Don't leave me, Mama. I'm awful fearful of dying. I don't want to die alone."

I continued stroking his hair, murmuring, "I won't leave you. I'll stay with you. I promise you won't be alone."

He looked at the sky again. "I ain't but 19, Mama. I ain't lived my life yet, ain't even been with a woman …"

I watched as his eyes lost their luster and his chest ceased to rise. I reached out and closed his eyes, thinking how sad it was he had lost his life at such a young age and for such an unjust cause. I heard Abbie shouting and looked up to find her waving at me. I got to my feet and ran.

It was sheer luck she found Josh, his body under that of a Union soldier, right on top of him. I helped Abbie pull the man off, crying out when I saw Josh, covered in blood, his face ashen and eyes closed. I knelt beside him, placing my fingers on his carotid artery, sighing with relief when I felt movement. "He's alive," I told Abbie.

"We got to get him to the hospital, Lizzie," she said, kneeling beside me. "I can't tell if that's Josh's blood or the soldier what was on top of him, but there's a right lot of it."

I stood, yelling as loud as I could for help, stifling a sob when I saw two young men headed our way. Between the four of us, we managed to remove Josh from the battlefield and to the hospital, which was being emptied as the wounded were being loaded onto wagons. Dr. Blackstone, washing his hands outside, ran to help carry Josh inside and place him on a cot. I stepped back, watching as Dr.

Blackstone cut Josh's shirt off him, placing my hand over my mouth when I saw the bloody tear in his shoulder.

"Is it a bullet wound?" I asked, thinking if so, Josh would lose his dominant arm.

Blackstone shook his head. "Looks like a bayonet wound." He grabbed a bandage and placed it over the wound, pressing down, then glanced at us. "When did this happen?"

I shook my head.

Abbie said, "He's been gone over 36 hours. We liked to never found him, some Union soldier was laying right on top of him."

"That might have saved his life."

"What do you mean?"

"The soldier's body might have put enough pressure on that wound to slow the bleeding. A wound like this," he waved his hand at the injury, "bleeding like that for several hours could be fatal."

"Is that why he ain't awake?" Abbie asked.

Blackstone ran his hands over Josh's skull. "He's been hit on the side of the head, may be concussed," he muttered to himself, ignoring us as he studied his bloodied fingers. He seemed to realize we were still standing there and looked up with a belligerent gaze. "Go get me bandages, a needle, sutures, whatever you use to disinfect a wound. Now."

Josh came around as Dr. Blackstone was stitching the wound. He looked groggily at the doctor then at Abbie and me. "Isaac?" he asked softly.

"He died last night," I said, squeezing his hand.

He closed his eyes, tears leaking from the corners. "I was hoping to get back to him before he did." He sighed. "I never did find Alphonso."

Once assured Josh would live, I stepped outside to watch the activity as we prepared to retreat in heavy rain. I had been told it would take hours to fully account for the wounded and load the wagons, and this became obvious when I learned that the wagon train consisted of hundreds of Conestoga-style wagons along with over 10,000 animals, wagon loads of provisions and a small herd of cattle.

I felt sorry for the injured men being loaded into the backs of the wagons, lying on the hard boards of the beds with little or no straw beneath them to cushion the jostling of the wagon. The overhead canvas didn't provide adequate cover against the cold rain falling down, and they were quickly drenched.

Abbie joined me and we stood in the downpour while Elijah and several men gingerly loaded Avery's coffin into a quartermaster wagon. Sensing movement beside me, I was startled to see Josh nearby. I put my hand on his arm, studying his pallor, the way he seemed to sway on his feet. "You need to lie down, Josh."

He shook his head. "I'm going with Elijah. It's the least I can do, see my friend Isaac safely home."

"What about your position in the Army?"

"I've been mustered out." He glanced at his arm, secured tightly to his body in a sling. "Not much use to anyone if I can't shoot or write or even ride a horse proper." He turned to me. "You and Abbie will go with us, won't you, Lizzie? I can't stand the thought of being without you, not knowing if you're safe or in harm's way."

I smiled, placing my hand on his cheek. "Of course. But you need to ride in the wagon with Isaac. We'll get the horses and ride alongside."

He nodded and this slight motion caused him to stumble. He would have fallen if Elijah hadn't caught him. We eased Josh onto the bed of the wagon, beside Isaac's coffin. Abbie stepped inside the hospital and fetched a blanket, which we put over him. I feared the jostling of the wagon would open the wound in his shoulder but he was too weak to ride his horse or sit beside Elijah.

The head of the column didn't leave until four that afternoon, with rain still falling heavily. I could hear the moans of the wounded men, some calling out for someone to show mercy and kill them, others calling for their mothers or loved ones. Dr. Blackstone joined me for a few moments, telling me that only about one in 100 had been treated for their wounds, and many were traveling with legs and arms shattered by minie balls, bullets in their faces, arms, legs or torsos, their clothes clotted with blood. Most had not eaten for 36 hours. "We'll lose a good many before we reach our destination, I'm afraid," he said with a grimace before leaving to go to the surgeons' wagon.

We told Elijah to go on ahead, that we would collect our horses and join up with him. As we were preparing to leave, I noticed Tavia staring after the wagons going by, a lost look on her face. I grabbed Abbie's hand and guided her over to the young woman, still wearing her bloody Confederate uniform. Tavia gave us a look so filled with grief it brought tears to my eyes.

"I wanted to take my brother back with me to Tennessee but they won't allow it. They say they'll bury him here."

I looked at the passing wagons bearing men injured and dying piled next to one another and felt sick to my stomach. "We have horses, Tavia. Why don't you come with us? Our friend Josh is wounded and you can ride his horse until you get to your destination or you can come with us if you'd rather."

She turned back to me and gave me a curt nod. "I thank you, Lizzie."

We easily caught up with the ambulance transport I was later told was 17 miles long and began that sad journey home in the pouring rain, our spirits about as heavy as the moisture that fell. Imboden's orders were that he not stop until he reached his destination and we pushed on endlessly. Wagons that broke down were abandoned along with some of the critically wounded men, who were left behind on roadsides, with the hope that local civilians would find and take care of them. This troubled me immensely. I feared leaving them behind would be leaving them to their deaths at the hands of Union troops but Imboden would not listen to my pleas. He did allow Abbie and me to do what we could for the men, which was never enough. We would leave them, watching us with pleading eyes, in pain and great fear, and I never felt more helpless or hopeless.

As we made this slow, miserable march, we were constantly harassed by civilians and small bands of Union troops. Early one dawn, we were ambushed by civilians in

Greencastle, who attacked the wheels of the wagons with axes until they were driven off. That afternoon, Captain Abram Johns led 200 Union troops in attacking the wagon train. They captured 134 wagons, 600 horses and mules, and 645 prisoners, half of them wounded. I began to despair not only for our lives but that we would never reach our destination. This, along with my constant worry about Josh, who remained weak and feverish, fueled my anxiety to the point where I found it hard to keep myself composed enough to deal with the wounded soldiers.

Rain and heat and humidity followed us on that slow, arduous trip and we had merely gone 60 miles or so when we reached the small town of Williamsport, Maryland, only to learn that the Potomac was at flood stage and that the rising waters had destroyed the pontoon bridges. The water was too deep and treacherous to cross so we were stuck until a bridge could be built or the water level subsided enough to ford. Although it had been reported that the Federals occupied a large force in Williamsport, this proved to not be true, so the town was taken, churches, homes and schoolhouses claimed for hospitals, and the wounded removed from the wagons and housed so the surgeons could treat them, with the citizens being instructed to cook for them.

We once more found ourselves engaged in battle, this time from Union cavalry generals John Buford and Judson Kilpatrick. General Imboden hastily organized an artillery battery of as many wounded as he could who could operate muskets, which upped our number of defenders to less than 3,000, with it being reported that the Union had twice that number. The troops were told that unless they could repel the attack, we would all become prisoners and that the loss of his whole transportation would ruin General Lee, as it would take months to replace, if the Confederacy had the means to do so. This rallied the troops and they were enthusiastic about fighting but we probably would have been defeated if not for the arrival of an ammunition train from Winchester and later the appearance of General JEB Stuart from Hagerstown, forcing the Union troops to retreat in what came to be known as the Wagoner's Fight. Abbie and I, along with the doctors and nurses accompanying the wagon train, once more found ourselves nursing the wounded and dying in makeshift hospitals, the horrid sounds of battle all around us. Unable to shoot, Josh carried supplies to the soldiers and helped reload their guns.

I lost sight of Tavia but later found her in our improvised hospital in a church, bleeding from a wound to the gut, abandoned against the wall to die. With a cry of disbelief, I knelt beside her and took her hand. "Tavia, can you hear me?"

She opened her eyes and gave me a sad smile. "They put me against the wall, Lizzie. I reckon I know what that means."

"They're just busy and have no space," I lied.

"You're awful kind, Lizzie, but I've seen enough injuries like this to know what's gonna happen."

Tears flooded my eyes. "Oh, Tavia, I'm so sorry." I looked around for Abbie, hoping she could stop the blood, but didn't see her anywhere. I quickly examined Tavia, closing my eyes when I realized not even Abbie could save her. The wound was too mortal. She probably would not have been saved in my time.

She grimaced when she saw my expression. "It's for the best, I reckon. I'll be with Truett again."

I sat beside her, ignoring the screams and shouts around me. "Tell me about Truett," I said, trying to take her mind off her injury.

She grimaced with pain, her voice coming in gasps. "We were twins. He was born first. Our ma swore I came out holding on to his leg." I squeezed her hand, smiling at that image. "We were inseparable even as babies. Never knew our pa. He took off when he found out our ma was whelping. She died when we were five, I can't remember what from. Our grandparents raised us and they were good to us, but Truett and me, we were our own little family. He always looked after me first, said it was his duty to protect me, see no harm came to me." Tears filled her eyes. "I'm glad I'm going. I wouldn't know how to make my way in the world without him."

"I had hoped you would come live with us, Tavia," I said. "We would have made a nice home for you."

She shook her head. "I don't reckon I'd ever be happy without my brother, seems like I'm not a whole person without him." She looked at me, her expression a mixture of sadness and guilt. "I been thinking about ending my life just to be with him. Reckon the Union did it for me."

"Oh, Tavia, I am so sorry."

She lapsed into silence for a bit. I bathed her perspiring forehead with my apron, continuing to hold her hand. When she opened her eyes, she gave me a beatific smile. "I been talking to my brother, Lizzie. He says he's waiting for me." Her eyes moistened. "He's whole and healthy again and says he's in a good place."

"Oh, Tavia, that's wonderful." I blinked hard, trying to hide my tears. Why did so many young men and women have to die? I asked God. Like the young soldier in the battlefield, Tavia hadn't had a chance to live her life yet, meet a young man, fall in love, get married if she wanted, have children.

As if sensing my thoughts, she said, in a low voice, "It's all right, Lizzie. I reckon I'm at peace with it. And I'll be with someone who loves me. That's all I ever wanted in this world was to be with my brother, who loved me more'n anybody else. When he went off to war, I couldn't bear the thought of staying behind, not knowing what happened to him. So I joined up too and never once regretted it." She closed her eyes. "I'm awful tired. I reckon it won't be long now."

I didn't know how to respond to that so simply stayed with her, holding her hand until she died. Afterward, I claimed her body for burial.

The rain, along with the hot summer weather, was not conducive to a decaying corpse, and due to the offensive odor and fear of infectious diseases such as cholera and typhoid fever, it was deemed best to bury the dead in Williamsport. Josh and Elijah reluctantly agreed to leave

Isaac behind but made a vow to one another they would return at a future date to bear it back to Swan's Pond.

Abbie and I stood silently by while Josh and Elijah buried Isaac's coffin in the Riverview Cemetery, a small graveyard overlooking the Potomac River. They were kind enough to bury Tavia in the same cemetery under a beautiful old chestnut tree. Afterward, we held small services over each grave, saying prayers and singing Amazing Grace. Before we left, I gathered a bouquet of wild flowers from nearby and placed them on Tavia's grave.

The next day, Josh, Abbie and I were on the bank of the Potomac, watching as soldiers busily tried to build another pontoon bridge. I had never seen one of these before. In my time, most bridges were iron and steel and concrete. This pontoon bridge consisted of a row of boats lashed side by side together over which a bridge made of planks was laid.

Abbie and I sat on a blanket, leaning back against a large oak tree while Josh lay with his head in my lap. Although his wound was healing well and he was no longer feverish, he had lost weight and was still weak. I idly ran my fingers through his hair, liking the heavy weight of it as he watched the activity, occasionally closing his eyes.

"In my time," I said, "we have boats that can zip across the water faster than a horse can run."

Josh squinted up at me.

Abbie smiled. "Like them cars you told us about?"

"Yes. And we ski behind them."

They gave me identical looks of confusion.

"They're like these wooden sticks…" I picked up a twig and drew a pair of water skis in the dirt "… and we stand on these and ski on top of the water behind the boat." I quickly sketched in a ski boat with a person on skis being towed behind.

"Do they go as fast as the boat goes?" Abbie asked.

"Yep."

Josh shook his head. "I can't imagine," he said.

"I can," Abbie said. "Lizzie's told me so much about what the future holds, I reckon nothin would surprise me."

Josh smiled at her.

Abbie spied a young soldier she had treated walking along the riverbank. He looked frail and weak and as if he would fall down at any moment. "I best go see to him," she said, rising and heading off.

Josh and I were silent a long time. I thought he had gone to sleep but he finally stirred and looked up at me. "I think I killed a man, Lizzie," he said.

I simply nodded. I had known since the battle that something was troubling him but had prayed it would not be this.

"Was it the man we found on top of you, Josh?"

He shrugged, looking away. "Probably. He was trying to kill me with his bayonet. I don't remember much, only fighting with him, trying to keep him from stabbing me with that thing. When he did, I fell back, taking him with me, and managed to get it away from him. He was fighting something fierce, and I recall him picking up a rock and hitting me with it. And just before I passed out, I remember sticking that bayonet in him." He shuddered. "I can feel it, the way it just slipped inside his body, like a knife through butter. Blood was everywhere, I didn't know if it was mine or his and was so tired and woozy I didn't really care."

I stroked his hair. "I'm sorry, Josh, but it wasn't deliberate, you know that."

"I didn't go to war to kill," he said in a low voice. "I'm going to have to live with that for the rest of my life."

I wished I had paid more attention to what had killed the soldier when we found Josh but had been so concerned for him, nothing else mattered to me. "But you may not have killed him, Josh. There were soldiers fighting everywhere. Someone could have come along and bayoneted him."

He shook his head. "I guess I'll never know." His voice was so anguished, it broke my heart.

Leaning down, I kissed him lightly then watched the soldiers building the bridge for a moment. "That battlefield was filled with blood, Josh. I've never seen anything like it and pray I never do again."

"Me too."

"I was so afraid of losing you," I said, my eyes tearing.

He rose up and stared at me. "You didn't. You won't."

But we both knew that was a false assurance. This was a brutal war and place, and nothing or no one was safe.

Once the bridge was in place, we began our journey home from there, leaving the wagon train as soon as we crossed the newly built bridge.

I was happy to return to my cabin but the memories of that battle stayed with me. I'd often wake at night, seeing that young soldier dying on the battlefield or Tavia in the hospital, hearing the anguished cries of those wounded men in the hospitals and wagon beds, begging for mercy, the dying screams of men and horses on the battlefield. It seemed Josh had nightmares of his own to contend with, although he would not share them with me. I had no idea what he saw during the battle but suspected it had to have been more horrible than what I had seen. I made him promise me he would not return to the war, and he assured me he had no plans to. The bayonet wound had done damage to the muscle in his shoulder and Dr. Blackstone had warned him he may never be able to use that arm as well as he had.

So Abbie and I went back to our lives, doing chores around our homestead, treating the mountaineers, holding our clinic, occasionally being called to Camp Vance to tend to the sick or injured, helping Josh when he needed it with the Underground Railroad. I listened to everyone around me praying daily that this brutal war would end, knowing that would not be for another two years but unable to say so.

Chapter Eleven

Late Summer 1863

Let Me Wrap You in My Warm and Tender Love

Spring and summer were always busy times for us, the great majority of our time being devoted to not only planting, weeding and harvesting our vegetable garden but gathering herbs from which we made tinctures, poultices, salves and teas. The summer had been brutal, with high humidity and heat, and on a day when we felt, for what felt like the first time in a very long time, the refreshing hint of a cool breeze, Abbie and I decided to walk to Sarie's to deliver ginseng root which we knew she needed. When we arrived, we found one of the conscripts from Camp Vance standing on her porch, looking around.

"Can we help you with anything?" Abbie said, as we drew closer.

He nodded as he stepped off the porch, then seeming to remember his hat, snatched it off his head with a jerky motion. When I noticed the faint dusting of peach fuzz on his cheeks, I wondered if he was one of the junior reserves. "Dr. Glover's sent me to fetch Miss Sarie. Said to tell her he has a patient he wants to consult with her about." He looked back toward the door of the cabin. "I been knocking but nobody's answerin."

I smiled to myself when he mentioned Dr. Glover. I had noticed the good doctor seemed fascinated with our Sarie, always seeking her out the times we visited the hospital at Camp Vance, escorting her around, listening with deep interest to her diagnoses and treatments. At first, Sarie had been her usual brusque self with him, acting as if his very presence annoyed her greatly, but eventually began to warm up to the man, I suspected more from his persistence than anything else. I even saw her smiling at him once, which shocked the devil out of me. Sarie rarely smiled, but when she did, her beauty shone through like rainbow prisms through a glass.

Abbie turned away from the house and yelled, "Sarie."

We heard Sarie's muffled voice from the barn and all walked that way, watching as she and Amanda May stepped out of the barn, pitchforks in hand.

Abbie gestured at the soldier. "This man's come from Dr. Glover. Says he needs your help with a patient."

I watched Sarie's face closely at this news, expecting her usual frown of disgust at mention of a man, but was a bit surprised at the slight change in her expression, as if this was not unwelcome news, which she quickly replaced with her usual stern look. She nodded as she leaned her pitchfork against the outside of the barn. "I'll get my medical bag and be right with you."

"Do you mind if I tag along?" I asked her as she passed by. Like Dr. Glover, I liked seeing Sarie in action. She had a brilliant mind for herbs and was a superb healer, although her brusque bedside manner could use more than a little attention.

"If you've a mind to," Sarie said, without looking at me, as if it didn't matter to her one way or the other.

Abbie smiled at Amanda May. "I'm on my way to the Gibson farm to see about their billy goat. He got kicked by their mule t'other day and is in bad shape, poor feller. You think you might want to come along and help me tend to him?"

We all knew Amanda May would say yes. It seemed she much preferred animals to humans and I admit to more often than not feeling much the same way. Like Abbie, Amanda May had a special way with animals and Abbie usually took her along when she was treating one that was hurt or sick. I suspected it wouldn't be long before Amanda May became our local veterinarian.

Amanda May's face lit up. "I'd be glad to help you, Abbie," she said, hurrying after Sarie to fetch her own medical bag.

As Sarie, the soldier who finally introduced himself as Joey Kingston, and I rode down the mountain, Sarie asked him what the trouble was.

He glanced her way with a shrug. "I reckon Dr. Glover wants to ask you about Buford. He got cut by a bayonet and the wound looks awful ferocious. Dr. Glover's wantin to cut off the leg but Buford's set on keepin it. I reckon the doc hopes you'll be able to fix it afore he has to cut it off."

Sarie simply nodded while I began to shuffle through the information in my mind about how best to treat such a wound and save the leg.

The camp, as usual, was in disarray, with garbage and detritus littering the pathways, the smell of the latrine hanging heavily in the air. I noticed what looked to be a dead possum near one of the tents, dead feet in the air, its innards exposed and covered with buzzing flies busily laying larvae.

The large canvas tent which had originally housed the hospital had now been replaced by a wooden structure which had been somewhat hastily and shabbily built by the soldiers at hand, many of whom I suspected didn't know the first thing about carpentry or building. It looked to lean to one side but at least had windows and doors that closed, and was not as drafty or as moldy-smelling as its predecessor. The floor planks were a bonus which, if swept and mopped regularly, kept dirt and dust from drifting through the air, contaminating wounds and medical equipment. As usual, upon stepping inside, I gazed around the hospital, checking for unsanitary conditions that could prove detrimental to its inhabitants, but everything looked neat, tidy and clean. I suspected this was the only edifice in the whole camp that was somewhat hygienic.

Dr. Glover looked up when we stepped through the door, his face brightening at once when he spotted Sarie. I glanced at her and didn't miss the slight upturn of her lips. As if she felt me watching her, she turned and glared at me before walking toward the doctor.

"Miss Sarie, Miss Lizzie," he said, cordially, nodding to each of us before focusing on Sarie.

"You got a soldier with a bayonet wound needs tending?" Sarie said in her usual curt manner.

He nodded. "A thigh wound, not too deep but not shallow by any means. Buford, that's the name of the soldier who's injured, didn't think it was serious so tied a handkerchief around it, thinking that'd stop the blood, and didn't think to come here until it got infected. I've done all I can but the infection is getting worse and has begun to putrefy. Buford claims he'd rather die than have his leg amputated but I see no other recourse. Naturally, I thought of you, Miss Sarie, and hope you might have an alternative means of treatment."

"Well, let's have a look."

Dr. Glover didn't respond right away, his eyes focused on Sarie. I glanced her way, curious at what the doctor saw. She was awfully pretty, with silky blond hair and blue eyes, her complexion what was called peaches and cream in my time. If she'd only smile more, I thought, she could have any man she wanted. But then, Sarie didn't want a man, claimed she had no use for them, that they were more trouble than they were worth. The reason why was understandable, of course, but no one other than me knew the circumstances. And knowing this, I doubted if I'd have much of a desire for a man after what her father had done to her.

I watched as Sarie waited expectantly for the doctor's reply, finally clearing her throat and shifting her body in an impatient way.

He blinked as if startled. "Yes, quite right." He reached out as if to take her elbow but quickly withdrew his hand. "This way," he said, tilting his head toward the back of the building.

He led us to a small curtained-off area, and as soon as we stepped through, the odor of decaying flesh was so powerful, I resisted the urge to cover my nose. Buford lay on a cot, a thin blanket covering his groin area, leaving the injured leg exposed, the wound covered by a bandage soaked in pus and blood. His face was red with fever and he looked emaciated, his ribs seeming to strain against his skin, his abdomen concave, his face all sharp angles. I watched his breathing, shallow but steady, and wished for a stethoscope to listen to his heart.

Sarie leaned over, removed the bandage, and studied the gash.

Buford raised his head slightly and when he caught sight of her said, "You better not be here to cut off that leg, ma'am. I ain't about to lose it. I done told the doc that. I'll kill anybody that tries." He pulled out a hand from under the blanket, gripping a lethal-looking hunting knife. His hand shook as if he could barely hold the knife and his eyes kept closing as if keeping them open was too exhausting.

Dr. Glover glanced at us. "Don't know why he's so intent on keeping it if it could kill him but I promised we'd try."

I felt sorry for Buford, knowing he didn't have the strength to defend that leg if the doctor decided to remove it. "How'd it happen? Was he wounded in battle?"

Dr. Glover shook his head. "During a training exercise. Apparently Buford was too slow in getting out of the way of a zealous charge by one of his colleagues."

Ignoring the knife, Sarie turned her head toward me and raised her eyebrows. I immediately got the message and joined her.

I studied the pus-filled wound, checking for signs of gangrene. Resisting the impulse to gag, I leaned forward and sniffed but detected no sweet smell. "It's not gangrenous yet but will be soon, I think."

She nodded. "We got herbs that will help with infection but I fear this is too far gone."

"I remember reading in olden times, they would pour boiling wine over infections such as this," I muttered, wondering whether that would actually work.

Sarie nodded. "I seen it done. Sometimes it works, sometimes it don't."

By this time I had gotten used to the smell and leaned closer. "Lots of dead tissue there ..." I stopped, remembering the maggots on the possum. My eyes met Sarie's.

"Maggots," she said as if reading my mind.

"Yes, maggot debridement therapy."

She raised her eyebrows.

"Medical term," I explained. "That might help. I saw some larvae on a dead possum as we passed by one of the tents."

Dr. Glover leaned close, nodding. "I've heard of surgeons using it on the battlefield. Never occurred to me to try it."

"We got to make sure they're the right kind," Sarie said. "Needs to be from a blowfly."

The common housefly, commonly called the green bottle fly. They would only eat the dead tissue and leave the healthy tissue alone. Since neither Sarie nor the doctor seemed inclined to go collect them, I raised up, saying, "I'll need tweezers or something to remove them."

Dr. Glover nodded. "I have some here. I'll go get them."

Sarie straightened up, eying me. "You ever done it afore?"

"No, but I've studied it." I lowered my voice. "In my time, we don't usually do that, we have antibiotics, stronger medicines to fight infection."

She gave me a wary look. Sarie still seemed disinclined to believe I had come from 110 years in the future. I thought this was due more to her practical nature than anything else. To her, everything was black or white, there were no gray areas between, no ghosts or mystical beings, no supernatural events, no lights to step through and be transported to another time and place. I wondered how she reasoned my insistence I was not from this time and suspected she simply told herself I had either amnesia or was delusional. It explained the cautious looks she sent my way from time to time.

Dr. Glover returned with a long-handled pair of tweezers and glass jar. I took them from him, saying, "Thanks," then left him to Sarie. Maybe he'd find a way to worm his way into her heart, I thought, with a smile as I left.

I found the possum, still decaying by the tent, the strong odor of rot overridden by that of the nearby latrine ditch and all the refuse and horse manure littering the ground. I was relieved to see dozens of green bottle flies lighting on the body then lifting after depositing their larvae. Waving them aside, I set to work to capture a couple of dozen busily devouring the decaying innards of the possum, ignoring the disgusted and confused looks of soldiers passing by. None stopped to ask what I was doing or if they could help, however. When the jar was halfway filled, I rose to my feet and returned to the hospital.

Sarie and Dr. Glover were bent over the leg of an injured soldier, deep in conversation. When I joined them, Sarie was pointing at the young man's bruised and swollen foot, explaining to the doctor about the benefits of using leeches to help with the bruising and swelling. This was something she did quite often which worked remarkably well. They looked up as I approached and Dr. Glover smiled at me, saying, "Let's get to work."

As I inserted the larvae into the wound, I couldn't help but quote what I remembered from my studies. "They're beneficial for tissue debridement, disinfecting, stimulation of healing, and biofilm inhibition and eradication."

Sarie gave me a curious look. "What's biofilm?"

"A thin, slimy film of bacteria that adheres to a surface. The maggots secrete digestive enzymes that break down the dead tissue and liquidize it, which they ingest. Their secretions increase the wound PH which inhibits the growth of bacteria." I stopped, realizing germs and bacteria weren't taken seriously at this point, although Sarie had heard me talk about them enough not to be bothered by it.

"We'll keep em in the wound for two to three days," Sarie said. "We can either place a bandage over it or let em roam free. They'll leave when they're done."

Buford, who had become more alert and was watching this with trepidation, said in a weak voice, "Will it hurt?"

"More'n likely tickle a little," Sarie said, "but it shouldn't hurt too bad."

He lay his head back down. "Don't matter to me one way or t'other long as you don't take that leg off." He looked at Dr.Glover. "You promised, Doc, you'd honor my wishes."

Dr. Glover patted his hand in a consoling way.

"Why is it so important for you to keep your leg?"I couldn't help but ask.

Buford turned his attention to me, his eyes barely focused. "I got me a girl back home I'm plannin to marry, and I made her a promise I'd come back in one piece." His eyes slid shut and he began to doze.

"I wonder what he'd do if he woke up and that leg was gone," I mused.

Dr. Glover shook his head. "Told me he'd take that knife and slit his throat, after slitting mine."

Sarie ignored us, rummaging in her medical satchel. She pulled out garlic roots and handed them to Dr. Glover. "Might help to make a poultice out of this and put it over the wound. Don't reckon it'll bother the maggots none, but if it does, take it off and keep the maggots. If he can stand it, make him eat raw garlic." She nodded at me. "Lizzie can tell you what it does. I ain't too familiar with her medical terms."

Dr. Glover looked at me. "It's both an antibiotic, meaning it kills germs, and an antibacterial, meaning it kills bacteria. It should help him. If not, there are other herbs we can use. Honey also works wonders fighting infection."

Dr. Glover nodded. "I've heard you talk enough about bacteria and germs while you're here, I reckon I've come to respect what you're saying. Makes sense, seeing the difference you ladies have made in treating our men. Since I've instructed our staff to wash their hands between patients, sterilize our equipment after each use and use clean bandages, our mortality rate has significantly decreased."

I smiled at him, glad to see a forward-thinking doctor. I glanced at Sarie, wishing she could unbend a little. Dr. Glover would be a good match for her.

Sarie pulled her satchel over her shoulder. "We'll be back in two days to see how he's doing. You send somebody to fetch us if anything changes."

Dr. Glover smiled at her, his feelings so clear on his face. "I'll do that, Miss Sarie. I can't thank y'all enough for coming and tending to Buford."

Sarie gave him a curt nod before turning on her heel and leaving.

I smiled at the doctor before following her.

When I returned home, I found Abbie and Amanda May sitting on the porch, drinking apple cider. I accepted a cup from Abbie and sat down on the porch, leaning against the corner post to sip the refreshing drink. Unable to resist, I shared with them my views about Dr. Glover and his attraction to Sarie.

Abbie gave a short laugh. "I reckon I noticed the same thing, Lizzie, but you know Sarie and her dislike for men. Shoot, he might as well give up now 'cause I doubt she'll ever return his feelings."

I smiled at her. "I don't know," I said in a singsong voice, and told them I suspected Sarie was beginning to soften toward the man. I shrugged. "Who could resist the adoring looks he gives her? Or do you think she even notices?"

We were all quiet, considering this.

"Maybe someone should tell her," Amanda May suggested.

Abbie and I exchanged looks. "Let's not," I said. "Might scare her off. Let's wait and see what happens."

"Well, one thing about that, it'll sure be fun to watch," Abbie said.

As Abbie and Amanda May began to talk about the billy goat they had just treated, I watched Abbie's dogs Billy and Bob playing with the piglet we had been given in payment for tending a family suffering from food poisoning. I called the pig Elmer but Abbie didn't like the name until I explained to her the cartoon character Elmer Fudd. Most of our payments were either in produce, milk, eggs, or animals. We had so many chickens, I couldn't keep up with them, and three barn cats who were constantly trying to get at the chickens. A fourth cat, acting as if being in the barn was too undignified for him, had moved into the cabin with us. Since

Billy, Bob and Elmer got along well with him, we let him stay. We also had a billy goat and pregnant nanny goat as well as a wild boar Abbie had found wounded in the forest when he looked to be barely a few weeks old.

As if sensing I was thinking about him, Pudge, the house cat who had come out of the cabin to lie in the sun, climbed on my lap and began to purr. I stroked his back, enjoying the feel of his silky fur, and found myself in one of those rare moments on the mountain when I was content with my life. As always, this was short-lived when the thought of how my life would change when I returned home entered my mind. I began to wonder what would happen to these beautiful animals if Abbie and I went through the light. When Amanda May laughed at something Abbie said, I looked at her and knew the answer to my concern.

As Amanda May prepared to leave, I told her I'd accompany her back to Sarie's. Abbie debated going with us but decided to stay behind and replenish her medical satchel. While Amanda May and I walked on the well-used pathway from our cabin to Sarie's, I decided to tell her the truth about where and when I came from. She listened to me silently, never interrupting, and when I finished, stopped and looked at me. "So you're a traveler?"

I could feel my mouth opening in shock. "You know about people like me?"

She nodded. "My great-granny was a traveler. Said she came from over 200 years in the future."

"Miss Lilly, the one who brought you here?"

"Yes'm."

I grabbed Amanda May's hand. "Did she try to go back, do you know?"

She shook her head. "Said she didn't want to. She told me she preferred it here."

I couldn't believe this. "But why? It's so primitive here, so hard. Life is so much easier in the future, so much better."

Amanda May gave me a concerned look. "Not her future, Lizzie. She told me there was a great war here in America. She said America wasn't America anymore, and people lived in worse conditions than they do now."

151

"What?"

She nodded. "She never talked about it much, said she didn't want to, but told me another country had invaded America and there was war everywhere."

"We have that now, Amanda May, here in America, among our own people."

"Yes, but she said this future war is worse because there are ..." she trailed off, trying to find the word "... weapons, advanced weapons that can kill thousands at once."

I immediately thought of a nuclear attack. "Oh, God."

"She said there were small groups of Americans who hid out in the mountains." She waved her hand around us. "Like here. She was only 16, but was a soldier, a ..." she frowned, searching, "... guerilla fighter, fighting for America when she accidentally stumbled into one of the lights and ended up in this time."

We began walking again. "Can you think of anything else she told you?" I asked.

"I'll try to remember, but like I said, it wasn't much. She didn't want to talk about it."

"What I wanted to ask you," I said, returning to my concern, "is if I go back and Abbie goes with me ..."

Amanda May gave me a sharp look.

"I haven't really talked to her about it but hope she does. Of course, you're welcome to come too, if you're with us when we find the light."

She shook her head. "I like it fine here."

"If Abbie goes back with me," I said, "will you see to our animals? Maybe live at the cabin and take care of them for us?"

She smiled with delight. "Of course, Lizzie, I'd love to." She stopped once more, reached out and hugged me. "But I hope you don't go back, Lizzie. I'd miss you and Abbie so much."

I returned her hug, tears in my eyes. I'd miss more than a few people here, I realized with sadness, even Sarie.

When Sarie and I returned to Camp Vance two days later, Buford's fever was down and the larvae had performed magnificently. The putrefaction was much better and the wound looked like it was beginning to heal. Dr. Glover, expecting our arrival, had sent a couple of soldiers out that morning searching for maggots feeding off a dead animal and they'd returned with a jar of the white larvae.

Buford was more alert and seemed happy to see us. "Dr. Glover told me y'all saved my leg. I'm much obliged to you," he said with a smile.

Dr. Glover gave us a look, which I interpreted to mean he had told Buford this to make him feel better. But I was beginning to think the leg would be saved and was happy for Buford and his bride-to-be.

We watched as Dr. Glover replaced the larvae, and after further instructions, Sarie told him we would not return unless he needed us to. The disappointment on his face was so clear, I didn't think even our practical Sarie could miss it. Somehow she managed to ignore it, bade him goodbye in her usual curt manner and left without lingering.

I couldn't resist whispering to him before leaving, "She's a hard one but I think she'll come around if you keep trying." I smiled at his shocked expression.

Chapter Twelve

Late Fall 1863

Soul Sacrifice

Abbie and I were awakened early one morning by a young black slave who asked us to come quick to the plantation of Sandy Blair. When Abbie asked him if anyone was hurt or sick, he shrugged, saying, "Miss Lisa said to fetch y'all right quick. She was in a state, she was, and that's all I know."

We immediately dressed, grabbed our medical satchels and rode down the mountain to the Blair plantation, huddled in our coats, wondering what had happened. I had met the Blairs at church, and Sandy was hard not to notice, the way he "strutted around like a bantam rooster", as Abbie liked to say. The man seemed likeable enough, always friendly and smiling to everyone, although it seemed that smile never quite reached his mud-colored eyes, while his wife Lisa would stand next to him, her head usually lowered, as if patiently waiting for him to give her permission to move or talk.

After the first time I met Sandy, when I told Abbie I got a bad vibe from him, she looked at me, confused. "What's a vibe?"

"A feeling. There's something off about him, Abbie."

She nodded, saying, "You ain't the only one thinks that,

Lizzie."

He was a handsome enough devil but I had eyes only for Josh and that wasn't why I began to watch him. It was the way his wife held her body, huddled into herself defensively as if afraid. The way he made sure she was always by his side, watching her like a hawk if she moved one step out of reach. The way she flinched when he would touch her sometimes, as if in pain.

Walking home from church with Josh and Abbie one day, after I had observed Lisa walking stiffly and sitting with her back not touching the pew, I told them I feared Sandy Blair was physically abusing his wife.

Josh and Abbie exchanged a glance. Abbie finally sighed. "I reckon the whole mountain suspects it but can't do nothin about it. Ain't no law against it, far as we know."

I glanced at Josh. "Is that right?"

He gave me a sick look. "I'm afraid most look upon a wife as the property of her husband. I know it isn't like that in your time, Lizzie, but that's the way it is here."

I shook my head in disgust. As a woman from the Summer of Love and the early stages of the feminist and civil rights movements, I had eagerly embraced all this foretold, and it angered me that at this time in America, women and blacks were treated so poorly without any rights or defenses.

"Besides," Josh went on, "there's no proof even if it was illegal."

"That's only because he probably beats her everywhere but her face and neck so others won't know or suspect," I said bitterly. "He's a typical abuser, nothing but a bully and the lowest scum there is."

They both gave me looks of commiseration but didn't say anything. I vowed to myself I would try to help Lisa get away from that man, no matter what it took.

The Sundays we attended church, I tried countless times to seek Lisa out, to find a way to tell her she didn't have to put up with this sort of behavior, but Sandy never gave me the chance to speak to her alone. He made sure she was always within arm's length and when I would approach her made sure to greet me first, his arm protectively around his wife's shoulders. So as we made our way to the Blair plantation on that cold, frosty morning, I suspected we were going there to treat Lisa, who had been injured at her husband's hands.

Sandy had inherited the place from his father and it looked to me to be more of a farm than plantation. The gray, bleak day did nothing to enhance the looks of it, I thought, as I noted the house was a box-like, one-story white clapboard with peeling paint and a wide front porch that looked badly in need of repair. The nearby slave cabins were scattered close to a shallow, meandering creek which I knew would freeze solid in the winter. The fields behind the house were rutted and bare, and I briefly wondered what Sandy grew there.

Lisa stood waiting for us on the porch of their home, shivering in a shawl pulled tight around her nightgown. I glanced around for her husband but didn't see him anywhere. She immediately hurried down the steps to meet us as we dismounted, her distress only enhancing her beauty. As shallow as I felt for feeling so, I envied Lisa her ivory-colored skin and chestnut-colored hair, dark-blue eyes framed by thick, black lashes, thinking in my time, she would never need to worry about wearing mascara or makeup.

"It's Patsy," she said, grabbing hold of my arm. "I think she's dying." She turned and set off at a near-run toward the slave cabins. Abbie and I glanced at each other, wondering who Patsy was, then rushed to keep up with her.

When we stepped into a small, one-room shack, the closest one to the house, I immediately drew back at the coppery scent of blood which hung heavy in the air. On a mattress against the far wall lay a young black girl, limbs akimbo, her eyes showing a slit of white sclera. She didn't register us as Abbie and I approached, which alarmed me even more. I heard a slight plopping noise and looked down to see bright red blood pooled under her thighs, soaking through the thin, corn-husk mattress and dripping onto the floor.

"What happened?" I asked Lisa over my shoulder. When

I noticed the bloody knitting needles lying next to Patsy, I drew in a sharp breath. "Oh, no."

I immediately lifted her tattered white gown, stained red from the waist down, and put my hand between her legs, which came away slick with blood. "Did she ..." I glanced at Lisa as I put my hand on her carotid artery, searching for a pulse.

She nodded. "I didn't know she was ... I didn't know she'd try to do something like that." There were tears in her eyes. "She's only 13, she's too young to ..." She covered her mouth with her hands and began to cry.

I reached over and closed the young girl's eyes. "I'm sorry, Lisa, she's gone."

"Those are my knitting needles," she said, her voice high, tears streaming down her face. "She must have taken them from ..." Her voice trailed off at the sound of footsteps and we all glanced up when Sandy stepped into the cabin.

"What the hell's going on in here?" he said, glaring at his wife. He barely glanced at the young girl on the bed before focusing on Abbie and me, anger flaring across his face. He turned to Lisa, jabbing a finger our way. "What'd you send for them for?"

"To see if they could save her," Lisa screeched at him. Her face was beet-red, her fists clenched in anger. "You did this to her," she said, her voice low and raw, as she pointed at the bed. "She's just a child and you raped her and put that baby in her belly and she was too young to live with it. This is your fault."

Sandy stepped closer to her, his fists clenched. "Shut your mouth," he said, as he punched her in the belly.

She immediately sank to the floor, gasping for breath. Oh, I remembered how that felt, when Constable Jackson had done the same to me, the panic that overtakes you when you think you'll never be able to draw another breath, the effort to get air into your lungs when none will come. Abbie crouched next to her, mumbling to her, and I moved in front of them when Sandy reached out to his wife, I assumed to pull her to her feet so he could hit her again.

"You touch her again, I'll kill you," I said.

He sneered at me. "She's my wife, I can do anything I want to her. Just like that gal over there." He pointed at Patsy's body as if she were nothing but a piece of furniture.

Oh, the anger I felt hearing him say those words. I wanted to rake my nails down his face, cut his despicable tongue out.

He put his arm out as if to push me aside. "Get out of my way or I'll do the same to you."

Silently thanking Sarie for insisting we carry knives, I reached into my apron, drew mine out and raised it in the air, close to his face, showing it to him. When I spoke, my voice was low and harsh. "Touch me or her, I'll use it. If I knew I could get away with it, I'd use it anyway."

His expression revealed surprise, a touch of fear maybe before anger dropped over it like a grotesque mask. He made a point of giving me a look of bemusement. "I don't reckon you got the guts for it."

"And I wonder how much guts it takes to beat a defenseless woman and rape a child," I said.

His fists clenched but he remained where he was. We stared at each other for a long moment before he finally spoke. "You all ain't got no business here. Get off my property now or I'll send for the sheriff."

"After we see to her," Abbie said in a calm voice, standing and coming to join me. "We need to see to her properly, Mr. Sandy. As you know, there are certain things to be done for her, and I don't reckon you want your wife to have to deal with that. We'll go after that."

His attention shifted to Lisa, doubled over on the floor, and he gave a curt nod. "Deal with her then get off my property." He jabbed a finger at me. "But I'm warning you, I better not see you here ever again." He turned on his heel and left after sending a malevolent glare toward his wife.

Lisa remained on the floor while we tended to Patsy, sobbing into her hands. We ignored her as we took off the young slave's nightgown, washed her body, then redressed her in a shabby dress, the only other article of clothing we found. She was a beautiful girl, her silky skin the color of dark cocoa, with high cheekbones and almond-shaped eyes.

She looked too young to bear a child and I had to force my mind away from the thoughts of what that man had done to her. She should have been playing with other children, enjoying life, instead of living the life of a slave, doing some cruel man's unwanted bidding.

It was cold in the shack, and we shivered as we worked. I looked at the cold dirt floor, the large gaps between the planks of the cabin, the thin, threadbare blanket at the foot of the bed, wondering if the slaves faced bitter winters like this. The slave cabins at Josh's father's plantation had the same gaps, but once cool weather moved in, they would pack the cracks with mud and horsehair which Josh assured me helped insulate the cabins in the winter. Once the weather was mild enough, they'd chip out the mortar so cool air could flow into the cabin through the gaps.

Lisa eventually roused herself and joined us. She looked down at Patsy's still body, taking her small hand in hers. "She was so sweet," she said, tears running down her face. "I loved her so."

I touched her upper arm. "I'm so sorry, Lisa."

"He's a brute," she said, her voice low, as she stared at Patsy. "He likes them young, boys and girls alike. He rapes them all. She isn't the first one he's gotten with child, she won't be the last." She glanced away, toward the door. "And if he's not raping them, he's whipping them or beating them." She swallowed and her eyes met mine, filled with defiance. "Or me if it's more convenient." Without saying a word, she dropped her shawl and unbuttoned the bodice of her nightgown, sliding it off her shoulders. Abbie and I gasped at the bruises that covered her chest and abdomen, some bright purple and black, others fading to a sickly yellow and green. She turned around and I felt sick at the welts on her back, caused by a whip or belt.

"He did that to you?" I blurted out.

She only nodded as she turned back around and rebuttoned her gown, then picked up her shawl and wrapped it around her. "Killed the baby I had in my belly," she said. "Beat me so bad, I thought I'd die right along with it." She glanced at me, her expression wretched. "He'll kill me one day, I know it in my heart. He's already killed a couple of the slaves, whipped one boy to death, beat the other one, made us all watch, and all over some suspicion he had they stole from him. Which they didn't!"

I clenched my fists, livid. "You don't have to take that, you don't have to live like this," I said, my voice harsh.

She laughed bitterly. "Oh but I do, don't you see? Where would I go, what would I do? I don't have family to take me in, help me." She glanced toward the door. "He's brutal and evil and gets satisfaction from hurting people." She turned back to me. "I wish him dead," she hissed. "We all wish him dead."

Not sure how to respond to that, I glanced at Abbie, who was watching Lisa closely.

Lisa chewed her lower lip, as if contemplating something, then grabbed one of my hands and one of Abbie's. "You're healers, you would know how to, to ..." She looked out the door again before saying, her voice low, "Help me."

I turned to Abbie, unsure what to say. She stared at me for a moment then touched Lisa on the shoulder. "I'll talk to Sarie," she said in a calm voice. "She knows a way. He won't be hurting you or nobody else much longer if'n that's what you want."

"But how ..."

"You'll have to do it yourself but Sarie will tell you what to do. Nobody will know, they'll only think he died of a heart attack or some such thing."

Lisa grabbed Abbie in a hug, whispering, "I know it's a sin, I do know that, but I'd rather burn in hell than live with what he does to me and our slaves. He's evil, Abbie."

"I know," Abbie said. Her eyes met mine. Hers seemed to be asking me if I was all right with this. I looked at Patsy's body, thought of Lisa's back, her dead baby, and nodded.

We were reluctant to leave Lisa, afraid that Sandy would beat her after we left. Lisa only smiled and hugged us as if trying to reassure our troubled minds. For the first time, I saw hope in her eyes. "Perhaps for the last time," she said. "Tell Sarie I'll be at church Sunday, if she can be there. I'll try to find a way to talk to her."

Once home, sitting in front of the fire to warm up, I asked Abbie if there was anything we could legally do.

She gave me a sad look, shaking her head. "They're his property, Lizzie, that's what the law says. I reckon he's got the right to do anything to them he wants."

I sighed, feeling so helpless and desperate. "Not for much longer. The only good thing to come out of this war will be to end that kind of ownership. At least as far as the slaves are concerned." I had told Abbie a good deal about my time and she knew about the civil rights movement and how blacks had suffered. "Things won't be much better, Abbie, but at least it will put an end to slavery."

We were quiet for awhile, then I had to ask. "Do you think she'll do it?"

Abbie stared at the fire for a long moment before shrugging. "If she wants to live, I reckon she has to, don't you?" Her eyes met mine. "You know he's gonna eventually kill her, Lizzie, like she said. Rupture her—is it the spleen you told me that can cause somebody to bleed to death from a beating?"

"Yes, or the kidneys, well, any vital organ."

"What would you do if you were her?" she asked me, her eyes troubled.

I considered this for a long time. "Here, at this time, I'd find some way to kill him," I said softly, shocked when I realized I actually meant that. Oh, how this era had changed me, I told myself, and not for the first time. But in my time, women had more rights than they did now, weren't considered a man's property to do with as they wanted. They could divorce their husband or bring charges against him. But not here, not now.

The following Sunday, Lisa seemed to move more carefully and Sandy hovered closer than ever to her, occasionally sending me threatening looks. I watched as Sarie simply walked by Lisa, who had her hands behind her back, slipped a package into one palm, and walked on, without speaking to her or Sandy. Sandy, busy talking to another congregant, didn't even notice the exchange or Lisa tucking the packet up her sleeve. I suspected what Sarie gave her was an herbal tea she made to help ease terminally ill patients who were in a great deal of pain into death, those that asked her to do it. Knowing Sarie's abuse at the hands of her father and the way she felt about such men, I doubted she even thought twice about giving Lisa the tea. I had queried her more than once about what was in it but she refused to tell me. I doubted even Maggie and Abbie knew.

As I witnessed all this, ambivalent about what was going to happen, I began to think of all the people that man had damaged through his actions. I wasn't God but felt strongly that someone like Sandy shouldn't have the right to continue on without any kind of repercussion.

Within a week, we learned that Sandy Blair had died, Josh telling us that the doctor in Morganton claimed it seemed to be from a heart attack. I had told Josh about finding Patsy dead and what Lisa told us but had not relayed her request to us to help her murder her husband. When he gave me a questioning look after telling me of Sandy's death, I glanced away, unable to meet his gaze. There were nights when I would lie awake, wondering if I should have stopped it, then telling myself it was either him or Lisa and more slaves who would suffer at his hands. I kept seeing Patsy's still body lying on that blood-soaked mattress, which helped assuage my guilt at times. But there were times when I thought that not only had Lisa sold her soul to the devil but also Abbie, Sarie and me.

At the funeral, Lisa played the part of a grief-stricken widow beautifully, looking pale and teary-eyed, crying openly when the casket was lowered into the ground. Standing over the burial plot, when our eyes met, she gave me a brief nod, mouthing, "Thank you." I looked away. I could have stopped it, knew I probably should have, but didn't and I would have to live with that for the rest of my life.

Chapter Thirteen

Early Winter 1863

Helplessly Hoping

It had been a busy fall and winter for the sisters and me, with many on the mountain suffering from colds, bronchitis and pneumonia, and I realized with a start one morning at breakfast that more than a week had passed since I'd visited Pokni. I usually went to see her at least a couple of times a week, sometimes more, often accompanied by Abbie. I always looked forward to spending time with Pokni, listening to her stories of the Catawba while gathering and learning about herbs. Over the past year, I had watched her grow more and more frail and feared she was not long for this world. She had made it clear to me more than once that she was ready to leave this Earth and join her husband and I was fearful this mindset would only hasten her death. Feeling an urgent need to see her, I sent Abbie out alone to help Sarie, Maggie and Amanda May, telling her I wanted to check on Pokni.

Abbie nodded, looking worried. "Like I told you, I don't see much when it comes to ones I love, but she's been poppin into my mind ever since last night. I'm glad you're goin. As soon as I can come, I'll join you."

Having learned never to dismiss Abbie's feelings, I

kissed her on the cheek, picked up my medical satchel and left in a rush. I found Pokni in her hut, lying on her pallet, her face pale, her drooping eyelids revealing her weakened state. Her wolf Nashoba rested close to her, as if trying to offer his warmth. Nashoba whined when I stepped into the hut, giving Pokni a look of grave concern. This alarmed me more than anything. Nashoba wasn't the first canine I had known who was alert to his companion's health condition.

A brief smile touched Pokni's lips when she turned her head to see who had come to call.

I knelt down beside her and took her hand in my own, automatically placing a finger on her wrist to feel her pulse, weak and thready. "How long have you been sick, Pokni?"

She shook her head as if it didn't matter, saying, "I am not sick, only dying. I will be leaving soon, I think."

Tears sprang to my eyes. "Pokni, no. I can't stand the thought of losing you."

She cupped my cheek with her other hand. "There is no need to grieve, Daughter. I won't be leaving you, only this old, frail body. I will continue on my life's journey but will come back to look in on you from time to time." She winked at me.

I tried to stifle my sobs as I held her hand. Finally able to speak, I said, "Is there anything I can do for you? Anything to make you comfortable?"

She shook her head. "I have the warmth of my wolf, a loved one with me, I have all I need."

She closed her eyes and seemed to doze. I got up, put more wood on the fire, riffled through my satchel trying to find something to give her, but had no idea how you treated someone who claimed to be dying. I didn't doubt she was; she knew her body better than anyone and had been ready for this for some time. I finally decided I'd make her Mullein or bunny's ears tea, which was good as an expectorant. She had sounded a bit phlegmy to me.

I glanced up when I heard what sounded like thunder outside. We had occasional thunderstorms in the winter but it was rare.

Pokni opened her eyes. "Did I tell you the story of

Heloha and Melatha?"

Tears rolled down my face as I said, "No," thinking this would probably be the last Choctaw legend I heard from her. "I'd love to hear it, but first can you try to drink some tea?" I held a cup out to her.

After she nodded, I helped her sit up. When I held the cup to her mouth, she inhaled deeply then gave me a slightly amused look.

"You sound a bit congested," I said.

She only smiled as she took a sip. I could barely get her to take a couple more before she lay back down again, her hand, the skin paper thin, its back marked by knarled blue veins, automatically resting on the head of her wolf. "You will take care of him," she said.

"Of course, Pokni. I love him as I do you."

Without preamble, she began the legend. "Heloha and Melatha were two gigantic Thunderbirds. Since they were very intelligent, Nanishta gave them the task of finding a way to warn the People about the approach of storms. Heloha, the female Thunderbird, decided she would lay enormous eggs which would roll around on the clouds, causing the rumblings of thunder, while Melatha, her mate, would catch the eggs before they fell off and plummeted to Earth, flying so swiftly his movements would be seen as flashes of lightning." Finished, she sounded breathless.

I squeezed her hand. "I do love your legends, Pokni. I've written them all down. I don't want them to get lost after you …" I couldn't say the word.

"They will live as long as people like you continue to tell them," she said, her voice barely a whisper.

We were silent for a long time, Pokni passing into and out of dozing, me silently grieving. There was so much I wanted to say to her but didn't know how to put into words. When I heard a rustling outside, I glanced toward the door. Abbie appeared, looking anxious and a bit wet.

"Is it raining?" I asked. I hadn't even noticed.

"Not as hard as it was." She knelt beside me, studying Pokni. "How is she?" When she looked at me, her eyes were wide and frightened.

"She says she's dying." My voice choked.

"Oh, Pokni," Abbie said, reaching out and touching the old woman on the face.

Pokni opened her eyes and smiled at Abbie. "Don't be sad, little one. I go to join my warrior soon."

Abbie smiled at her, tears running down her cheeks. "You speak of him often, Pokni, but however did he die? I've always been meanin to ask you that."

A look crossed Pokni's face, one of fierce hatred and the need for revenge. "The white man killed him."

Abbie and I drew back, stricken. I wondered how in the world this old woman could be so loving with us, knowing that my kind had murdered her husband.

"What happened?" Abbie and I asked together.

"It was after the Great Removal," Pokni said, looking beyond us, as if seeing a vision. "As I told you, we hid here in the mountains. He was out hunting one day and the agents of President Jackson ..." she turned her head and spat as if that name were poison on her tongue "... were tracking those who did not follow the Trail of Tears. They came upon him and shot at him without saying a word to him." She sighed, a tear rolling from the corner of her eye. "He managed to get away but was badly injured. He made it back to the cave where we hid but my medicines could not help him. He died the next day."

I pressed my other hand over hers. "Oh, Pokni, I am so sorry."

She nodded, her eyes closing. "I think I lost my mind," she said in a low voice. "I gave his body to Hashtali, the sun god, who sent his buzzards to take away his earthy remains. I collected the bones and kept them with me until I moved here, then buried them at the edge of the forest under the large chestnut tree." She looked at us, her eyes fierce. "You will bury me beside him," saying this in a demanding way.

"Of course, we will, Pokni," Abbie said, patting her reassuringly. "Whatever you want, all you have to do is tell us."

"Yes," I said, "just tell us."

She nodded as if relieved then fell silent, falling back into a doze. Abbie and I sat side by side, holding hands, constantly reaching out and touching Pokni. She finally stirred and looked at me. "I dreamed of you last night, Daughter."

"You did?"

"You found a light you thought was yours, but it was not. You went through it to a time in the future, beyond your time even, to one much worse than it is here. A time of great war and many deaths." She reached out one frail hand and grabbed mine, squeezing hard. When she spoke, her voice was fierce and determined. "If you see a light, make sure it is yours before you go through. Promise me."

I swallowed, fear crawling up my spine like spiders. This sounded like the future world Amanda May told me her great-grandmother had come from. "I promise, Pokni. I'll take the time to make sure."

She released my hand, her gaze going to the ceiling of her small hut. Smiling the most beatific smile, she said, in a voice filled with awe and wonder, "My warrior waits for me." She reached toward the ceiling with one hand. "He will accompany me on my journey. We will be together once more." Abbie and I couldn't help but look up, at only the ceiling, then at each other, fear and sadness in our eyes.

Pokni's hand dropped to her side and she stuttered out a breath. Nashoba whined as he looked at his companion, then let out the most awful, grievous howl. Abbie and I clutched each other, crying when we realized she had left us.

I'm not sure how much time passed after that as Abbie and I silently grieved, watching the shadows move across the hut as the sun began its journey home.

Abbie finally stirred. "We need to stay with her tonight, Lizzie, in case the Raven Mocker comes, then bury her tomorrow."

I nodded, feeling numb and dazed. "She asked me to take care of Nashoba." I glanced around. "Where is he? He was here a minute ago."

Abbie shook her head. "He left shortly after she passed, Lizzie. Didn't you see him go?"

"No." I began to cry and lay down beside Pokni, putting my hand on hers, noting her body was already cooling. Abbie lay down on the other side of Pokni, and we stayed that way through the night, protecting our beloved Grandmother.

The next morning, we washed Pokni's body with scented oils, wrapped her in her best dress, one she told us she had worn as a maiden, made of beautiful buckskin with brightly colored beads, and braided her thick, gray hair. Afterward, we wrapped her in a blanket then picked her up, carried her slight body outside and gently lay her beside the chestnut tree where she had marked her husband's grave. The rain had softened the ground enough that it didn't take us long to dig the grave. Afterward, we placed Pokni's body inside then filled it in, mounding the dirt neatly. Abbie went into the woods and came back with a clump of purple asters she'd dug up which we planted at the head of Pokni's grave in place of a tombstone. Nashoba appeared suddenly, standing beside us as we sang *Amazing Grace*. He whined and howled, sniffing at the dirt, which saddened me even more. I tried to console him but he would have none of that. After Abbie said a prayer over Pokni's body, I turned around, looking for Nashoba, but he was gone, so we went back to the hut to wait for him. He never returned.

Chapter Fourteen

Spring 1864

We're Not Gonna Take It

Time flowed, and before I knew it, almost half a year had passed and the war still raged on, bloody and brutal. At our clinic, we saw more and more soldiers dealing with amputated limbs and ill-treated wounds, and tried to help those who suffered from what came to be known as combat trauma. We heard so many horrific stories, I wondered if I'd ever be able to forget them, even if I made it back to my time, which seemed to me now more a dream than a reality. I had been on this mountain almost five years and had begun to doubt I would ever find my light and return. But I was determined more than ever to go back so welcomed the spring of 1864, when the day's light lengthened and the temperature warmed, conducive to more strenuous and numerous searches for my light.

On one such night, after Abbie and I had been searching on the mountain longer than normal and had returned home tired and depressed, a loud booming noise woke me from a deep sleep. I sat up, clutching the quilt to my chest, looking around with alarm. Abbie slid out of bed, wrapped an afghan around her and went to the door, seemingly unperturbed at this loud intrusion. She opened it, letting in a cold draft of air smelling clean and fresh, stared for a second, then without a word swung it open. I shivered at the chilly influx but welcomed the way it seemed to scrub away the smoky scent lingering in the room from the small fire we had earlier.

Josh stepped inside, followed by three men with hats low over their faces. Seeing me in bed, Josh stopped at once, ignoring the jolt when the man behind him collided with his back. He swept off his hat, saying, "Lizzie, Miss Abbie, I'm sorry, I didn't want to wake you but we need help."

"It's fine, Josh." I wrapped the quilt around me and tried as gracefully as I could to climb out of bed. Josh, being the gentleman he was, averted his eyes. Two of the three men silently watched me while the other simply stared at the floor. I joined them, saying, "Is anyone hurt or ill?"

Josh moved away and it was then I noticed the man staring at the floor swaying on his feet. I gestured toward the table. "Get him in the chair over there." Josh and one of the others helped the injured man over to the chair and eased him into it. He immediately slumped forward, his chin bumping his chest. Without saying a word, Abbie went to the fireplace and began stoking the fire in case we needed to boil water. I surmised from her actions, measured and calm, that she had done this sort of thing before.

I tilted the man's head back and opened one eye. "It's too dark to see anything, can someone please light the lantern?"

While Abbie did the honors, I turned my head and took a deep breath. The odor coming off the man was a sharp coppery smell mixed with acrid sweat and feces, meaning blood and injury, possibly severe. After she handed the lantern to me, I gave it to Josh. "Hold it above his face." My fingers brushed over the man's black-stubbled cheeks as I checked his pupils, relieved that they were not pinpointed or dilated. "He apparently hasn't been hit on the head. I looked at the two strangers. "What happened?"

The man who had helped support his cohort answered for the group. "He's been shot. Josh said you'uns was healers, could mayhap help him."

I nodded. "I'm Lizzie, that's Abbie. And you are?"

He drew back a little, seeming surprised at this. "I don't reckon that's something you need to know." His tone was curt and harsh. The other man, who had hung back during all this drama, stepped up next to him and jabbed an elbow in his side, causing him to grunt and stand straighter, but he got the message, saying, "Keith Blalock." He gestured toward his assailant, whom I thought looked more like a boy than man due to his small stature and slim build. "That there's my wife Malinda."

"Sam," she said, taking off her hat and nodding at me. "You can call me Sam."

Abbie and I stared at this person with her hair cut short like a boy's, wearing a man's shirt and riding britches. I bit my tongue to keep from asking Abbie why we hadn't thought to wear pants. Luther had left a few behind and with some alterations by Abbie they would fit well enough. It'd sure make doing chores around the farm a heck of a lot easier.

Abbie snapped me back into focus, saying, "Where's he been shot at?"

"In the stomach," Josh said, with a grimace.

I dropped the quilt, ignoring everyone's look of surprise, figuring my heavy cotton nightgown was thick enough to conceal anything that needed covering. "Let's lay him out on the table." After Abbie cleared it off, we managed to get the man onto it with some difficulty. As I washed my hands, I said, "What's his name?"

"John, that's all you need to know," Keith said in a brusque manner, ignoring his wife's exasperated sigh.

I overlooked this, thinking he was probably anxious about his partner's condition. "Get that coat off of him." Returning to the table, I unbuttoned John's shirt and pulled it open. Then stepped back, sensing Abbie joining me as we both studied the wound. Aided by Josh, I turned John on his side, looking for blood. "There's no exit wound, the bullet's still in there."

"He ain't gonna live," Abbie said simply, as Josh gently lay the man on his back.

I gestured for Josh to hold the lantern above John's torso then prodded at a small bullet wound in his abdomen, right below the belly button. "How long since he was shot?"

When no one responded, I pointedly looked at Keith, wondering why he was so reluctant to reveal anything. He finally shrugged. "Near about a day. We been hiding out, hoping he'd get better but he didn't. Lucky we found Josh here, who said he might be able to help us."

I glanced at Josh. "They were holing up in Scarborough's barn."

I nodded. Our own hiding place when we needed to conceal a runaway slave before taking him or her on to the next station.

"I'm pretty sure it went into the intestine, Abbie." I studied John's skin, pale as watered milk. "Has he lost a lot of blood?"

"A right fair amount," Sam said. I studied her for a moment, noticed she didn't seem as upset about the injury as her husband did.

"Can you do anything for him?" Keith said, wringing his hat in his hands.

I maneuvered the area around the wound, trying to feel the bullet, but it had apparently gone too deep. "I can try to get the bullet out but in doing so will probably do more harm than good. If it's in the intestine, it's a fatal wound. I don't have the right kind of instruments or sutures to operate."

Sam shook her head with disgust. "I told you John weren't up to it, Keith," she said with great irritation. "Told you in private so the others wouldn't hear and think me, nothing but a woman, was telling you what to do, when we both know I got more sense than you ever thought about. Don't know why you won't listen to me. Just 'cause you're a man don't make you any wiser."

A feminist in the 1800s, I thought with suppressed glee. We all waited in silence for Keith's response, which ended up being a shrug of acquiescence. Finally he turned back to me. "What can we do for him?"

I shook my head. "I'm sorry but there isn't much. If it's penetrated the intestine, which I suspect it has, giving him something to drink for the pain will only make things worse. As it is, bacteria are probably leaking out of the intestine which will cause peritonitis and septicemia and eventual death." I glanced up, noticed their expressions. "That's like gangrene of the intestines, or blood poisoning." I hesitated. "It's not a peaceful death. He could linger for a bit and will be in a lot of pain."

Keith and Sam looked at one another. I was shocked when Keith said, "You reckon you can just go ahead and end it for him?"

I shook my head. "I won't kill him."

Keith hung his head and walked away.

Sam sighed. "Well, I reckon we just wait then." She scooted out a chair and sat with an expectant air.

"I'll make tea while you all decide what to do," Abbie said, looking flustered. I'm sure she felt the same as I did. I didn't want a man dying on our kitchen table.

I picked up the quilt from the floor and wrapped it around me once more. "Is he wanted? Running from anyone or thing?"

Sam nodded. "He's a deserter from the Confederacy and was helping us."

I raised my eyebrows at this.

"We're pilots," she went on. "Help deserters or prisoners of war, those that want to join up with the Union 'stead of the Confederacy. We get em over the mountains to the Union headquarters in East Tennessee."

"Much like we do with the Underground Railroad," Josh said. "Except with soldiers, instead of slaves."

I found this interesting. I looked at Sam. "And you do it too?"

She nodded. "Never was one of them women waits on their man at home, keeping the home fires burning, doing chores and sewing, cleaning, cooking and such. I like to be where my man is."

I smiled, thinking I liked this woman.

By this time the room was beginning to warm. Sam took off her hat and coat, hung them on the back of her chair. She turned back to me. "Keith and me are partners. We hunt and fish together, do everything together, and it don't bother him none that I like wearing pants more than skirts."

I looked around the room for Keith, found him leaning against the door, staring at his feet. "However did you get involved with being a pilot?" I couldn't help but ask.

Sam leaned back in her chair, getting comfortable, obviously in the mood to talk. "Keith took it upon himself to join the Confederacy sometime back when they passed that Conscription law, although he and me was for the Union from the start. But this is a Rebel state and you got to be careful about which side you choose. Keith thought about running off to Kentucky to join the Union but it's a far piece and they'd've hung him if he got caught. So he figured he'd join the Confederacy, get his ten dollars and a new musket when he joined. Then after he was trained as a soldier and sent up to Virginny, why, it weren't but a short trip to the Union lines. So off he went. Wasn't long afore I knew I couldn't just sit and wait for him to come back so I cut my hair, bound myself up, put on my britches and went looking for him. Joined the Army in Lenoir under Colonel Zebulon Vance, who's now our governor, as you probably know." She made a face of distaste at that. "I claimed I was Keith Blalock's brother Sam and meant to join up with him. Finally found him and we been together ever since."

"Did y'all desert as well?" I asked, smiling at Abbie when she handed me a cup of tea.

"Nope. Keith didn't take well to the Army, didn't like all them rules and regulations, so he went and rolled his whole body in poison oak, poison sumac and poison ivy. Oh, he was a sight with his eyes all swole up and red bumps a-festering all over his body. Sergeant took one look at him at roll call and sent him to the camp doctor at the infirmary. The doctor couldn't figure out what he had so Keith told him it was the Unaka fever from back home and was liable to spread like wildfire. They didn't want nothing to do with a man what looked so ill and contagious so discharged him."

I smiled at that image. "And what about you? How did you get them to discharge you?"

"I went to see our camp commander, Zebulon Vance, told him my story and proved it by raising my shirt and undoing the wraps that bound me in. Figured he'd get mad but he only smiled, had his adjutant release me from military service, and me and Keith left."

I couldn't help but laugh at this, didn't miss Sam's smile. "Are y'all from around here?" I darted a glance at Josh, who was watching Sam with something close to fascination.

"No'm. We're from over Grandfather Mountain way. A-course, once the Home Guard learned Keith was healthy enough, they ordered him to reenlist so we started hiding out with other draft dodgers till we joined up with Colonel George Kirk and started helping soldiers nearby get over into East Tennessee." She nodded at John, still unconscious on the table. "Like I said, John was a-helpin us."

"Where are the soldiers?"

"Holed up in that barn he told you about." She tilted her head in Josh's direction.

I looked at John, who moaned softly. I didn't know what to do for the man. I couldn't give him anything oral for pain because of the gut injury but knew when he gained consciousness his pain would be unbearable.

Sam stirred in her chair. She finally straightened up, saying, "Well, I reckon we know what needs to be done, Keith. Get on over here and help me get him up and outside."

Abbie and I exchanged panicked glances. "What are you going to do with him?" I asked.

Sam pulled on her coat, stuffed her hat over her head. "I reckon we'll strap him to his horse, keep him with us till he dies."

"He's going to be hurting something awful. Riding a horse will only make it worse for him."

She turned to me, looked me in the eye. "When he comes around, what happens to him is gonna be his decision. Till then, we ain't got no choice but to continue on. The Home Guard will be out looking for those soldiers, and if we don't get moving, they'll find em pretty quick. Desertion's a hanging offense for them, and us helping them will send us to the same fate."

I looked at Josh, who seemed as unsure what to do as I was. His eyes met mine for a long moment. "I reckon it's their decision, Lizzie," he said. "We can't stop them, and if those soldiers are caught in Papa's barn, you know who they're going to suspect put them there." He pulled his coat on and opened the door. "Besides, it's safer for you and Abbie if they're not found here. You know that."

I could only watch as they carried John out the door. After it closed behind them, I looked at Abbie. "I wish we could have helped him in some way, Abbie."

She shook her head. "He was doomed the minute he joined up with them two. They was nothin either one of us could have done for that man." With a sigh, she climbed in bed. "Turn down the lantern, Lizzie, and come to bed. It's not yet dawn."

I did as she asked, saying a silent prayer that John would not suffer too much and that Josh would return home safely, then remembered what Sam had said. "What do you think she meant, Abbie, about it being John's decision when he came around?"

She yawned before answering. "I reckon they'll let him decide whether to die right then or wait till the angels decide to take him."

I gasped. "You mean, they'll kill him?"

"Probably let him do the deed himself, Lizzie." She sighed. "It's the merciful thing, don't you think?"

I honestly didn't know how to answer that so simply turned on my side and stared into the darkness for the rest of the night.

The next afternoon, Abbie and I were sitting on the porch, where Abbie was altering one of Luther's britches. She had eagerly agreed to my suggestion that we dress in pants while doing chores and such around the house, although was terribly worried about what Sarie would say. "Shoot, she'll probably like the idea as much as we do," I told her. "Sarie's a real tomboy."

Abbie squinted her eyes at me. "What's a tomboy?"

"A girl who isn't all girly-girl, you know, like Charlotte, Josh's sister, who only seems interested in clothes and hairstyles and wouldn't think it ladylike to not ride a horse sidesaddle or even do such a horrid thing as put a saddle on a horse." I made a face.

"So we're tomboys too," Abbie said with a smile.

"Sure are and proud of it." We both glanced toward the forest at the sound of horses' hooves and watched a quartet of men ride into the yard, reining up when they spied us. Brett and his men, I thought with resignation. Abbie and I glanced at each other, knowing their reason for being here.

I stood, watching as they dismounted. Since Sarie had shot the bushwhacker, and I had been with her, Brett's suspicion of us had lightened some, but I knew one wrong move on our part would put him back on our trail again. "Good morning, Brett. There anything we can do for you?"

"Might be. We been trackin some people and looks like their trail leads right to you."

I tensed. "You still working for the Home Guard?"

"Yes'm. They made me cap'n." He gave us a proud look before continuing. "As y'all know, it's our duty to round up deserters, fellers hiding out from enlisting, escaped prisoners of war and such, and bring em to justice."

"And you're looking for someone, you said?"

"Got a bloody trail leading right into your yard here," he said. "You had any visitors lately? Got anybody hiding out in that cabin we don't know about?"

Abbie rose to her feet, joining me. "We had some folks come through last night seeking our help but we couldn't do nothin for them. We're healers, as you well know. They didn't give us their names or what business they was up to."

"What kind of help was they needin?"

"One of them had been shot," I said. "A gut wound. They wanted us to do something for him but we aren't surgeons and could only tell them he'd die from his wound so they rode off."

He squinted his eyes as he studied us. "You mind if I come on up there and check that cabin out, make sure they ain't hiding in there?"

"You don't believe us?"

"Ma'am, whether I do or not don't matter here. I have to make sure. You can give us permission, but if you don't, why, under law, we can come on up there and check it out anyway. You don't got any say in the matter, I'm only askin to be polite."

I stepped aside, making a sweeping gesture with my hand. "Then by all means, check the cabin."

Abbie and I stayed on the porch while they conducted their search. It only took minutes, and when they stepped outside, three of the men went into the yard and to their horses while Brett remained on the porch with us. "You get a good look at em?" he asked, glancing from me to Abbie.

"It was dead of night," Abbie said, "and they woke us up bangin on the door. I lit a lantern but it was too dim to see any of em real clear. I remember they called the man what was shot by the name John."

Brett's eyes darted to his waiting men. He turned back to us. "Anything else?"

Abbie and I acted as if thinking long and hard. I finally said, "Well, they all wore hats low on their heads and had scarves around their necks. One was kind of tall and one real short. The injured man, I don't know. They carried him to the chair and put him in it so I couldn't tell you how big he was. We asked them their names but the one who seemed to be the leader told us we didn't need to know that." I made my eyes go wide. "Do you mean to tell me they were deserters? Here in our cabin?" I grasped Abbie's hand. "We could have been in danger, Abbie."

"I reckon so," she said, in a frightened voice.

Brett watched us closely. He must have believed us because he finally relaxed. "Might be a good idea to keep that door locked and not answer it if somebody comes knockin in the dead of night."

"Well, we have to answer," Abbie said. "Somebody on the mountain might need our help, might be a birthing going on, or a sick young'un."

"Then mayhap you should ask who's there before you open the door."

Abbie shrugged. "I reckon that's a right good idea, considerin what's going on."

I smiled as charmingly as I could, which I doubt was

convincing, since my lips were quivering with anxiety.

Brett nodded his head and doffed his hat, his eyes narrowing with suspicion. "Well, best get back to that trail. If you see them folks again, you best let us know else we might begin to think you're helping deserters and such."

"Well, if we'd known they were deserters and such, I'm sure we would have reported them," I said snippily, thinking, we got rid of Constable Jackson and all his superstitions and here we go again.

He narrowed his eyes at me but didn't comment, instead nodded before stepping off the porch and mounting his horse. He gave us a long, measuring stare before riding off. I looked at Abbie, raising my eyebrows.

She shook her head. "Brett ain't got the sense of a grasshopper, but as you know, he's as mean as a striped-eyed snake. Can't tell if he believed us or not." She sighed. "Ain't no use to worry about it now. Time will tell, I reckon." She sat back down and went to work on the pants.

I eased into my rocker. "I only hope we didn't replace Constable Jackson with that guy. He looks like he's enjoying the power the Home Guard's placed on him more than ever."

"Shoot. Whoever made that decision must've been half asleep or drunk." She gave me a wary look. "We best be careful around him, Lizzie."

Chapter Fifteen

Late Spring 1864

With a Little Help From my Friends

Although Amanda May was Melungeon, many mistook her dusky skin color and curly black hair for that of a Negro or Mulatto and assumed, wrongly, that she was Sarie's slave. Amanda May had been brought to Sarie in 1859 by her great-grandmother, Lily, who had died within an hour after they arrived and before we could find out the reason they came to us all the way from Virginia, something she hadn't confided in Amanda May. Since Amanda May's great-grandmother was a healer and knew Sarie to be such, Sarie assumed she had brought her to the sisters to be bound to them to learn the art of healing. At that time, a girl or boy whose parents or guardians couldn't take care of them would often give them to another person, usually a businessman or some sort of tradesman, for seven years so the child could learn a trade.

Though the sisters and I told this to everyone we introduced Amanda May to, more than a few congregants of the church we attended, for some reason, refused to believe she was anything but a slave and insisted Amanda May should attend a church specifically for such. I wasn't even aware there was one, to be honest, and the injustice of this—in regards to Amanda May, let alone any slave, being barred from a Christian church—irked me to no end. I was not above letting my feelings be known, along with Sarie, to no avail. If our pastor's wife, Freda Hennesy, hadn't interfered and insisted that Amanda May was most definitely not a slave and more than welcome in her husband's church, I'm sure she would have been banned, a terrible affront to this sweet girl's self-esteem. In any event, whereas before I had looked upon Freda as a busybody and gossip, I now gained a new respect for her as someone who would not stand idly by at anything she considered unjust.

Amanda May had been bonded to Sarie at the age of 12, and now, five years later, had blossomed into a lovely young woman with a petite build and silky black hair curling around a heart-shaped face encompassing the most beautiful blue eyes I'd ever seen. I, however, wasn't the only one who was struck by her beauty, as several young men hovered around her like bees around a honeycomb.

I looked upon Amanda May, who was shy and timid, as a fragile young woman, and my first instinct was to protect her, so I eyed these young men with suspicion, knowing Amanda May would in all probability be unaccepted by their families. Two stood out, both sons of plantation owners. Tommy White was 17 years of age, a tall, lanky youth with shaggy blond hair and gray eyes and a large build that promised to morph into muscularity as he matured. He seemed smitten by Amanda May, always seeking her out, escorting her here and there, looking at her with what I could only term adoration. I had heard gossip that his father had threatened to disinherit him if he didn't stop "courting" Amanda May but Tommy ignored this, supposedly telling his best friend he'd live in a cave with Amanda May if she'd have him. Donald Sharp was 19 with a shorter and stockier build than Tommy, with chestnut-colored hair, dull brown eyes, and a face scarred by acne. Although not handsome by any means, enough young, single women seemed to find him appealing, I suspected due more to his father being a plantation owner than his looks or personality. Donald didn't interact with Amanda May as much as Tommy simply because Tommy was around her most of the time, but when he did would stand close to her, almost touching, whispering in her ear, many times causing her to look uncomfortable. What troubled me to no end was the way he would watch her from afar with a calculating look in his eyes. Sarie and I both warned Amanda May to stay away from Donald, who was arrogant as well as a bully and braggart. I also thought him a coward, as he had managed to convince an alleged doctor, as no one seemed to recognize the man's name, to provide a faux medical reason exempting him from being conscripted. I knew this because he had approached the sisters and me, asking for the same thing, which we refused. I feared he would take what he wanted from Amanda May and leave her broken and of ill-repute.

Knowing Sarie's dislike for men, I was surprised she didn't intervene and put a stop to any young man courting Amanda May but Tommy's determination seemed to gain some respect from her and we were all intrigued by his protectiveness of Amanda May. He made it clear to one and all how precious he found her and would token no discourtesies made to her. So, Tommy eventually wore us all down, including Amanda May, who began to look back at him the same way he did her. I expected there would be a wedding in the future, Tommy's inheritance be damned.

It wasn't long before I noticed a man appearing to be in his 20s who began accompanying Donald to church. Both young men would stand at a distance, trying to covertly watch Amanda May, which they did not succeed at, while looking to be discussing her. I pointed this out to Sarie, who didn't show any outward sign of apprehension but I caught a flash of alarm in her eyes, as she told me she would keep a close eye out. I couldn't figure out why these two were so interested in Amanda May until one Sunday after church, when Tommy appeared out of nowhere sans Amanda May, looking distraught. I fleetingly thought of Donald and his friend before Tommy said a word.

The day was so beautiful, Abbie, Josh and I had decided to lead our horses and walk for awhile as we made our way back to my cabin, enjoying the verdant scenery surrounding us along with the warm breeze lifting the hair off the napes of our necks, carrying with it the blooming scent of honeysuckle. The horses jerked at their reins and made startled noises when Tommy came crashing out of the brush, breathing heavily. We waited with alarm while he put his hands on his knees, bent over and tried to catch his breath, knowing the news could not be good. Tommy's complexion, usually ruddy and healthy-looking, was a pale shade of milk and his hands trembled as if with palsy. When he finally could talk, he straightened up and gasped, "Amanda May's gone. I can't find her anywhere."

"Maybe she's with Sarie," Abbie said.

Tommy shook his head. "I already asked her. She's gone to Maggie's to see if she went off with her, but on my way here, I saw Micah Jacobson and he told me he saw Donald and some man he didn't recognize put her in a wagon between them and off they went." His eyes were wild with panic. "Micah said she looked scared and they were bullying her something awful."

My eyes met Josh's. "What would he want with her?" I asked.

Josh thought a moment then his eyes narrowed. "Where's Donald's brother Joseph?"

Tommy swallowed hard. "I reckon he's headed home from church."

"Let's go," Josh said as he mounted his horse and held out his hand for Tommy to get on behind him. I climbed on Beauty while Abbie got on Jonah and we hurried after Josh, me praying all the while that Donald and that man hadn't taken Amanda May off to rape or murder her.

Josh's horse was faster than ours, and when we caught up with him and Tommy a mile or so past the church, they had found Joseph and had him backed up against a tree, pressuring him for answers about what his brother was up to. Joseph, who had apparently been bullied by his brother all his life, was a meek boy and I felt a pang of sympathy as he hunched his shoulders and cowed, as if afraid Josh or Tommy might strike him. As upset as Tommy was, it wouldn't surprise me if he did. His face was now beet red and his fists were clenched, his stance rigid, spittle flying from his mouth as he threatened Joseph.

I dismounted, grabbed Jonah's reins and led our mounts close to Josh's horse and another I didn't recognize, grazing passively nearby. When we joined them, Joseph was saying, "I only heard them talking the once and they were discussing what kind of price they could get for such a ..." his voice trailed off for a moment as if trying to find the right word, one I assumed he meant to replace the one actually used "... an attractive slave."

"What?" I said, my voice rising. "They mean to sell her?" Josh glanced at me. "But they don't have any papers."

He grimaced. "I'm sure there are ways around that."

"Where did they go?" Tommy yelled, his face inches from Joseph's.

Joseph flinched, pressing harder against the tree, as if hoping it would absorb him. "They're headed toward Asheville is all I know. They got a man there, owns a big plantation, who's interested."

"They can't be too far ahead of us," Josh said. He turned to me. "I'll go after them. You and Abbie go into Morganton, get Sheriff Brittain, tell him what's happened."

I shook my head. "I'm going with you. You're going to need help."

"I am too," Tommy said with determination. He glanced at Joseph's horse. "I'm taking your horse, Joseph. I'll return him to you later." He leaned closer, glaring at him. "It's the least you can do."

Joseph nodded, his face reddening with shame. "I hope you catch up to them and put a stop to this," he said, his voice low. "I knew I should have told somebody but my brother, he's, well, he'll kill me if he finds out I told y'all what he's doing."

"Not if I kill him first," Tommy said. In that instant, I saw the man he would become, a powerful one with a hard core who would not let any harm come to those he loved.

Abbie, looking frustrated, said, "I want to come with y'all but I'll go find Sarie then we'll both go get the sheriff. We won't be far behind."

I hugged her quickly then mounted Beauty. As soon as Josh and Tommy were on their horses, we were off at a gallop.

As we rode, I put my hand into the pocket of my skirt, thankful I had my knife there. I patted my saddlebag, containing a Colt Pocket Revolver Sarie had given me. Although guns frightened me, since the beginning of the war, Sarie had insisted that we all carry weapons with us in case of bushwhackers or raiders, and Josh had spent hours teaching me how to load, shoot and clean my weapon until I was fairly comfortable with it. Abbie and the sisters were well acquainted with guns, having been taught to shoot by their father when they were young, but Amanda May was a novice like me and was so frightened of them, Sarie eventually gave up trying to convince her to carry one, much less shoot it. Instead, she taught her how to properly use a knife to stop or even kill someone, although we all suspected our passive, sweet Amanda May would never utilize it in that vein. Even so, I prayed she had her knife with her and would use it if those two despicable men tried to harm her.

By nightfall, we hadn't caught up with the kidnappers but our horses were lathered and tired so we stopped at an inn several miles past Marion, North Carolina. Josh estimated it was close to 60 miles to Asheville from Morganton and I feared Donald and his cohort would travel through the night but Josh felt they would stop, as well, possibly in Black Mountain, which wasn't far ahead of us.

Near midnight, I heard a commotion downstairs and, wrapping a shawl around me, went down to investigate, finding Abbie, Sarie and Sheriff Brittain milling about. The sight of Sheriff Brittain relieved my anxiety at once as we now had an official witness who could verify that Amanda May was not a slave nor the property of Donald and/or his partner in crime. I invited Sarie and Abbie up to my room and led Sheriff Brittain to the room where Josh and Tommy were staying. After a brief conference with Josh, we agreed to leave out at dawn the next morning.

We ate a quick breakfast of biscuits and honey washed down with coffee then saddled up and rode out, intent on catching up with the two men. Sheriff Brittain insisted he be in the lead, and I was glad of that as I wasn't sure what Tommy would do once we caught up with Donald and his cohort. He hadn't spoken much since we left the previous day and the look in his eyes was speculative and hard. I feared if Amanda May was hurt in any way, someone would end up dead because Tommy would not let it pass.

As we rode west, the rising sun felt warm on my back and I glanced behind me a time or two to catch the sight of it cresting the mountains, painting the sky a beautiful rose and gold color. I remembered traveling through Western North Carolina on my way to Woodstock over 100 years in the future and wished I had taken time then to view the scenery in more detail as I was curious just how much it had changed. Since being here, I had grown to love the beauty of the mountains although would never bear any affection or longing for this time, the reason I was on my horse at this early hour riding as fast as I could a legitimate basis for this.

We stopped to let the horses rest shortly before noon, taking time to eat more biscuits, this time with preserves. I doubt we took more than 15 minutes before Sheriff Brittain instructed us to mount up. I feared greatly that Donald had had time to reach Asheville and we would never find him, but luck was with us, as not more than an hour later, we topped a rise to see a wagon ahead of us, three people swaying on the seat. Tommy made a clicking noise to his horse, touching its sides with the heels of his boot, and shot past Sheriff Brittain, who looked startled at this. With a determined look, he encouraged his own horse into a full gallop, shouting at us as he flashed by to stay back. Josh, seeming to catch their excitement, ignored this and rode after them.

Abbie, Sarie and I hung back a little at first, reining in and staring at one another. Sarie finally shrugged, saying, "It's best to let the men handle it but I'll be damned if I'm gonna let that bastard get by with what he's done. I mean to see to it he pays for this." She clicked to her horse and was gone, Abbie and me not far behind.

When we reached the men, Sheriff Brittain was riding alongside the horse leading the wagon, his hand on its halter, forcing it to slow down with his own horse, trying to eventually bring it to a standstill. Tommy and Josh were on either side of the wagon, yelling at Donald, who was driving, to stop. Donald ignored them, his eyes on the road, as if thinking if he didn't acknowledge them, they couldn't stop him. But the Sheriff finally got their horse under control and halted. Once he did, Tommy, riding beside Donald, put his hand on the lever for the hand brake and pulled it, then one-handed yanked Donald off of the wagon seat, jumping out of his saddle and landing on him, where he began to whale away. Sarie had by this time dismounted and was running for Amanda May. Abbie and I followed suit, impatiently waiting as Josh pulled the other man off the wagon seat, then we all clambered up onto the wagon, touching and hugging Amanda May, who was crying with relief. We ignored the clamor on the ground, Tommy pounding away at Donald while Sheriff Brittain tried to restrain him, Josh getting in a punch or two of his own at the other man before tying his hands behind his back with rope he seemed to produce out of thin air.

Once Sheriff Brittain got Tommy off of Donald, he yanked him to his feet with one hand, holding Tommy back with the other while yelling at Josh to bring him some rope. Although Donald outweighed Tommy by a good 30 pounds or so, Tommy's fury managed to do some damage to Donald's face. His nose, pushed to one side, looked to be broken, blood ran down his chin from a split lip, one eye was already swelling shut, a cheekbone was inflamed and beginning to bruise, while a cut on his forehead leaked blood into the one good eye. Tommy, other than skinned knuckles, looked none the worse for wear. Once Tommy realized the situation was out of his hands, he climbed up onto the wagon, rudely pushing Sarie and me aside, and took Amanda May into his arms. She clung to him, crying openly, and we watched as he rocked her like a small child, saying soothing words to try to calm her. For the first time, I realized how much larger he was than Amanda May, who appeared tiny in his arms. I turned to Sarie, who caught my eye and nodded at me. Yes, this man would do for our sweet girl.

Abbie, Sarie and I climbed down off the wagon, giving Tommy and Amanda May some privacy, watching as Sheriff Brittain and Josh manhandled Donald and the other man into the back of the wagon. Donald landed on his back, his hands bound behind him. The other man managed to keep his balance, staring at Josh sullenly, as if he wished his hands were free so he could give back what he had been given. Once Donald was upright, the sheriff asked him where he was going.

He tried to smile, which I'm sure wasn't too comfortable with a busted lip. "Taking a trip to Asheville," he said in a haughty, although snuffling manner due to his broken nose. "A man's got a right to do that, don't he?"

"Not when he's kidnapping a young woman, with the intent of selling her as a slave," Sheriff Brittain retorted.

Donald tried to look offended. "I had no such intention, sir, and whoever told you that is a liar."

Sheriff Brittain turned his attention to the other man. "Who are you?"

The man jerked his eyes away from Josh with some reluctance. "Name's Arnold Gunthry and I don't know nothing about selling anybody as a slave."

"Bet you know a bit about kidnapping, though," the sheriff said, his voice low and cold.

"No, sir. Like he said, we was taking a short trip to Asheville, that's all. As for the young lady ..." he glanced in Amanda May's direction, "... she asked to come along and we figured there'd be no harm in it."

The sheriff stepped back, an expression on his face as if disgusted with this farce. He looked at Amanda May, who had calmed down by now and was listening to all this, shaking her head while Tommy held her in a fierce grip.

"What say you, Amanda May?" Sheriff Brittain gestured to Donald and his cohort. "These gentlemen invite you along for their little trip to Asheville?"

Amanda May straightened up with a determined look on her face, and for the first time I realized she was not as fragile and timid as I thought. "No, sir, they didn't. They kidnapped me with the intent of selling me as a slave to a plantation owner down in Asheville."

Donald gave her an indignant look. "That's a lie." He looked back at the sheriff. "Besides, you gonna take the word of that ni—"

Tommy reached down and swatted the back of his head, causing Donald's head to jerk forward and his teeth to click together. "Watch your mouth or I'll pull your tongue out and you'll never say another word again."

Amanda May jutted her chin in a pugnacious way, and I had to hide the smile this brought. I felt so proud of her. "Look at the paper in his coat pocket, Sheriff. The one says he owns me and has the right to sell me."

"That so?" Sheriff Brittain reached forward and tried to tug open Donald's coat but he jerked away. Josh grabbed him by the lapel and yanked him closer to the sheriff, who pulled out a folded piece of paper. Josh pushed Donald away and he fell on his back again.

Sheriff Brittain unfolded the paper and studied it for a long moment. "Looks like she's telling the truth." He glanced up at Donald, then Arnold. "Looks like you two are gonna be spending a long time behind iron bars, boys."

Arnold's mouth opened in shock. He glared at Donald. "He told me he owned her, said he had the right to sell her. I was just taking him to the man who wants to buy her. That's all I done, nothing else."

I stepped forward. "He's lying, Sheriff. I've seen him at church with Donald several times, always watching Amanda May. He knew she wasn't a slave."

Sarie nodded. "I seen the same thing. We was watching him because we suspected them two was up to somethin." She turned concerned eyes on Amanda May. "I'm so sorry, sweetheart, I thought you was with Tommy. I didn't know they'd taken you or I'd've stopped em with a gun."

Amanda May gave her a sweet smile. "It's all right, Sarie. I knew you and Tommy would come. I knew it in my heart."

Tommy drew back, looking at her. "Did they hurt you, darlin? Do anything to you? Anything at all?"

We all knew what he meant.

Amanda May patted his arm. "No, sweetie, but only because he told the man I was pure, said he was gonna get a higher price for me because of it."

Tommy's face grew red and he moved to grab Donald but Sheriff Brittain stopped him, yelling, "You got your revenge, he's mine now. I'll see to it he pays for what he done."

Amanda May took Tommy's hands in hers, kissed the bruised knuckles. "Get me down from here, Tommy," she said in a low voice. "Take me home."

Tommy swung down from the wagon seat then reached up and picked her up like a baby doll, holding her in the air and putting her gently on her feet. He put his arm protectively around her.

Sheriff Brittain said, "Josh, help me truss these two so they can't escape. I reckon I'll tie my horse behind and drive the wagon back to Morganton. Y'all can go on ahead or wait and ride with me if you've a mind to. It's up to you."

"I reckon we'll all ride back with you, Sheriff," Josh said.

We watched as he and Sheriff Brittain made sure the ropes binding the two men's hands behind their backs were secure, then tied their feet with more rope, looping the hands and feet together. For the first time I realized what hog-tied must mean. Both men looked uncomfortable and I hoped they were. I hoped that wagon jostled every nerve and muscle in their bodies as Sheriff Brittain made his way back to Morganton.

Once done, Sheriff Brittain and Josh joined our little group. Tommy and Amanda May were a short distance away, holding hands, talking to one another in whispers. "Y'all about ready to go?" Sheriff Brittain yelled. "Amanda May, you can ride in the wagon with me if you want."

With a glance at Amanda May, Tommy led her over to our group. "I reckon she'll ride with me, Sheriff." He turned to Sarie. "But first I got something I need to say."

Sarie stiffened a bit but didn't reply.

Tommy shifted his feet, looking uncomfortable. He swallowed before beginning. "Miss Sarie, I reckon you know how I feel about Amanda May. Why, I don't reckon it's a secret to anybody in Morganton or Brown Mountain, for that matter."

I smiled to myself, thinking, oh, no, this can't be happening, not here.

"And," he went on, "I'd like to ask your permission to marry Amanda May and marry her soon. I turn 18 in two months and I'm obligated to go and join the Confederacy but I want her to have my name and be under my protection before I go."

"But what about your inheritance?" Abbie said. "We all heared how your pa said he'd disinherit you if you continued to court our Amanda May."

Tommy looked at her and smiled. "Why, I'd give up my life for Amanda May, Miss Abbie. That money and that plantation don't mean a thing to me. The only thing I care about is being with Amanda May and taking care of her, making her happy. She's my life."

I looked at Josh, who was watching me. I smiled at him, my eyes bleary with tears. He reached out, took my hand, put it to his lips and kissed the back of it.

We all waited for Sarie to speak. She took her time about it but finally stirred and said, "Well, Tommy, I reckon you've proved you'll take good care of her. If'n she'll have you, why I reckon you have my blessing."

We all turned to Amanda May, who was smiling at Sarie. "I'll have him," she said softly. "He's all I've ever wanted in my life, Sarie. I'll be right proud to marry you, Tommy," she said turning to him.

There was much whooping and laughing at this as Tommy swept Amanda May into his arms and kissed her.

Abbie interrupted this joyous occasion by saying, "But where will you live if'n your pa throws you out, Tommy?"

Sarie interrupted before Tommy could answer. "Why he'll live with us. Amanda May has her own bedroom in the loft. I reckon it's big enough for the two of them. And she'll stay with me while he's gone away to war and however long it takes them to decide where they want to live."

"Why, I'd be honored to share your home, Miss Sarie, and I thank you," Tommy said, before turning and kissing Amanda May again.

"I reckon we've celebrated enough," Sheriff Brittain said after a few moments as we all looked anywhere but at Tommy and Amanda May. "We best get on the road if we want to make any headway toward Morganton before nightfall."

As we mounted and began the trip back to Brown Mountain, I felt happier than I had in a long time, knowing our Amanda May would be protected and cared for. I glanced at Josh, feeling his own love for me in the way he looked at me, knowing wherever we ended up, *whenever* we ended up, this man would love and protect me as well.

Chapter Sixteen

Late Spring – Early Summer 1864

All in a Day

Until 1864, Brown Mountain remained physically untouched by the war, other than the constant controversy between those who were for secession and those against, which kept us busy treating the victims of those who thought they could convince others of their conviction by fists, knives or guns. And, of course, the sporadic raids by bushwhackers looking for food and arms or simply to cause trouble. The sisters and I continued on with our biweekly clinic at the church and were occasionally called to Camp Vance when illnesses broke out requiring more help than the medical staff could handle. I wished more times than I could count that I had studied what happened in the mountains of Western North Carolina during the Civil War but that proved to be wasted energy and effort so was on alert at all times for the sounds of battle or any news travelers might bring while passing through.

Josh found me at the clinic one Thursday in late May, bandaging the amputated arm of one of the mountain boys who had just returned home. I heard Josh's voice before I saw him, inquiring of Abbie where I might be, and when I looked up, became alarmed at the look of panic on his face. I smiled at him to let him know I was aware of his presence and after reassuring the young man that he could come to us at any time with questions or concerns, then instructing his wife on how to continue to change the bandages, making sure they were clean and as germ-free as possible, I stepped outside, where Josh was waiting on me. He immediately took my elbow and guided me away from the building.

It was a beautiful day, the sun warm on my face, a light breeze blowing, the scent of pine and nearby wildflowers heavy in the air. I fleetingly thought it would be a lovely day for a walk but the look on Josh's face told me he had come to tell me something serious. I fought a rising sense of panic, wondering if he had decided to join the war effort once more. His shoulder had healed although it still gave him problems but I hoped the brutality he had witnessed would stay any desire to go back into battle.

Once we were beyond anyone hearing us, he stopped and turned to me. "I just got word from my source in New York, Lizzie. He said a colonel who goes by the name of George W. Kirk …"

"Is that the same one who's been leading raids into Mars Hill and Warm Springs? The one the Blalocks work for?"

He nodded. "The very same one and he's a traitor to the South at that. I'm told he initially enlisted in the Confederate Army but opposed secession, which isn't an anomaly here, as you well know, but due to his Unionist views deserted. He served as a guide for the Union Army in East Tennessee and Western North Carolina, aiding deserters and recruiting Unionist guerillas, before joining the Union Army. Seems he's made a name for himself and his regiment, called Kirk's Raiders, and has been ordered by Major General John Schofield to raise 200 men and move along the railroad into Virginia, destroying trestles, cars and water tanks, and burning bridges."

"The railroad? You don't mean …"

"Yes, the one that ends here in Burke County."

I stepped back. "You think he's coming here?"

He nodded. "Makes sense. The Confederacy utilizes the railroad system to move supplies and soldiers, so what better way to immobilize it than to lay waste to one of its major modes of transportation? More importantly, Camp Vance is here, and it's strategically important to the Confederacy. It houses hundreds of conscript soldiers as well as serves as a temporary prison camp for Union loyalists and deserters of the Confederate Army before sending them on to the Salisbury Prison Camp. He may decide to attack Camp Vance simply because so far no Union Army has been able to win any victories in these mountains. If they do, that could be a major win for the North."

"And major defeat for the South. Josh, he has a terrible reputation as a raider. I've heard him called a partisan guerilla fighter and that his men are mostly deserters and bushwhackers. Some of the things I've heard they've done, destroying and burning ..."

Josh took my hand. "I can't stand by and let them descend on Morganton or Brown Mountain, Lizzie. But I can't let it be known how I got this information."

"Do you have any idea when he plans to attack?"

"The order was given in February and this is May. He's had plenty of time to put together enough men to begin his march. He's at most 70 miles away, at worst, right outside our door."

"We have to get word to the camp's commandant, Major McClean."

"I agree. But how?"

I thought for a moment. "I'll do it."

"Lizzie—"

"I've been there countless times, they won't think it strange if I show up. I'll take Abbie with me, she can check in with the hospital while I see the commandant. You can't go, Josh. What would you tell them when they ask how you came by that information? They know I treat soldiers at our clinic. I could simply tell Major McClean that I treated a Union deserter who passed the information on to me before leaving. That I have no idea who he was or where he came from but felt they should be aware of an impending attack on the camp."

Josh looked away from me as he considered what I said. He finally turned back to me and nodded. "I don't think they would question you, Lizzie, if you tell them that. But if for any reason they suspect you of anything, tell them I was the one who told you."

I put my hand in his. "They won't, Josh. If anything, they'll appreciate I passed the warning on to them."

The next morning, Abbie and I rode down to Camp Vance to see the commandant, Major Jesse McClean. When we entered the camp, she veered off toward the hospital while I made my way to the major's headquarters, a small wooden building hastily built for that purpose. It had been some time since we had been called to the camp, but as always, I checked out the condition of the place, which looked even more primitive than ever. It seemed my continual warnings about sanitary conditions were taken seriously for sporadic periods of time but now the living conditions had become wretched at best. Garbage littered the ground and I could smell the stench of the distant latrines and corral. Most of the men I saw looked desolate and depressed, as if they didn't want to be there. I couldn't blame them.

When I stepped inside the building, I found the major sitting behind a rustic wooden desk, studying papers. He glanced up at me, seemed startled, then rose to his feet. "Miss Baker, I wasn't expecting you," he said, tugging at his jacket. One thing that had surprised me about this time was how short the men were—I suspected the average height was close to my own—and Major McClean was no exception. In fact, he was a bit shorter and I always felt as if I towered over him. He gestured toward a chair in front of his desk and waited for me to sit before resuming his seat.

"Is there a problem at the hospital?" he asked, looking concerned.

I shook my head. "I've learned some information that might be important and felt it imperative to come here and tell you," I began and told him about Colonel Kirk and the impending raid.

He gave me a suspicious look. "How did you come by this information?"

"As you know, the sisters and I have a clinic at the church. Yesterday morning, I treated a soldier who had just come from East Tennessee, where he was stationed with the Union. He wouldn't give me his name but said he was a deserter and was telling me this in secret. He was on his way to Virginia, where he lives, and I suppose as a thank you for our helping him, he felt obligated to let us know there's trouble coming this way."

Major McClean sat back in his seat, looking off in the distance. "Is the young man still here?"

"No, he left right after. I imagine he's well on his way by now."

He nodded. "It's a most unfortunate time," he said, as if to himself. "Our conscripts are members of the junior reserve garrison and are waiting for issued weapons to arrive. We have little arms to defend ourselves."

I stared at him in shock. How could a Confederate training camp not have weapons, I wondered.

As if answering my question, he said, "The Confederacy is very limited on funds, it seems. We are suffering the consequences."

I nodded. "Aren't the junior reserves boys aged 17?"

"Yes, that's right."

I felt sick to my stomach. "Maybe you should speak with the Home Guard," I suggested. "I'm sure they can help." I immediately regretted saying this because Brett Galloway would become involved, and as suspicious as he was, he would want to know more about my alleged confidential informant.

Major McClean considered this. "I can alert them, I suppose." His voice trailed off. He thought a moment longer then turned his attention back to me. "In any event, I do thank you for coming to me with this. We can only hope the young man might have been misleading you with a false rumor but, if not, pray that our weapons arrive before Kirk

197

and his raiders do. I'll see to it that we have extra guards posted and aware of what might be headed our way."

I rose to my feet, more concerned than pacified. The major quickly stood. He was respectful if nothing else. "Yes, I do pray this proves false, Major." I turned to go then looked back at him. "I wish you luck."

He nodded. "I do thank you, Miss Baker." He picked up a piece of paper off his desk and began to study it, dismissing me.

When I told Josh and Abbie about my conversation with Major McClean and my concern that he didn't seem overly concerned, they agreed with me there was nothing more we could do than wait and pray Kirk would not raid Morganton. But that was not to be.

On the morning of June 27th, 1864, Abbie and I were paying a medical call at the home of James and Beatrice Peterson in Morganton. I had helped Beatrice with morning sickness five years earlier when she was expecting her first child. She suffered from the same problem with her second pregnancy, so we had come down the mountain to check on her. Abbie and I were sitting with Beatrice and her husband in their parlor, drinking ginger tea while admiring their young son, when a man I recognized as William Waightstill Avery stormed into the house in a state of great agitation. I was quite shocked at this as I was used to seeing him looking melancholy and glum, which I always assumed was as a result of having killed a man in cold blood after the man whipped him in public. Although Mr. Avery was acquitted of the charges, I felt he paid the price in the way it seemed to have affected him.

James rose to his feet when Avery stormed into the room. "What is it? What's happened?"

Ignoring us, Avery said, his words clipped and fast, "Get your gun and come with me."

James gaped at him.

"Whatever for?" Beatrice said, her voice high and edged with fright.

Avery spoke to James, as if he hadn't heard her. "Early this morning, Colonel George W. Kirk and over 100 Yankees crossed the bridge where the Loudermilk family lives, heading toward Camp Vance. The Loudermilks were able to raise an alarm and some men managed to escape but there were close to 300 men present in camp, including conscripts, prisoners and deserters." He grimaced with disgust. "For some reason, Major McClean was not present when Kirk marched out of the woods with a flag of truce, demanding the camp's immediate surrender and offering that all prisoners of war would be paroled and no destruction of personal property would take place. After a bit of a skirmish, with one officer killed from what I understand, Lt. Bullock, the senior officer present, conceded. Kirk, the bastard ..." He glanced at Beatrice, Abbie and me, mumbling, "Excuse me, ladies. Kirk broke his agreement, placed the young men under arrest as prisoners of war and proceeded to burn the camp, leaving only the hospital intact, after which he destroyed the railroad depot, a locomotive and four train cars. I was told by one of the conscripts who managed to escape that Kirk planned to capture a train, go to Salisbury to release the Federal prisoners confined there, arm them, and bring them back, but when he learned from his scouts that Confederate detachments were converging on Morganton he withdrew, heading back to Tennessee, taking with him 40 of the conscripts who had surrendered at Camp Vance who elected to join his regiment rather than return to Confederate service." His face twisted with disgust. "The traitors!"

James glanced at Beatrice, who looked shocked, before saying, "I'll get my gun and hat and catch up with you."

Avery gave him a curt nod. "Ladies," he said, tilting his hat at us, and left.

James hurried out of the room and when he returned had a gun strapped to his waist. He quickly kissed Beatrice, nodded at Abbie and me, and followed Avery out the door. By this time, Beatrice was wringing her hands in agitation and crying, in an obvious state of shock. It took quite a while for Abbie and me to calm her down. Anxious to get back to our cabin to take make sure the raiders hadn't done any damage and to take care of our animals, we finally turned her over to their servants Hannah and Bill, with directions to administer valerian tea. Abbie and I mounted our steeds and rode as fast as we could up the mountain, alert for any signs of Union soldiers or outliers. Relieved to find our cabin intact and our goats chewing away at scrub brush, the chickens bustling here and there, looking as if they had much business to attend to, our cats sleeping peacefully in patches of sun in the barn or house, and Billy and Bob and the two pigs peacefully dozing under the porch, we moved on to Sarie's cabin, then Maggie's, accompanied by Sarie and Amanda May. We debated whether we should move our animals to our hidey-hole but Sarie convinced us she had learned from one of the mountaineers on his way to join the Confederates riding after Kirk and his men that Kirk was well on his way back to Knoxville and so far as he knew hadn't left any soldiers behind. So Abbie and I retired to our homestead, guns and knives at the ready, in case any threat still lingered, while Sarie and Amanda May rode to Camp Vance to check on the hospital. I suspected Sarie actually wanted to make sure Dr. Glover was alive and well and hadn't been taken prisoner.

I didn't know until afterward that Josh had been drafted as well. He told me he and about 64 others, most of which were old men and boys, under the command of Colonel George Love, caught up with Kirk 14 miles from Morganton. Kirk placed prisoners taken from Camp Vance in the front line as a human shield, and when the Confederates fired at Kirk and his men, yelled, "Look at the damned fools, shooting their own men." One prisoner was killed during the skirmish and another wounded. Kirk and his men managed to escape, but 21 miles from Morganton, another skirmish ensued with the Morganton Home Guard, this time resulting in the fatal shooting of Colonel Avery with Kirk escaping back to Knoxville, Tennessee, having lost only one man.

This was a stunning blow to Western North Carolina, proving that their mountain defenses could be penetrated. The Confederate loyalists were angered and embarrassed over Kirk's success, with the Unionists being emboldened by the raid, interpreting the incident as a sign that Confederate control over the western counties was frail.

Whereas before, the mountaineers had felt relatively safe from invasion by Union forces, we all knew this was a false security and our days may be numbered at best. This only made me more frantic to find my light with Josh and Abbie and leave.

Chapter Seventeen

Late Summer 1864

Heartbreaker

It might be foolishness, at least I suspected Sarie would call it that with a disapproving sneer in my direction if she found out about it, but after that horrific raid on Camp Vance, I convinced Abbie and Josh to search more diligently with me for my light. We all knew Kirk's victory had proved to the Union they could bring the war to our mountain and the air was filled with tense anxiety as Morganton waited for what would happen next. I became frantic to find my light so I could get out of this vicious, violent time and prayed constantly Abbie and Josh would go with me if we found it. Although Josh had told me he wanted to go, I at times questioned this, knowing how hard it was to leave loved ones behind. I had hinted to Abbie about going with me but never broached the subject outright, hoping she would make the decision herself.

Perhaps it was nothing more than a foolish dream on my part, but I refused to believe they wouldn't both be happier, certainly more content, more comfortable if they were away from all this violence and these primitive living conditions. In a place, a time where we would all be safe. Who wouldn't want that? I asked myself. That one question circled through my head endlessly as we traipsed around the mountain night after night.

Time, as always, passed, and before we knew it, fall, with its promise of setting the mountain afire with glorious color, hovered on our doorstep waiting for summer to give way to cooler days and chilly nights. Like time, the war kept going until it seemed to me it would last forever, but I knew it would end in less than a year, shortly after the death of Lincoln which occurred sometime in April of 1865, if I remembered right. Thankfully, there had been no major fighting in Morganton except for a few minor skirmishes between people on opposing sides of the war and occasional raids by small gangs of bushwhackers, but we all knew the war could come to us at any moment.

I'd only been keeping track of one date as we moved through that summer, the fifth anniversary of the day in August when I'd impulsively reached my hand out, touched one of the Brown Mountain lights and traveled back in time 110 years. As it moved closer, I despaired I would never be able to find my way back and agonized that I would be stuck here forever. I eventually began to wonder if perhaps we were going about finding the light in the wrong way. Maybe I needed only to go back to where Abbie and Sarie had found me that long ago night to find my light again. The more I thought about it, the more convinced I became that was the solution. To go back to the exact spot at the exact time—or as close to it as possible—on the same day five years later.

Who knows, maybe it had been that simple all along.

Near dusk on the day of my fifth anniversary, Abbie and I sat on our porch, waiting for Josh to meet us for another search. It had begun to sprinkle and I hoped this would not turn into a summer storm which could leave us drenched in seconds. As we waited, I made small talk about the weather, the full moon, anything I could think of, working my way up to the question I really wanted to ask.

"Abbie, do you remember where you found me when I came through the light? It wasn't far from Sarie's cabin, was it?"

"Close enough, I guess."

"Can you take us there tonight?"

"I reckon I could. Hard to forget the place we found Belinda and her baby's skulls." She shifted to look at me. "What are you thinkin, Lizzie?"

I hesitated, saying a quick prayer I would be able to convince her to agree with my plan. "It's been five years now. You know how homesick I am and how much I want to go home. I'm wondering if maybe the date had something to do with it." I shrugged. "Probably just wishful thinking on my part but ... we've searched, as far as I can tell anyway, everywhere else on the mountain and we only saw it that one time when Constable Jackson kept me from touching it. Other than then, we haven't found it yet so maybe tonight we should look in the same place I came through. I mean since it's the anniversary of when I came through and all," I finished lamely.

"Is that what you really want?" she asked.

I could all but feel her displeasure, her lack of enthusiasm, in the words. Still, I nodded. "I'm sorry if that hurts you but I do. I feel like I should at least try, anyway. I love you and Josh, Maggie, Amanda May, all our sweet animals. Shoot, I'll even cop, uh, admit to loving Sarie a little bit but I need to go back if I can." After a brief pause, I went on. "I'm hoping you'll go with me but I understand if you won't. Josh too."

Abbie considered me for a long moment. "All right, I'll take you there. I love you too, Lizzie, but ..." She broke off, cocked her head then pointed to the edge of the forest. "I reckon that's Mister Josh comin this way."

I don't think he saw us as he rode into the clearing and toward the barn. After dismounting, he tied his horse to a post then began to walk toward us, his booted feet shredding the mist that had started to gather along the ground. My heart pounded in my chest as I watched him in silence. I loved him so and didn't know if I could bring myself to leave if he decided not to go with me.

Shivering, I remembered the popping sounds of gunfire, the booming of cannons exploding at Gettysburg. I could still clearly hear the dying screams of men and horses, the agonized moans of those wounded. As it always did, the remembrance brought back the chill of worry about Josh. For a moment, I thought I smelled gunpowder and the acrid stench of ozone that had seemed to linger in the air for days, along with the bitter, coppery scent of fresh blood and fear … and death.

A small gasp of breath then a deep inhale cleared the scent from my nose as Josh noticed us and raised his hand to wave. The memories were only a product of my overactive imagination, of course, but they were powerful enough to remind me of my determination to get back to my own time and to take Josh and Abbie with me if I could.

Josh, wearing a gun riding low on his hip, smiled as he moved nearer to us. When he stepped up onto the porch, I threw my arms around his neck, kissing him as if he were a long lost love returning from war—or a cherished lover going off to war.

When I finally let him go, he looked into my eyes. "What's all this? Are you all right?"

I shook my head. "No. I mean, yes. I really missed you."

"Well, it has been a couple of days," Abbie said with an indulgent smile.

Josh laughed. "You ladies look ready to do some serious searching."

Abbie, dressed as I was in an old pair of Luther's pants, a loose flannel shirt of a dark, dingy plaid, with her hair tucked up under a man's hat of rusty dung brown, pointed in the direction of Sarie's cabin. "Lizzie wants to head over in that direction, where she was after she come through the light that time."

Josh only nodded though I saw understanding come into his eyes. "All right. Since it's close enough to walk, I'll unsaddle Boomer and put him in the barn with Beauty and Jonah." Afterward, he smiled at me as he took my hand. "Let's go." As we walked along, he said, "Do you remember where it was, Miss Abbie?"

"Like I told Lizzie, it's hard to forget where you found a couple of skulls. Somethin like that just sticks right in your mind."

"I'd say it would." His hand squeezed mine. "Are you all right, Lizzie? You're shaking a bit."

"Josh, I ..." I shook my head again, knowing it wasn't fair not to tell him. Willing the shaking to stop, I said, "I'm fine, a little nervous is all. I, um, have a feeling we're going to find my light tonight. I've been here five years today and it just feels like tonight is when I'll be able to go back." I couldn't control another shiver. "I need to know that you and Abbie will go through it with me. I don't know if I'll be able to without you." A tear trickled down my cheek. Wiping it impatiently away, I took a deep breath then choked out, "I don't know if I can go through it without both of you."

He leaned toward me, gave me a kiss on the cheek. "I told you I would, didn't I? Of course, I can't speak for Abbie."

Abbie didn't respond to that and this spoke volumes to me. How could I convince her to go, I wondered frantically.

Josh intruded on this thought, saying, "Lizzie what about Ben? I don't know if I could stand seeing you with another man."

I battled back more tears, knowing they would weaken him. It wasn't fair and I knew I wouldn't be able to cope with thinking that was the only reason he agreed to come with me. "I'll admit I love—loved—Ben but not the way I love you, that's the God's honest truth, Josh. What I feel for you is so much more and I have a feeling it'll only grow with time. I don't want to give you up but I know it's not fair to ask you or Abbie to give up your home and family for me so I'm not going to. I'm selfish enough to do it anyway but instead I'll just say I love you both very much and don't want to lose either of you."

Abbie's hand reached out for mine, gripped it hard as Josh laid his cheek on top of my head. "I love you, too, Lizzie, deeply enough to go, to give us a chance for a life together. I'm sure Abbie feels the same way."

We both looked at her. "I ain't for sure, Lizzie. I like my life here just fine, but you need to go if'n that's what you want and you think that's where you belong, just like this is where I belong. If I had my 'druthers, you'd stay here with us but I know that's not the way you want it."

Disappointed, I squeezed Abbie's hand, turned to kiss Josh's cheek. "I guess that will have to do me for now, Abbie."

She gave me a curious look. "What if the light won't take y'all? I keep thinkin of that, can't stop thinkin about it, even though I want you to go if that's what will make you happy."

I didn't know what to say; she had voiced my worst fear.

She sighed. "I reckon all we can do is see what happens if'n we do see your light."

Twilight deepened as we walked on. When we spotted the light from Sarie's cabin, smelled the smoke from her fire, Abbie led us off the trail, deeper into the dark of the forest. The mist that had hugged the ground rose up as it often did on the mountain, muffling the sound of our footsteps and making it harder to see anything even with the full moon that peeked through the quickly thinning clouds hovering low in the eastern sky.

The pattering rain lessened to a thin drizzle as we moved in silent tandem on the trail. We veered into the trees when we heard something coming toward us. Josh motioned us to silence as he peered through the slender branches of a young maple tree. I prayed whoever or whatever it was would pass us by without detecting us.

"Only a deer," Josh said then stepped back onto the path, motioning us to follow.

As the trail widened, Abbie moved up beside us and in a quiet voice, said, "What the devil's got you so nervous, Mr. Josh?"

He shook his head. "Not nervous, just cautious. I ran into Brett Galloway who told me the Home Guard's been put on alert about a band of outliers who've been causing more trouble than usual the past few nights. We need to be careful, is all."

I gave him a questioning look. I could tell by the sound of his voice he wasn't telling us everything he knew and wondered what this group had done that had him so concerned.

When the path forked, Josh stopped then turned to Abbie. "Which way now, Miss Abbie?"

She thought about it for a minute, staring in both directions, before pointing to the right. "I reckon that way would get us closer to where we need to go. It ain't far now."

I did my best to relax, or try to. Josh might not be nervous but I sure was. I began to worry about all the things that could happen before we got to wherever Abbie was taking us, what might take place when we got there, if we would actually find my light, and what would occur when we touched it. Would it only take me? Where would I end up if it did? Back to 1969 or to some other time, possibly into the future or maybe further back into the past? Did I dare take the chance of that happening?

I would find out soon enough, I told myself. All I knew right at that moment was I had made up my mind if for no other reason than I needed to do something, to take my life back if I could.

As the mist thickened around us, I caught the faint scent of dying leaves and pine needles—the familiar smell of approaching fall on the mountain. I listened to the sound of our footsteps, muffled by the moss and damp undergrowth on the trail. The chirps of insects and night birds shut off momentarily as we passed by.

Just as I relaxed my tight grip on Josh's hand, Abbie said in a low voice, "Let's move off the trail into the woods now. Somebody's comin toward us."

Josh stopped so he could listen better. After a couple of seconds, he nodded to Abbie. Apparently he heard them too.

"What are you thinking?" I asked him.

He lowered his voice to a whisper. "I'm thinking whoever it is will catch up with us soon. We need more cover. Right now the most important thing is to get us off this trail. We won't be quite so visible but we have to walk as quietly as possible. With a little bit of luck, whoever it is will stick to the trail and go right by us."

Josh took my hand, his voice barely audible. "Hold on to Abbie. Try not to make any noise if you can help it." He looked up at the sky. "Should be full dark soon which will make it easier and those clouds might shroud the moon if we're lucky but we have to be careful. Don't let go of either one of us."

With that, he moved off into the trees, not exactly tip-toeing but stepping slow, placing his feet carefully in order to be as quiet as possible. I tried to imitate his every move but wasn't always successful. I winced, cursing silently in my head at every snap of a twig, knowing in my heart that might be enough to give us away to whoever was nearby. Abbie, behind me, seemed to have the same Daniel Boone skill as Josh did.

It felt as if we crept through the forest for hours, moving into and out of shadows cast by the moon playing hide and seek with the frisky clouds but I'm sure it was only minutes.

"Josh?" I whispered when he stopped suddenly and I bumped into his back.

"Just getting my bearings," he said, looking around. "Which way now, Miss Abbie?"

From behind me, she pointed slightly to the right. "Keep goin that way, Mister Josh."

He nodded, but before he could start moving again, we heard the sound of hushed voices. He gripped my hand then crouched down, pulling me down with him. I did the same with Abbie.

We stayed that way, listening to more than a few men urging each other on for several minutes, long enough for my legs to tingle in protest. One of the men remarked as they passed close by, "Gonna have me a girl tonight, don't make much difference to me who she is or what she looks like." The other men laughed at this and made crude comments, agreeing with their cohort. It sent shivers up and down my spine, hearing this, and I inadvertently stepped back, my foot snapping a twig. The forest was silent, birds and small animals hovered down, waiting for the intruders into their space to pass, and the sound of that snapping twig seemed to echo across the mountain. Josh gripped my hand tighter as we heard one of the men shush the others in a harsh, warning tone.

I peered through the trees, trying to get an idea of how many there were, whether they were Confederate or Union soldiers, or the bushwhackers Brett warned Josh about, but I couldn't see a thing, not even the flash of a saber or glint of a knife or rifle. The only thing I knew for sure, judging by what the one man had said, was that they were trouble and wouldn't mind it a bit if they ran across a woman or girl along the way. It was obvious what they planned to do with them if they did.

I had spent almost every second of the last five years wishing I could find the light that had brought me here, hoping it would take me back to my time, back to where I belonged. In all that time, I don't think I'd ever prayed for it more fiercely than I did at that one moment.

They finally began to move away. I peered into the trees, once again caught the faintest glimmer of light from Sarie's cabin, and my blood froze as a scene from an old World War II movie flashed into my brain. The British, huddling behind blackout curtains so the German fighter planes couldn't see where to target their bombs.

"Blackout," I murmured.

"What, Lizzie?" Josh whispered at the same time Abbie said sotte voce, "What does that mean, Lizzie?"

I pointed. "We need to get to Sarie and tell her to turn off—douse the light. If we can see it, so can those men. It'll lead them straight to her and Amanda May."

Josh tensed but didn't say anything as he stood up. After Abbie and I had gained our feet, he leaned over to whisper in my ear, "No more talking, we can't risk it. Move as fast as you can but try to be quiet. We're not in the clear yet."

I nodded before whispering the same in Abbie's ear. I knew from the way she gripped my hand she was terrified for her sister and Amanda May, for what those men might do if they came across two unprotected women alone. I squeezed her hand, hoping she would get my message of reassurance. Sarie, in my opinion, was one of the bravest women on the mountain, or anywhere else for that matter. I'd seen her in action several times, knew she wouldn't go down without a fight and would do whatever she could to protect Amanda May.

After a few yards, a cloud blanketed the moonlight completely and Josh moved Abbie and me behind a couple of big oaks that had begun their life so close together the trunks had merged together, forming one trunk wide enough to shield two people.

"Stay here," he whispered. He gripped Abbie's hand in his free one, looked her right in the eyes. "Right here, you hear? I'll go see what's going on. Promise me, both or you."

Without waiting for our response, he moved back toward the path. Although I desperately wanted to find my light, Sarie and Amanda May were more important so I held hands with Abbie, hiding behind the connected oak trees, and waited. The air grew cooler as the breeze picked up and I imagined Abbie was praying her heart out. I know I was.

I jumped at the harsh roar of a gunshot. The light in Sarie's cabin blinked out and everything went quiet.

Abbie screamed, wrenched her hand from mine and took off running through the woods.

I ran after Abbie, catching up with her in a few steps but only because she stumbled. My heart pounding, I went down on my knees when I all but fell over her prone body. "Abbie, Abbie, are you all right? Oh, God, Abbie, say something."

She groaned, and although I knew better, I immediately pulled her up to cradle her in my arms. "Are you okay, Abbie? Oh, please tell me you're okay."

"I think I broke my ankle or maybe I just sprained it real good. It hurts like the very devil." She hitched in a breath when I hugged her tight.

"Is your back okay? Please tell me I didn't just paralyze you."

"I'm all right," she said impatiently as she pushed at my arms. "Leave me be, Lizzie. We got to get moving. Sarie and Amanda May might need help." She held her hand out. "Just help me up. Let's see if'n I can walk."

I stood, pulling her up with me as gently as I could. "Okay, how does that feel? Try to take a step if you can."

She did as I asked, testing the foot carefully as I stood beside her, holding on.

"Stop a minute. You should let me check it first before we try to go farther."

Shaking her head, she hobbled a few steps on her own. "Best leave it be, Lizzie. I 'spect it'll swell up a bit but my boot might keep it from swelling too bad. I can move my ankle around, so at least it's not broken, just sprained like I said. I can walk on it, I just have to go slow."

I slipped an arm around her waist. "Lean on me as much as you can. Maybe that will help."

She nodded then pointed forward. "I want to go on over and check on Sarie and Amanda ..." We heard crashing through the woods and both grew silent, waiting to see who it was, praying it was Josh.

Two men stepped out of the trees, smiling when they saw us. One was very tall and lanky, the other short and squat. They were filthy looking, their clothes spotted with dark stains and grime, their long hair and beards matted with dirt and bits of twigs and leaves.

"Well, lookit what we got here," the tall one said, as they advanced toward us. Abbie and I backed away and turned to run but Abbie's injury slowed us down and they easily caught up with us. When they were within arm's distance, the tall man grabbed the back of my shirt, pulling me back toward him. He moved so fast, I didn't even see his hand before he yanked the cap off my head, my hair spilling out and tumbling around my shoulders. Seeing this, he turned and winked at his cohort. "Didn't take near as long to find me a woman as I thought it would."

The other one, holding Abbie by the arm, gave her the once-over before casually knocking the cap off her head. "Looks like I got me one too," he said.

I fleetingly thought the two men must be mentally challenged, as they'd released us to remove our hats. Without communicating with each other, Abbie and I turned and began to run, stumble, actually, away from them. When Abbie faltered, I put my shoulder under her arm and my arm around her waist and, taking most of her weight, pulled and tugged her along with me.

The men easily reached us, each one grabbing and yanking us back. I staggered a few steps but Abbie fell to the ground. I wrenched out of my captor's grip and knelt beside her to help her up, wishing I'd brought along my gun. But I did have my knife. Hearing him approach from behind, I put my hand in my pocket, pulled it out. When he grasped my arm, I turned and slashed at him, catching him across the cheek, watching as a thin red gash opened, blood pouring down and dripping off his chin.

The tall man cursed, knocking the knife out of my grip with one hand, cupping his cheek with the other. Backing away, I glanced around for it but couldn't see where it had gone. Abbie, still on the ground right beside me, was struggling with the other man, who had straddled her. I forgot about the knife as I kicked him in the left kidney, glad I wasn't wearing a skirt which would have impeded my actions. He yowled in pain and rolled off her.

The one I had slashed grabbed me again, pulling me toward him, saying, "You're a fierce one, ain't you? Well, that don't bother me none, I like a fighter." His breath was fetid, smelling of spoiled food, rot and gum disease.

"Let them go!" we heard from behind us. We all turned to see Josh nearby, his gun in his hand.

My captor released me, shoving me away. In my peripheral vision, I saw his partner quickly gain his feet, one hand rubbing at his back. It was disconcerting that neither man looked particularly concerned at the sight of Josh. With swift movements, they each had guns in their hands, pointed at him.

"I reckon you're outnumbered," the taller one said, his voice mild. "Put it down."

Josh shook his head. "You best leave now if you value your lives. The Home Guard's on the way. You don't want to be here when they get here."

Both men snorted with derision. "We took care of em," the shorter one said. He waved his gun at Josh. "Put it down or you're dead."

I backed up as I looked at Abbie, hoping she got my message. She nodded as if she understood, and quietly rose to her feet. Moving almost synchronistically, we each shoved the man in front of us as hard as we could. They stumbled forward as Josh ran toward them. He kicked the shorter man in the knee with his boot heel, and we all heard the sickening crunch as it broke. With a cry of pain, his leg collapsed under him and he went down, dropping his gun. Josh tackled the other man and they began to roll around on the ground, struggling with one another, fists and curses flying.

Without even thinking about it, I quickly searched the ground, well aware a forest floor is always littered with fallen limbs, found a sound one, picked it up and swung it like a baseball bat, hitting the man on the ground searching for his gun on the back of his head. He collapsed on his face and didn't move. Within five steps, I reached the man fighting with Josh, struck him a solid whack below his shoulder blades. When he collapsed against Josh, I raised my weapon in the air, brought it down as hard as I could, and clubbed him on the back of his head, grimacing at the explosion of blood that followed the arc of my weapon when I raised it. His eyes rolled back in his head, his whole body went limp, and Josh dropped him on the ground.

Josh got to his feet, giving me a crooked smile as I dropped the limb with revulsion. "Well done, Lizzie," he said breathlessly.

We heard crashing through the trees, men's voices as they drew near.

Beside me, Abbie said, "Lizzie, look. Do you see it?"

I turned to where she pointed and froze when I saw the light. "Is it mine, Abbie? Oh, God, is it?"

She shrugged, her eyes so wide I could clearly see the whites. "I reckon you'd know better than me."

Josh was watching the woods as the sounds grew closer. "We have to go," he said, in a frantic tone. "More are coming this way." When we didn't answer, he turned, following our gazes to the light. He faltered, watching its advancement with a look of amazement and shock.

Torn between the impossible decision of staying here and helping Sarie or going toward the light, my mind went blank. Shaking my head in an effort to clear it, I watched as it moved quickly toward us, dodging in and out of the trees as if playing a game of peek-a-boo. It took the sound of multiple voices to jolt me back to attention. I glanced toward the trees but my gaze was immediately drawn back to the light. I couldn't stop watching it.

Abbie tugged on my hand. "Lizzie, we need to go. They're coming and Sarie needs us."

"She's right," Josh said, "they'll be on us any minute now." The urgency in his voice as he touched my arm broke my focus on the light.

We began to run in the direction of Sarie's cabin, Josh ahead of us, the light moving parallel to us.

"It looks like it's coming right here for you, like it's been waitin for you to find it again," Abbie wheezed as she followed the path of the light with her eyes. She squeezed my hand hard enough to hurt. "What are you gonna do, Lizzie? You have to decide."

We both stopped running. I glanced at her, unsure what to do. She stared at the light, now with a slightly dazed look on her face as if she sensed what I did—a distinct pull, almost a sense of urgency drawing me toward it. It felt to me as if I had no choice but to go it, to accept whatever happened next. This, I thought, is your fate, your destiny. But I hesitated as I stared at it, wondering if it was the right light. It had an orange tint around the outside circle, but hadn't my light's been brighter? Remembering Josh, I looked around and saw him struggling with another man as at least half a dozen more boiled out of the woods. How many were there, I wondered crazily.

"Josh," I screamed. "The light, it's here." I glanced at the light again. "It's—I think it's the right one."

"Go to it," he yelled back, punching the man in the stomach then kicking him away. "I'm right behind you."

But I couldn't move. I couldn't leave him, so waited, watching as the light drew near. When I could clearly see its pulsing inner circle, the feeling spread through me, yearning, wanting, even craving to touch it.

I looked back at Josh, who was running toward us, the men hard on his heels. Panic skittered up my spine. If they got their hands on us ...

The light stopped in front of Abbie and me, hovering as if waiting patiently for us to step into it. Without regard to what she might feel or want, I took Abbie's arm and pushed her toward the center of the light, toward that seductive core. She struggled against me, saying, "No, Lizzie, stop!" but I ignored this, intent on getting us to safety. Then I remembered Pokni's dream and ceased at once trying to force her, focusing on the color pulsating around the outer circle. It was too pale, I thought, not bright at all. My mouth opened in horror and gooseflesh crawled along my arms as my inner voice screamed at me, "It's not your light!" But it was too late, I had pushed Abbie too close to the center and it was taking her.

She shrieked at me, her voice high with panic, "Lizzie, help me! No, I don—"

I yanked at her, trying to pull her out of the light, but it had her now, drawing her in, *sucking* her in. I screamed with frustration as I felt it latch onto my hand, still clutched in Abbie's. Looking back as the light slowly gathered us in then began to envelop us, I reached out with my left hand for Josh. "Josh, help us, it's the wrong light, Josh, please ..."

The last thing I saw before it completely took us was Josh, reaching for me, his fingers barely grazing my own, a man on his heels, grabbing for his shirt.

ACKNOWLEDGEMENTS

Ken Burns' documentary series, *The Civil War*

Burke: The History of a North Carolina County, by Edward W. Phifer Jr.

The Civil War in the Smokies, by Noel Fisher

Bushwhackers: The Civil War in North Carolina the Mountains, Volume II, by William R. Trotter

The Practical Herbal Medicine Handbook, by Althea Press

Plants of the Cherokee, by William H. Banks

Medicine of the Cherokee, The Way of Right Relationship, by J.T. Garrett and Michael Garrett

Liar, Temptress, Soldier, Spy, Four Women Undercover in the Civil War, by Karen Abbott

Looking for the Confederate War, Blog, by Michael C. Hardy, Burke County, NC

Below are links to online sources utilized in research:
https://www.history.com/topics/american-civil-war/battle-of-gettysburg

https://www.historynet.com/picketts-charge-gettysburg

http://genealogytrails.com/mary/washington/averyfamilystory.html

https://www.civilwartalk.com/threads/letter-to-colonel-isaac-averys-family-from-john-a-mcpherson-september-1863.117497/

https://archive.org/stream/bloodysixthsixth00iobs/bloodysixth
sixth00iobs_djvu.txt

https://ehistory.osu.edu/exhibitions/cwsurgeon/cwsurgeon/a
mputations

https://www.crwflags.com/fotw/flags/us%5Ehosp.html

We'd like to thank the following people for their help in
creating this book:

Sherry Cannon, our Beta reader, for her sharp eyes and
great suggestions.

Kimberly H. Maxwell, our cover photographer and designer,
for such outstanding work.

Dave Billings, Historian, History Museum of Burke County,
Morganton, NC, for research assistance.

Laurie Johnston, Librarian, North Carolina Room, Burke
County Public Library, Morganton, NC, for research
assistance.

Tavia Stroud, for allowing us to use her very unique and
beautiful name for a special character.

Our husbands, Mike and Steve, for their understanding as
we go through the creative process and for handling all the
grunt work at the festivals, presentations and events we
attend. We love you guys and couldn't do this without you.

As always, our beloved readers, who continue to encourage
and inspire us in so many ways. We are blessed to share
this journey with you.

ABOUT THE AUTHORS

CC Tillery is the pseudonym of two sisters, both authors, who came together to write the story of their great-aunt Bessie in the *Appalachian Journey* series. Tillery is their maiden name and the two C's stand for their first initials.

One C is for Cyndi Tillery Hodges, a multi-published, award-winning romance/fantasy author who writes under the name of Caitlyn Hunter.

The other C is for Christy Tillery French, a multi-published, award-winning author whose books cross several genres.

To find out more about their work or for more information on their joint writings, please visit their website at https://cctillery.com or their page at Facebook: https://www.facebook.com/cctillery or contact them at cctillery@yahoo.com.

BOOKS BY CC TILLERY

Appalachian Journey Series:

Whistling Woman

Moonfixer

Beloved Woman

Wise Woman

Brown Mountain Lights Series:

Through the Brown Mountain Lights

Seeking the Brown Mountain Lights

Into the Brown Mountain Lights

Made in the USA
Monee, IL
09 January 2020

20075580R00125